CAST OF CHARACTERS

Abercrombie "Filthy" Lewker. The about-to-be-knighted Shakespearean actor-manager and noted mountaineer, also a gifted amateur detective.

David Webhouse. Lewker's host for the weekend, an overbearing, domineering member of Parliament, also about to become a knight.

Clare Feckenham Webhouse. His attractive, much younger second wife.

Charles Feckenham. Clare's cousin, a lean and taciturn engineer in his thirties, about to be knighted for his engineering feats in Ceylon.

Sir Henry Lydiate. Another neighbor, an elderly Tory who is a bitter opponent of David Webhouse's upcoming hydroelectric power bill.

Anthony Cattespool. Their nearest neighbor, an aspiring novelist who fancies Clare and who was an explosives expert during the war.

Tansy Pauncefoot. The youngest member of the household, a bright and inquisitive 11-year-old whose older sister was Webhouse's first wife.

Mrs. Anna Pauncefoot. Tansy's angular, acid-tongued mother, who stayed on after her elder daughter's death to run the household.

Mr. Cutpursey. The Webhouse's ancient gatekeeper and gardener, a former quarryman.

Detective-Inspector George Grimmett. An old friend and ally of Lewker's from the war, now with Scotland Yard.

Sergeant Albert Pitt. A tall, hatchet-faced young man who possesses an astonishing knowledge of explosives.

Flora. A mischievous golden cocker spaniel, the apple of Clare's eye.

Plus assorted servants, police officers, and local people.

D1628298

The Abercrombie Lewker novels

The Detective Novels

Death on Milestone Buttress (1951)*
Murder on the Matterhorn (1951)
The Youth Hostel Murders (1952)*
The Corpse in the Crevasse (1952)
Death Under Snowdon (1952)*
A Corpse at Camp Two (1954)
Murder of an Owl (1956)
The Ice Axe Murders (1958)
Swing Away, Climber (1959)
Holiday with Murder (1960)
Death Finds a Foothold (1961)
Lewker in Norway (1963)
Death of a Weirdy (1965)
Lewker in Tirol (1967)
Fat Man's Agony (1969)

The Spy Novels

Traitor's Mountain (1945)
Kidnap Castle (1947)
Hammer Island (1947)

*Reprinted by The Rue Morgue Press

Death Under
Snowdon
by Glyn Carr

The Rue Morgue Press
Lyons / Boulder

Death Under Snowdon
© 1952 by The Estate of Glyn Carr
New material
© 2007 by The Rue Morgue Press
87 Lone Tree Lane
Lyons CO 80540

ISBN:978-1-60187-004-9

Printed by
Johnson Printing

PRINTED IN THE UNITED STATES OF AMERICA

The cover picture of Snowdon is from Wikipedia and
shows the mountain as seen from Llyn Llydaw.

About Glyn Carr

Glyn Carr was born Showell Styles in Four Oaks, Warwickshire, England, in 1908 and died at his long-time home in Wales in 2005. He did his first mountain trek at the age of three and spent the rest of his life scrambling on rocks, snow, ice and mountains. During World War II Styles used his shore leave from the Royal Navy to pioneer new ascents in North Africa and Malta. After he was discharged, Styles led two exploring and climbing expeditions to the Lyngen Peninsula, 250 miles from the Arctic Circle, where he climbed seven virgin peaks. In 1954, he led an expedition to the Himalayas to attempt a 22,000-foot peak in the Manaslu range in Nepal. He published numerous books on climbing as well as young adult fiction. If you look upon a mountain climb as taking place in a large, open-air locked room, then Showell Styles was right to choose Glyn Carr as his pseudonym for fifteen detective novels featuring Abercrombie Lewker, all of which concern murders committed among the crags and slopes of peaks scattered around the world. There's no doubt that John Dickson Carr, the king of the locked room mystery, would have agreed that Styles managed to find a way to lock the door of a room that had no walls and only the sky for a ceiling. In fact, it was while Styles was climbing a pitch on the classic Milestone Buttress on Tryfan in Wales that it struck him "how easy it would be to arrange an undetectable murder in that place, and by way of experiment I worked out the system and wove a thinnish plot around it." That book was, of course, *Death on Milestone Buttress*, which first appeared in 1951 and was published for the first time in the United States by the Rue Morgue Press in 2000. Upon its original publication Styles' English publisher, Geoffrey Bles, immediately asked for more climbing mysteries. Over the next eighteen years, Styles produced another fourteen Lewker books (fifteen, counting one last, currently lost manuscript) before he halted the series, having run out "of ways of slaughtering people on steep rock-faces."

CHAPTER I

CURTAIN UP

From the Daily Courier, *June 3rd*

The Birthday Honors conferred by Her Majesty are announced today. They include two viscounties, two baronies, and four baronetcies. There are sixty new knights bachelor. ...

KNIGHTS BACHELOR

FECKENHAM, Charles Ismay. For public services in Ceylon.
LEWKER, Abercrombie. For services to the British theater.
WEBHOUSE, David, M.P. For political and public services.

From the London Record, *June: Lord Brine's "Town Talk"* ... and of course the Arts are not neglected. All lovers of the drama—on both sides of the footlights—will applaud the knighthood bestowed on Mr. Abercrombie Lewker, acknowledged to be the greatest Shakespearean interpreter of the decade and an actor-manager in the tradition of Tree. Most of my readers will know that the Abercrombie Lewker Players, recruited entirely from men and women who saw frontline service in World War II, are trained and produced by Mr. Lewker. But I fancy few are aware that this versatile man, now in his fifty-first year, served with distinction in a certain Very Secret department of our Intelligence during the war, has assisted the police in the solving of more than one baffling murder mystery, and was, until (dare I say it?) age and amplitude intervened, an Alpine climber of note. His charming wife—who was, of course, Georgina May, queen of Variety in the 'thirties—is at present on the Riviera. She will return to London, I learn, before the actual ceremony of knighthood takes place. ...

Letter from David Webhouse, M.P.

Plas Mawr
Nant Gwynant
North Wales.
June 3rd

MY DEAR LEWKER,

I see your name is in the Hons. List. Hearty congrats. So is mine. I suppose you receive the accolade at the Palace same day as me, the 14th. If that is so, I suggest you visit Plas Mawr for a long weekend first. Charles Feckenham, my wife's cousin, is staying with us. He also bags a knighthood, which makes three of us on the carpet. Come in time for dinner on the 9th. My Daimler can take us all up to Town on the 13th.

Maybe you think this invitation's odd. I know we haven't met since the Climbing Club Dinner twelve years ago. I've a special reason for it, however—in addition to looking forward to the pleasure of your company. Fact is, I want your advice on a matter of some gravity, and want it urgently. It's rather up your street, I think.

You'll like Plas Mawr. It used to be Lord Capel's summer residence and stands close under Snowdon. We might get in a mountain scramble one of the days—the hills are looking fine just now.

My wife (my second wife, Clare Feckenham that was) is an admirer of yours and joins me in hoping that you will accept. I hear your wife is abroad. Hence this invitation to yourself. I most earnestly trust you will be able to come.

Sincerely,
DAI WEBHOUSE.

P.S. If transport is a snag, I'll gladly send the car for you.—D.W.

Air Mail Letter from Georgina Lewker

Hotel St. Martin
Antibes.
June 5th

DEAREST FILTHY,

Your cablegram came this morning, darling, and it *was* a thrill, even though I knew about it before. Don't you think "Sir Abercrombie Lewker" sounds a wee bit *ponderous*? Sure you haven't been hiding away a first name all these years, something knightish like Rupert or Percy? I played Lady Blakeney once, you know, and could quite easily get into the habit of calling you "Sir Percy."

Of course go and stay with the Webhouses, darling, if you want to. Isn't he the man they call "the quarrymen's M.P."? If he is, he married Hilda Pauncefoot who was in the chorus of *Girls Galore*—much too young for him—and she died a year later and they *said* backstage it was gin and he bullied her—but I can see your frown from here so no more gossip.

Did you see Sir Frederick Claybury gets a K.C.B.? Is that the effect of being transferred to Scotland Yard, do you think? And someone named Grimmett, George, is down for an O.B.E.—can it be our delightful detective-inspector?

I'm feeling *lots* better now and shall return on the 12th—you're *not* to bother about meeting me, I can find my own way to the Cleveland Row flat by now—and though I suppose I shan't be allowed into the Palace to watch you rising Sir Abercrombie I shall come and wait for you at the gate unless the sentry chases me away.

I'm *so* proud of you, Filthy.

All my love,
GEORGIE

Letter from Abercrombie Lewker

14A Cleveland Row
S.W.1.
June 7th

DEAR WEBHOUSE,

Permit me to reciprocate your felicitations. As Brakenbury observes in *Richard III*, speaking of princes, we have "an outward honor for an inward toil."

I find myself able to accept your kind invitation. It is my intention to drive part of the way tomorrow, completing the journey on the following day. Unless some untoward happening intervenes, therefore, you may expect my arrival between six and seven o'clock on the evening of the 9th June.

Yours sincerely,
ABERCROMBIE LEWKER.

CHAPTER II

ENTER A TOUGH

So the odd business which was to spring into headlines as "The Birthday Honors Murder" began with a journey.

Mr. Abercrombie Lewker (known to his wife and some few privileged friends as "Filthy") would have been pleased by this circumstance; it was his

contention that the best of the Sherlock Holmes stories began with jour-
neys—*"Watson, I fancy we have just time to catch the night train."* But as he
rolled westward at the wheel of his big Wolseley tourer, humming snatches
of the "Pastoral Symphony" like some Beethoven-minded bee, Mr. Lewker
was sublimely unaware of the "case" awaiting him and mindful only of the
joyful fact that he was heading for the mountains.

Mr. Lewker's car, which has been called one of the sights of London,
resembles its fond owner. Like him, it is squat, majestic, and slightly obese,
disdaining streamlining. It is thirty years since it left the workshops, but
(again like Mr. Lewker) it wears its seniority with a self-assurance that cares
nothing for the snarls of overtaking sports models or the sneers of passing
limousines. On this sunny June day the reflections of trees and fields slid
slowly across the immense silver curves of its great headlamps like an old-
fashioned diorama. Mr. Lewker drove with the hood down, his large bald
head heliographing to the skies, his halo of graying black hair straggling in
the breeze of his going. His pouchy and bulbous-nosed countenance was
dignified and rapt. That his passing occasioned chuckles in Chirk and laughter in Llangollen bothered him not at all. The commonality might not recog-
nize him, might even find his appearance comical. Let them. He was Abercrombie Lewker.

He had lunched in Shrewsbury and driven without haste. The afternoon
was well advanced when the big car topped the hill that looks down above
Bettws-y-coed. Through that leafy village it trundled, and up the long pull to
Capel Curig, where the Beddgelert road swings left from the A5 to steer its
tortuous route into Nant Gwynant through the heart of the mountains. Sharp
shadows threw the wayside boulders into relief and the triple summits of
Snowdon stood bold and clear in a blue sky. Mr. Lewker's heart did not,
nowadays, leap up when he beheld a rainbow in the sky, but it never failed to
perform that Wordsworthian feat when he saw the mountains of Wales. When
he came over the last moorland stretch to Pen-y-gwryd, the lonely inn where
every great British mountaineer has stayed at one time or another, he brought
the Wolseley to a halt that he might greet his old friends in a more leisurely
manner.

Snowdon summit was hidden now behind the huge pointed peak of Crib
Goch that reared its shadowed crags beyond the intervening glen. From that
remote three-thousand-foot crest, as he knew from many a climb in the past,
a knife-edge of bare rock flung its gigantic scallops across space to join the
main Snowdon ridge, whence ambitious scramblers might cross Snowdon
top and return along the twin ridges of Lliwedd, thus completing the famous
traverse of the Snowdon Horseshoe. As he lit his short black pipe and stared,
little eyes screwed up under bushy brows, at the immensity of the hills, Mr.
Lewker felt a resurgence of youth. He wondered why he was not making for

some quiet and kindly Welsh farmhouse whence he might wander alone and unfettered among the familiar crags and cwms. He wondered, for the first time that year, why he did not come here more often. He wondered, for the first time that day, why on earth he had decided to accept David Webhouse's invitation.

The man was the merest acquaintance. Mr. Lewker remembered him vaguely as a large and noisy life-and-souler at the Climbing Club dinner, though he had heard much of him since, chiefly as a gifted slinger of mud from the opposition benches. An overbearing type, speaking "plain cannon-fire and smoke and bounce," a born demagogue. What he knew of Web-house, in short, he disliked. Yet here he was, bound for a long weekend at the man's house.

Mr. Lewker, who could deduce his own motives as well as those of others—a rare gift—decided that curiosity had led him to this pass. And Webhouse's letter had stirred that curiosity. A connoisseur of words and phrases (and Mr. Lewker was certainly one) could hardly miss the contrast between that slangy, hearty opening paragraph, so certain of its effect, and the uncertainty of the second; the descent from *come in time for dinner on the 9th* to *I most earnestly trust you will be able to come*; the spread lures of the house, the wife, the mountains, and—lastly—that extraordinary offer to send a car from North Wales to London for him. Undoubtedly Webhouse was almost desperately anxious that Abercrombie Lewker should come for the weekend, and almost as certainly it was that "matter of some gravity," on which he so urgently required advice, which was the cause of his anxiety. What that matter might be Mr. Lewker had no idea. It was, he remembered, "rather up your street." And it was unlikely to have anything to do with Shakespeare, theatre management, or Alpine climbing.

Mr. Lewker's few essays in detection had not previously been made public, but Lord Brine's babble in the *Record* might have caught Webhouse's eye. Taken in conjunction with the suggestion of anxiety, of uneasiness, to be perceived in the letter, that could mean that Webhouse—

With a deprecatory chuckle at his own folly, Mr. Lewker cut short these idle conjectures. His nose for mysteries was too apt to pick up faint and illusory scents. If Webhouse had some problem that would exercise his hobby of detection, that would be amusing. If not—well, the letter had mentioned the possibility of a mountain scramble. He started the car, and a moment later slipped out of gear and switched off the engine as the road began its three-mile descent into the wooded vale of Gwynant.

On his right the great hollow of Cwm Dyli opened beneath Snowdon's soaring peak. Below and in front the long mirror of Gwynant Lake gave back the sunlight and shadow of late afternoon. There was no sound but the rustle of the Wolseley's tires and the occasional passing song of a waterfall coming down the precipitous hillside on the left of the road. Mr. Lewker had coasted two-thirds of the hill, and had just remembered that he would arrive at Plas Mawr before his time, when a high-pitched cry came to his ears from the steeps above, a cry that ceased abruptly in a loud rattle of stones.

Mr. Lewker glanced up, and immediately applied his brakes. Bounding down the hillside in a minor avalanche of small rocks came a blue-and-brown bundle. It landed with a twang against the wire fence that separated road from mountainside and picked itself up.

"Hallo," it said brightly.

It was a small girl with a large grin. She wore a blue shirt and ragged blue shorts, and her thin brown legs ended in clinker-nailed boots. One of the legs was bleeding profusely from a considerable cut on the shin. Long pigtails of golden hair dangled on either side of a round sunburned face whose left cheek bore an ugly graze. Two critical blue eyes surveyed the actor-manager frankly.

"You're fatter than I thought you'd be," continued this apparition conversationally.

"Incapable and shallow innocent!" retorted Mr. Lewker, booming more than usual in his relief. "You are bleeding. Come here and be first-aided."

He got out of the car and began to rummage under the rear seat.

"I'm not hurt a bit, really and truly," declared the child, climbing over the fence. "I'm tough, because I'm going to be a mountaineer and you have to be tough, and I don't often slip like that because I'm very surefooted really, and anyway it's best to let the blood make a scab, Uncle Anthony says—"

"Maiden, approach!" roared Mr. Lewker firmly. He tore a piece of lint in two and smeared it with antiseptic jelly from a tube. "Look up at me." He dabbed the graze gently with the lint. "So. Now for the leg."

"Ow!" squeaked the child involuntarily. "Please scrub round that remark," she added hastily. "I don't usually cry out, because I'm—"

"Tough. I know. Sit down on the running-board. You have contrived to collect most of the mountainside in this cut. Tell me what I am to understand by this expression 'scrub round.' "

"They say it in the Navy," said the child, sitting down obediently. "It means sort of leave it out. Uncle Anthony told me, so it's right, 'cause he was in the Navy in the war. D'you always keep bandages and things in your car? Why d'you talk in that funny booming voice?"

"To question one, yes, I do. To question two, for the same reason you talk in that funny squeaky voice—we are tuned by what Viola calls 'Nature's own sweet and cunning hand.' "

"Is that Viola in Shakespeare? I like Viola better than Olivia, don't you? I like the Histories best, though—specially the bits like where it says 'wounded steeds fret fetlock-deep in gore.' That bandage 'll slip down to my ankle, soon as I start walking, so—"

"It will not slip," said Mr. Lewker loudly, "because you will not start walking."

He administered a final pat to the bandaged shin, picked the child up in his arms, and deposited her in the front seat of the Wolseley.

" 'Come,' " he declaimed, " 'sit thee down upon this flowery bed—' "

" 'While I thy amiable cheeks do coy,' " she chimed in eagerly. " 'And stick musk-roses in thy sleek smooth head——' "

" 'And kiss thy fair large ears, my gentle joy,' " finished Mr. Lewker.

They looked at each other with new respect.

"*Midsummer Night's Dream*," said the child. "I know lots of it."

"Have a chocolate," said Mr. Lewker, taking a box from the dashboard cubbyhole.

"Thank you very much. You have one too. How do they get this pink stuff inside? Have you tried to make the hair grow on your bald patch? Mr. Cutpursey puts mutton-fat on his. Do you really solve baffling mysteries, like it said in the paper? Are you—"

"Peace, ho!" bellowed Mr. Lewker, cutting short the flow. "It is high time," he went on less loudly, "that this conversation was placed on a proper basis. It is hardly etiquette for a young person to divulge so much of her aspirations, opinions, and literary tastes to a gentlemen to whom she has not been introduced. You will doubtless agree."

"But I know who you—"

"Pray allow me to continue. Knowledge of identity does not necessarily constitute an introduction. My name, which may not be unknown to you, is Abercrombie Lewker. I am charmed to meet you. As you infer, I can on occasion display some talent for detection, as I will now demonstrate. From the facts which you have—somewhat prematurely—divulged, namely, that you are tough, that you have an Uncle Anthony, that you know a certain Mr. Cutpursey who puts mutton-fat on his head—"

"He boils it first."

"His head?" demanded Mr. Lewker, momentarily deflected from his demonstration.

"No, the fat. He says it—"

"From these few but varied facts, I say," boomed Mr. Lewker resolutely, "I make a swift deduction, a miracle of pure reasoning. I deduce, my dear Tough, that you are the daughter of none other than Mr. David Webhouse, M.P."

His flourish had a quite unexpected effect. The child stiffened and sat bolt upright, small hands clenched and eyes flashing angrily.

"I'm not!" she cried. "I'm not his daughter! I—I wouldn't be his daughter for anything!"

Mr. Lewker, disconcerted, abased himself.

"Pray forgive me. I resign my detective's commission. You shall talk as long as you like and tell me who you are."

"All right." Her anger passed like a cloud-shadow. "I'm Tansy Pauncefoot, and I couldn't be Uncle David's daughter, anyhow, because he only married Hilda three years ago, and she died the year after that, and then he married Auntie Clare last year."

"I see. You are Hilda Pauncefoot's sister." Georgie's letter had not indicated how long ago Webhouse's first marriage had taken place. "And you live at Plas Mawr with Mr. Webhouse?"

Tansy nodded. "I call him Uncle David, but he isn't really. Hilda was twelve years older than me, you see. I'm eleven. My father died years and years ago, so when Hilda died Mother and me came to Plas Mawr to keep house for Uncle David. 'Course, I'm at boarding-school really."

"That fact is not immediately apparent," commented Mr. Lewker gravely. "Did you come rolling down the mountainside from boarding-school, may I ask?"

"You *are* silly. No—St. Olaf's has got chickenpox, so I'm on a sort of holiday. Isn't it lucky?"

"A most fortunate chance, i' faith. And where did you roll from? You were, I presume, gathering no moss?"

"Auntie Clare told me you were coming to stay," said Tansy, "so I thought I'd come and meet you, and I was too early, so I went up to practice climbing on those rocks up there. Uncle David says if it's fine he and you and Uncle Anthony and Mr. Feckenham—that's Auntie Clare's cousin—are going to do the Snowdon Horseshoe tomorrow but he doesn't think I ought to come. Will you make him let me? I do so want to come."

Her big blue eyes cajoled him. Mr. Lewker rubbed his chin and cautiously promised to use his influence.

"Who is Uncle Anthony?" he inquired.

"Oh, he's Mr. Cattespool, and he lives in the cottage above Plas Mawr and comes in to see us a lot. We'll be late if you don't drive on."

Mr. Lewker looked at his watch and pressed the starter.

"So we shall," he agreed as the car moved forward. "How is the wounded limb feeling?"

"Very comfy, thank you." Tansy settled herself and drew a deep breath. "This is a funny old car. Oo, look at the lake. Doesn't it make you want to bathe? Mr. Feckenham had a swim this morning. He's going to be a Sir for building bridges in Ceylon. You and Uncle David are going to be Sirs too, aren't you? Auntie Clare will be Lady Webhouse. Have you got a wife? I'm not going to be married, ever, 'cause I'm going to be a mountaineer like Hillary and Shipton. I've got a new windproof jacket—"

To this and much similar chatter Mr. Lewker lent a rather inattentive ear. On his right the loveliest of Welsh lakes reflected perfectly the greens and grays of the huge outline of Snowdon which—in evening shadow now— swept down to the craggy woods of its farther shore. The hydroelectric station that smirched the upper glen was out of sight, and the age-old peace of the valley lapped him round with welcoming arms, as it had first done thirty years ago. In those days, he reflected a little sadly, the sheer beauty of Nant Gwynant had moved him almost to tears; now he merely felt that a good dinner and a comfortable bed would round off the day nicely.

The road, which had wound pleasantly under the pines of the lake shore, curved round the foot of a rhododendron-clad hill at the end of the lake. A very tall old gentleman, bareheaded and wearing an old-fashioned tweed knickerbocker suit, was pacing along the road towards them. The evening sunlight, slanting through the trees, illumined scanty white hair and a pair of drooping mustaches like the White Knight's. Tansy waved to him as they passed, and the old gentleman responded with a stiff little bow.

"That's Sir Henry Lydiate," explained Tansy. "He lives at Plas Bach and he's coming to dinner tomorrow. Look—there's Snowdon."

The valley had narrowed at the lake end, but now opened to reveal a side valley on the right whose mountain-walls framed the summit-cone of Snowdon, remote and dreaming against the cloudless sky. Half a mile farther on another and narrower glen appeared on the left, a rhododendron-smothered vale whose northern wall was a massive bluff, precipitous and heathery, with bare rock-faces of considerable height scarring its flank. At the foot of this eminence, among the trees, rose the gables and chimneys of a large house.

"There's Plas Mawr," said Tansy, "and there's Uncle Anthony's cottage up above." She pointed to a little whitewashed building on the shoulder above the bluff. "Quick—turn left here, across the river."

"Thank you," said Mr. Lewker, swinging the car into a narrow lane and over a bridge. "You are an invaluable guide, Miss Tansy."

"I'd rather be called Tough than Miss Tansy," she returned, flinging back her pigtails. "Here's the gate, look. Blow your horn."

Beside a small lodge on the left of the road a pair of new and ugly wrought-iron gates flashed gilt convolutions in the sun. An old man in shirtsleeves, harsh-featured, with fluffy white hair fringing his baldness, came out of the lodge to open the gates.

"Hallo, Mr. Cutpursey!" shouted Tansy. "This is Mr. Abercrombie Lewker who's come to stay!"

The old man nodded grimly and closed the gates behind the Wolseley as they drove on. The drive was newly metalled, mounting a grassy hillside before twisting into an avenue between huge old rhododendron bushes.

"Mr. Cutpursey's funny," said Tansy, "but he's nice really. He goes off sometimes into the hills to watch beasties, and he calls it his three-gallon trip, and the mutton-fat doesn't make the hair grow *much*, does it? Here we are."

The car, emerging from the rhododendrons, halted on a wide gravel terrace in front of Plas Mawr.

The long gray stone house, built on a natural ledge of the hillside, was bowered in conifers and evergreen shrubs which rose steeply behind it to the foot of the bluff whose western facet of cliff towered sunlit above. The front windows of the house faced across the main valley to the green buttresses of Snowdon, shadowed now like the deep side-valley that penetrated them. The voice of the Glaslyn river flowing on towards Beddgelert and the sea was borne to the ear on the faint evening breeze. As a summer residence, Mr. Lewker decided, Plas Mawr was wholly admirable.

"Look," said Tansy hurriedly, "I'll have to go round the back—I'm not supposed to be seen in my mountain clothes. No, please—I can walk all right that far."

She bundled out of the car, hesitated, and then turned an unwontedly serious face to him.

"If you're really and truly a detective," she added, not without skepticism, "you can find out what's worrying Uncle David."

"He is worried, then?"

"Well," replied Tansy in a hasty and confidential whisper, "*I* think he's frightened of something."

She scuttled crabwise round the corner of the house as David Webhouse, roaring hospitably, strode from the front door to greet his guest.

CHAPTER III

THE CLIFF PATH

Dinner in the big dining room of Plas Mawr, oak-paneled like all its rooms, was materially satisfying but socially a trifle uncomfortable. Of the five people round the table only one (omitting Mr. Lewker) made any attempt at conversation. Clare Webhouse, her attractive figure sheathed in a green dinner-frock, did her best to entertain the new arrival. But she received no support from Charles Feckenham, a lean and silent man in his thirties, and little more from Mrs. Pauncefoot. David Webhouse's mother-in-law—Mr. Lewker supposed she might still be so described—closely resembled in appearance the boardinghouse landlady of the comic artists. Upright and angular, her thin graying hair drawn tightly back above a narrow forehead, she rarely opened her trap-like mouth except to ask for the salt or to throw an acid reprimand at the fat Welsh maid who brought in the dishes. Mr. Lewker caught himself thinking that the late Mr. Pauncefoot must have possessed large measures of good looks and determination to have begotten a child like Tansy upon this vinegary person. He wondered if her elder daughter, Hilda Pauncefoot, who was Webhouse's first wife, had been as attractive as Clare.

As for David Webhouse himself, both eye and ear could perceive that while there was food before him the presence of other people was a very secondary consideration. With his massive frame crouched above his plate and his elbows spread, he devoted himself noisily to Mrs. Pauncefoot's cooking.

Mr. Lewker's host had welcomed him warmly enough, with that domineering geniality which the actor-manager remembered of old. Webhouse was a rugged giant of a man, a head and shoulders taller than his young wife and probably more than twenty years older. His face, ruddy and faintly purple-veined, was the face of a bruiser gone to seed; his table manners were in keeping with his face. He had so far shown no sign of nerves or uneasiness, unless an odd sidelong glance, which seemed to be a frequent mannerism, could be so described. Mr. Lewker, descending the wide oak staircase just before dinner, had heard his harsh voice shouting down Clare's softer tones, and had gathered that an appeal against Tansy's dismissal to an early bed was being finally and angrily overruled.

Cheese—an excellent farm cheese—succeeded the sweet. Clare, who had been talking about detective dramas with (in Mr. Lewker's opinion) no adequate knowledge of stage matters, had changed the subject to books.

"I expect you could write an exciting autobiography," she was saying, flickering dark lashes at the actor-manager. "Why don't you? Anthony Cattespool, who's our neighbor, is writing a novel about the sea, and he—"

"Well, everyone done?" David Webhouse broke into the conversation with arrogant assurance. He massaged his thick lips with a napkin and flung it aside. "Anna, that was a damned good dinner."

"No need for profanity, then," retorted Anna Pauncefoot tartly.

Webhouse ignored her. "Coffee in the lounge, Lewker."

They crossed the wide hall from the dining room and entered a long drawing roomwhose tall windows admitted the last glow of evening. A golden cocker bitch flung herself madly at Clare, who picked the dog up and sank down on a sofa. Feckenham lowered his long body into a chair beside her. Mrs. Pauncefoot busied herself with coffeepot and cups.

"Cigar?" Webhouse motioned Mr. Lewker to an armchair and held out a large box. "Genuine Larranagas. Charles? You don't know a good thing when you see one, my lad. Does he, Lewker?"

"These are excellent," murmured Mr. Lewker, drawing reverently at the long cylinder. "I am quite unable to afford them myself."

Dai Webhouse dropped into a chair and ran a big hand through his mop of wiry gray hair.

"I like my luxuries out of the top drawer," he said with complacency. "I've earned the best and I get it. I tell my constituents up in the quarries, I'm no Communist, I tell 'em. Give every man a chance to get up the ladder—that's my sort of Socialism. If a man's got the character, the personality, and the will to work, he should have his due. Let him go for the good things of life, say I—the pretty things, if he wants 'em. And can keep 'em."

Mr. Lewker's sharp little eyes were on Webhouse as he spoke. They did not miss the glance the big man darted at his wife, a glance both possessive and jealous. It was natural that the actor-manager should look quickly at Clare and her cousin. Charles Feckenham had the lean good looks and half-contemptuous reserve that attract certain women irresistibly, and for all his apparent languor there was a hint of recklessness in his narrow-lipped mouth and in the gray-green eyes that were so seldom revealed. The eyes were veiled now as he lounged in his chair with a cigarette in his long fingers; but one corner of the mouth was drawn up in a faint but unpleasant grin. Clare's attention seemed to be wholly occupied with the spaniel.

"Poor Flora-flora," she was whispering. "Poor old bitchy-witchy Flora. Poor Flora's got a tight tum. Poor Flora doesn't like having tight tum. Poor—"

"I do wish you wouldn't get that dog up on the sofa, Clare," rasped Mrs. Pauncefoot like a file cutting into soft brass. "She dirties the covers."

Clare turned reproachful eyes, not unlike Flora's, on this critic.

"Poor Flora's not well, Anna," she murmured. "She's got a tight tum—haven't you, darling?"

"Nonsense," said Mrs. Pauncefoot tersely.

"Overfed little brute," Webhouse pronounced. "She eats any damned thing, Lewker. I've seen her eating string many a time—seems to like it. And Clare feeds her half a pint of milk a day, believe it or not."

"Well, you're a nice one to talk," countered his wife, without rancor. "Didn't I see you giving her something in a saucer on Tuesday?"

Webhouse seemed unaccountably embarrassed by this accusation. He shifted his feet and glanced sideways at Mr. Lewker.

"May have done," he growled. "Something I couldn't drink myself."

"It was half that glass of milk and soda I brought to the study for you," snapped Anna Pauncefoot. She began to collect coffee-cups noisily. "Wicked waste, I call it."

"The dog's always wandering up the cliff path," complained Webhouse. "She'll fall off it one of these days. Have to put a gate at the bottom."

"Flora hopes Anthony's coming down the cliff path," Clare murmured, playing with the dog's floppy ears. "Anthony takes us walkies, doesn't he,

Flora? We like Anthony, don't we, Flora? We think Anthony—"

"Oh, for Christ's sake!" shouted Webhouse. "I—"

He checked himself. Again his glance went quickly to his guest.

"Sorry," he said shortly. "Nerves aren't too good. Sorry, Clare."

"I should think so," nodded Mrs. Pauncefoot grimly. She picked up the tray of coffee-things and stalked to the door. "If you don't like Anthony Cattespool coming here, David, you should stop it," she added, and banged the door behind her.

Clare laughed softly and stood up, letting Flora slide to the floor. The roseate afterglow from the sky outside tinted her slim bare arms.

"Dai, you *must* stop swearing," she said. "I believe Anna thinks you're Antichrist. One of these days she'll kill you and they'll make her a saint."

Dai Webhouse looked up at her with a sudden jerky motion of his head. There was an odd little pause. Mr. Lewker, breaking it, felt that he was easing a tension.

"I fancy Mrs. Pauncefoot's brand of nonconformity does not canonize," he remarked.

"How clever of you!" Clare smiled at him. "But I keep forgetting your amateur 'tection. You're quite right—she's a Freewill Baptist or something." She turned to her husband. "I'm just going up to say good night to Tansy. She's awfully anxious about tomorrow—you'll let her go with you, won't you, Dai?"

"I've told you—" began Webhouse.

"Pray allow me to intercede for Miss Tansy," boomed Mr. Lewker, interrupting majestically. "I shall not enjoy my scramble round the Horseshoe if she is left behind."

"That decides it, then," nodded Clare, and went to the door.

The silent Feckenham uncoiled his semi-recumbent length with surprising quickness to open the door for her.

"You might have done that for Anna," Clare said as she passed him. "She had a tray."

"Anna can look after herself," said Feckenham.

He spoke quietly but with a certain emphasis, and Mr. Lewker's quick ear did not fail to catch the words. They were of no apparent significance, but he had already observed that Charles Feckenham rarely spoke unless he had something significant to say.

"Clare spoils that child," Webhouse was grumbling. "Tansy was sent to bed early as a punishment. No sense is being soft with her."

"Yet," said Mr. Lewker gently, "no child's punishment should outlast the night. Shakespeare—in *Titus Andronicus*, if I remember aright—has the line 'Sweet mercy is nobility's true badge.' It is not, perhaps, an inept quotation in our present circumstances."

Webhouse failed to catch the allusion, but Feckenham, who had resumed his chair and was to all appearances asleep, picked it up.

"We're not nobles yet," he grunted.

"Untitled for another five days, my boy," chuckled Webhouse, restored by this reminder to noisy geniality. "Make the most of it. Tomorrow we'll be aloft on the Snowdon ridges—three knights on a knife-edge. Not a bad head-line, that. Charles hasn't done much mountaineering, Lewker, but he'll be with us. So will Cattespool unless I'm mistaken."

"And Tansy?" put in Mr. Lewker.

"And Tansy, I suppose. Looks like being good weather for it, eh?" He stood up and went to the window. "Nice clear evening. What about a stroll round the estate? Coming, Charles?"

Feckenham was lazily unwinding a small coil of string he had taken from his pocket, while the spaniel Flora, head cocked and body quivering, watched him tensely.

"Still digesting," he drawled. "Stay here and entertain Flora."

Webhouse shrugged his ponderous shoulders and led the way through the hall and out of the front door.

"Queer chap, Charles," he said as they stepped out into the cool half-light of the garden. "Never think he'd done miracles of engineering in Ceylon, would you? Casual devil with money, too. He'd rather spend ten minutes letting that damned dog pull the end of a piece of string than sign a con-tract—Nice place, eh?"

Mr. Lewker had halted to admire the peace of the evening. Above the dark treetops that fenced the front of the house the jagged skyline rose, purple on fading gold. From somewhere in the firs behind Plas Mawr came the plash-ing of a waterfall. Flower-scent and the soothing breath of green things hung sweetly on the still air. He began to be glad he had come.

"Got it for a song when old Capel died," Webhouse said, jingling keys in his trousers pocket. "See the old coach-house down there? I've got a bit of a workshop there, as well as a garage. I've had the clock on the roof regilded, but the damned thing won't go."

It was fitting, reflected Mr. Lewker sentimentally, that the clock should refuse to go. Plas Mawr, built a century and a half ago, represented an era when private individuals as well as the state could afford to build spaciously and well. That era, with its grooms and coaches and class distinctions, was gone for ever. The tempo of living had quickened, and the old clock might well decline to tell the new and hurried hours.

"That business I wrote I wanted your advice on," Webhouse said abruptly.

Mr. Lewker came out of his abstraction with a jerk.

"My humble intellect is at your service whenever you require it," he returned.

"Yes. Well, I'm not going into it now. I'd rather you formed your own opinion first. You've a reputation for intelligence, Lewker."

"You think so?" Mr. Lewker felt patronized. "I trust my intelligence is sufficient to prevent me from forming an opinion without any evidence."

"All right," snapped Webhouse. "Let's walk up the cliff path."

They began to walk away from the front of the house, taking a path that wound through giant rhododendron bushes and climbed past a rock-garden towards the firs at the foot of the bluff. There was still light enough from the clear sky to see their way, and the bare rock-face that dropped into the trees behind Plas Mawr towered impressively overhead.

"My regular evening stroll," Webhouse announced. "Last thing before I turn in. Old Capel built this path to connect with the cottage on the hill above. See where it goes?"

He gesticulated with his half-smoked cigar towards the face of the bluff. Across the cliff, climbing gently from right to left, it was possible to make out an iron railing, presumably edging a footpath which ran like a ledge on the miniature precipice.

"Almost Alpine," commented Mr. Lewker.

"Continental, anyway. They say Capel kept a mistress in that cottage— Now, Lewker. What d'you make of this?"

They had reached a bend of the path, where it emerged from a belt of firs close under the steepening hillside. Webhouse had stopped by one of the outlying trees and was resting a forefinger on its trunk. The light was fast fading, but by peering closely Mr. Lewker could see that he was pointing to a dully-gleaming speck of metal embedded in the tree about four feet from the ground.

"It is, I fancy, an airgun slug," he ventured.

Webhouse nodded grimly. "It is. I was standing here when it passed my head, Lewker."

"Hum," said Mr. Lewker noncommittally. "You think it was fired at you?"

"I think nothing. I know it was fired and I know I didn't see or hear anyone. I yelled out, thinking it might be Cutpursey—the gardener, y'know, he's an old devil after rabbits—but he wasn't in the fir wood."

Mr. Lewker rubbed his chin. "Has Cutpursey an airgun?"

"I keep one in the coach-house, a pretty powerful thing. Cutpursey uses it sometimes. It's supposed to be Tansy's, but I've forbidden her to use it."

"This was a recent occurrence?"

"Five nights ago, June fourth. I was taking my usual evening stroll and happened to stop just here. Admiring the last of the sunset. Then that damned thing zipped past my ear."

"Past your ear," repeated Mr. Lewker thoughtfully. "It could have been accidental, could it not? The erring marksman, being human, might not wish to incur your anger."

"Could be." Webhouse was shifting uneasily from one leg to another. "Let's move on."

"You questioned Cutpursey, naturally," said Mr. Lewker as they walked on up the steepening path.

"No, I didn't. Didn't tell a soul about it—you're the first."

"Has Cutpursey, then, some reason to wish you ill?"

"Just the opposite, I'd say. I took the old chap out of a local quarry where he was working his guts out—he's a country-bred man, comes from Derbyshire originally—and gave him this job here at twice the wages."

"Then do you know of anyone …?"

Webhouse halted again. They had left the trees below and now stood on the heathery glacis at the foot of the bluff, and the stronger light from the evening sky showed his rugged face scowling and deeply lined.

"See here," he said. "Let's drop it there, Lewker. Want you to get an unbiased look at things—get me? We'll talk about it later."

"Just as you wish," returned the actor-manager doubtfully.

"I've not stopped my evening stroll since that happened—but I've locked up the gun. Here's where the cliff path begins."

The late Lord Capel, reflected Mr. Lewker as he followed his host, had evidently a turn for the romantic. There could have been no real necessity for carving this path across the face of a precipice, but it was undoubtedly spectacular. After bending well to the right to gain a natural ledge on the heather-tufted flank of the bluff, it swung left to climb steadily across the upper steeps. At first the mountainside above and below the path was not too steep for an active person to scramble up; but it grew quickly into a true precipice, and soon the path was a mere rock ledge running across a sheer wall. It was wide and well engineered, however, and the stout iron rail on the left hand had its stanchions firmly socketed in the rock. Looking out from this airy perch, one gazed above the falling green of the Plas Mawr woods, beyond the darkling valley with its stone-walled meadows and winding river, to the swelling bulk of hills which lifted Snowdon's huge silhouette into the sky of deepening gold.

"Capel's bridge-building wasn't much good," Webhouse said, stopping and pointing ahead. "Winter rains brought his stone arch down in January."

Mr. Lewker saw that the path had reached a ravine, little more than a vertical crack in the precipice. Down the back of this narrow trough fell a small stream, doubtless the waterfall whose plashing he had heard earlier. The square-hewn ledge of the path continued on the further side, but the masonry that had once bridged the short gap had fallen, and in its place was a wooden structure consisting of two broad planks with a handrail on the outer edge. This bridge was only eight or nine feet long, and its ends rested on the flat rock of the path on each side.

"It's only temporary," Webhouse explained. "I'm getting a good steel bridge made in Cardiff—should be arriving any day now."

"Suitable, as Baedeker would say, for those with steady heads," observed Mr. Lewker. He placed a foot on one of the planks; it gave gently beneath his weight.

"That plank's split at this end," said Webhouse, "but it's perfectly safe. I've crossed it every night since I've been home, and Cattespool uses it when he comes down."

"A wire rope braced to the rock would make it safer still," suggested the actor-manager.

"Well, it's only temporary, as I say. It'd take a charge of blasting-powder to shift it, all the same—it's a heavy thing." He stepped on to the bridge. "No one uses it except me and Cattespool," he added over his shoulder, "and that blasted dog, who's always smelling about up here."

Halfway across the bridge Mr. Lewker paused to look down. Behind him the little stream fell noisily in its groove. In front and below he saw it tumbling to white destruction on a fan of scree and rubble, a clear hundred feet directly beneath the bridge. Their fir wood came up to meet its dispersed runnels, and beyond the trees rose the chimneytops of Plas Mawr, so close beneath him that he fancied he could toss a pebble into them.

"Come on!" hailed Webhouse from the path above. "It's getting dark."

On the far side of the ravine the path quickly lost its spectacular character. It climbed to a heathery shoulder and flattened out where a dry-stone wall edged a high pasture above the bluff. Webhouse was waiting by an iron wicket-gate in the wall.

"That's the cottage," he said as Mr. Lewker came up, pointing to a small building that glimmered white in the dusk at the upper end of the sloping field. "And you can see a bit of the upper valley and the lake down there."

"I take it," remarked Mr. Lewker, panting slightly, "that the Anthony Cattespool mentioned by Mrs. Pauncefoot this evening lives there?"

Webhouse struck a match to relight his cigar. The orange flame revealed how dark it had now become; revealed also the sidelong glance he threw at his companion.

"Anna's a damned capable woman," he said, drawing strongly at the cigar. "She runs my house with the help of one maid and a daily woman, which takes a load off Clare. But she doesn't like me, and doesn't mind showing it. Narrow religious type of woman. Says things she doesn't mean, Lewker. She's my first wife's mother, as I expect you know—Clare agreed to her staying on here."

Mr. Lewker murmured affirmatively and wondered idly why his host should shy away from mention of Anthony Cattespool.

"No good calling on Cattespool now," went on Webhouse, as though he had heard the unspoken thought. "He's gone down to the coast for the day and won't be back till late. Took this place four months ago. He's supposed to be writing a book and wants peace and quiet, he says. Comes down to see us pretty often—Tansy's fond of him and it's company for Clare when I'm away addressing meetings."

"He comes climbing with us tomorrow?"

"Yes. And to dinner afterwards. Sir Henry Lydiate's coming to dinner as well—by Clare's wish. He's no friend of mine." He pointed to a dark clump of trees far below in the valley, where the tip of the lake glimmered silver in the dusk. "Plas Bach's in those trees. Very old place—Lydiates have lived there for centuries. The old man's the worst kind of Tory obstructionist. Time we went down," he added abruptly.

Mr. Lewker followed him obediently as he started down the path.

"Cattespool was in the Navy," Webhouse threw over his shoulder as they reached the bridge.

"So Tansy informed me."

"Did she? He did rather well—D.S.O. for demolishing some harbor wall in Norway or somewhere."

The last of the light was passing from the valley. The green dome of the sky darkened as though some heavenly electrician was dimming the lights of a vast theatre before the commencement of a drama. The path, where it turned and ran into the firs, was dark as the gangway of an unlit auditorium. On the soft carpet of fir needles their footsteps made no sound, and the sudden snapping of a branch in the depths of the copse was loud as a pistol-shot. It was not the noise that made Mr. Lewker jump, but the convulsive grip of Webhouse's hand on his arm, pulling him to a standstill.

For five seconds they stood motionless. Then:

"Is that you, Cattespool?" called David Webhouse hoarsely.

Heavy footsteps crackled among the trees and a figure, bent and gnome-like, stepped out on the path in front of them.

"Cutpursey." Webhouse sighed the name rather than uttered it. "What the hell," he demanded, suddenly blustering, "d'you think you're doing in there, man?"

"Settin' rabbit snares," muttered the gardener sullenly. "Ah'd no mind to skeer ye."

"Scare me, by God!" Webhouse checked himself. "Well—get along to bed, blast you!"

The old man turned without a word and shuffled away down the path. His employer pulled out a handkerchief and passed it quickly over his brow.

"Damned old idiot!" he said a trifle shakily. "Gave me a start. Thought it might be Cattespool—he sometimes walks up this way. Queer time to go rabbiting, isn't it?"

"Old countrymen—and you tell me Cutpursey comes from Derbyshire—sometimes set snares at night," replied Mr. Lewker.

They walked on. The path emerged from the trees and slapted down above a rock-garden to the graveled terrace in front of the house. The long yellow oblong of lights from the Plas Mawr windows showed the slight figure of Clare Webhouse walking slowly towards them with Flora.

"Is that you, Dai?" she called. "Someone's here to see you."

"Damn and blast!" growled her husband as they met. "I'll bet it's that old fool Lydiate. Why didn't you tell him I was out and push him off?" He threw his arm carelessly round her shoulders. "You'll catch cold, out here without a coat."

It was too dark now to see her expression, but Mr. Lewker thought she shrank a little from the caress.

"It *is* Sir Henry," she admitted. "But I couldn't possibly send him away, Dai. He's our neighbor—and besides, he knows where you go for your evening walk and how long it takes—Flora, *do* stop it!"

The spaniel had seized in her teeth the end of the lead, which dangled from her mistress's hand and was tugging furiously at it.

"Always pulling at things, that dog," said Webhouse irritably, taking his arm from his wife's shoulders. "Oh, well—suppose I'd better see what the old pantaloon wants. See you later, Lewker."

He swung on his heel and strode rapidly towards the house.

"I've put him in the study," Clare called after him.

Webhouse waved an arm and disappeared through the front door. Clare and Mr. Lewker followed more slowly and somewhat jerkily owing to Flora's intermittent braking.

"If you're feeling like bed," she said, "don't wait for Dai. Sir Henry's come to argue about Dai's hydroelectric bill and they'll be at it for hours—and it's twenty to eleven now."

"A little late for a call, surely," remarked the actor-manager.

"It is, isn't it? Flora!—*Naughty!*—But Sir Henry's like that. An old dear, really, but eccentric. Anyway, he won't let Dai get away for an hour."

"Then I think I shall take your advice. Like Bottom, I have an exposition of sleep come upon me."

"And you want to be fresh for this climb tomorrow. I'm not coming. So I hope you'll look after Tansy. Oh, for heaven's *sake*, Flora!"

She bent swiftly and slapped the spaniel, who yelped resentfully and was at once picked up and kissed.

"Clare didn't mean to hurt," cooed Clare. "Flora doesn't mind, does she? Not much?"

"I imagine Flora hardly minds at all," observed Mr. Lewker dryly.

"Flora doesn't like sarcastic people, does she?" murmured the girl. She held the spaniel towards him. "Make friends, Flora. I'm sure you like dogs really, Mr. Lewker."

"I like them if they like me." He stroked the silken head and received a wet lick on his hand. "Cockers are likable folk."

"This one is, although she's so mischievous. She's very young yet, you know."

She put Flora down and the dog immediately rushed madly up the steps and in through the front door.

"She's *so* funny," Clare added, leading the way into the lamplit hall. "She doesn't like Dai and he doesn't like her, and yet she's always taking things of his and burying them—look!"

Flora, with tail wagging and amber eyes shining, was trotting towards the open door with a slipper in her mouth. Clare rescued it with some difficulty and held it out.

"Dai's," she said triumphantly. "I told you. Of course she was off to bury it."

"Do you ever succeed in disinterring the buried treasure?" inquired Mr. Lewker.

"Oh, yes. She always buries her things in the same place—Cutpursey's rockery. He gets wild about it. Now, would you like a drink before turning in? Or is bed calling loudly?"

"My choice," said the actor-manager, who was feeling the combined effects of his journey and the mountain air, "is sleep, chief nourisher in life's feast."

"All right, then. It's oil lamps and candles here, as you see, until Dai gets his dynamo installed. Charles shall light you to your room."

She pushed open the door of the drawing roomand summoned her cousin.

Escorted by the silent Feckenham, Mr. Lewker mounted the wide staircase. From the landing the hall below looked like a dark pool, a pool where shadows might or might not be solid objects. Through Mr. Lewker's mind passed the odd fancy that he was standing on the verge of a similar pool of human affairs; the waters might be shallow and their shadows might be effects of lighting—or there might be strange objects in the depths.

The fancy faded and was forgotten as he followed Feckenham's gaunt shadow along a paneled corridor lit by a single oil lamp in a niche.

"Here you are," said Feckenham, opening a door and standing aside.

"Thank you." Mr. Lewker paused on the threshold, candlestick in hand. "You have been staying here for some time, I take it?" he said interrogatively.

The lean man showed no surprise at the question.

"Fortnight. Why?"

"I wondered if you had happened to notice anything strange in David Webhouse's manner."

"I have," said Feckenham coolly. "Man's afraid."

"You think so? Of what, may I ask?"

The shifting candlelight gave an added malevolence to Feckenham's twisted grin.

"Theft," he answered briefly, and stalked away along the passage.

CHAPTER IV

MOUNTAINEER'S DAY

"Where the devil's Cattespool?" demanded Dai Webhouse irritably, looking at his watch for the fourth time in ten minutes. "He'll make us late starting."

Clad in plus-fours and golf jacket, he was standing—or, more accurately, tramping jerkily about—beside his new Daimler, which glistened like a huge green beetle in the sunshine of a perfect June morning. Mr. Lewker, in very ancient tweed breeches and coat, and Charles Feckenham, in flannels and an anorak, sat smoking on the running board. The sun had only just come over the hills behind Plas Mawr and the shrubs and trees that bordered the terrace were steaming in the new heat. The glory of the morning, however, seemed to have an adverse effect on Webhouse's temper.

"The damned fellow's five minutes late already," he fulminated. "Upsets the schedule."

"The typical Socialist planner," drawled Feckenham with malice. "Plan perfect, individual idiosyncrasies ignored."

Webhouse's face deepened its shade of red.

"In my planning. Charles, I take men's characters into account—as you should know," he growled, glaring.

Feckenham, meeting the glare, dropped his eyes and smiled his twisted smile; but he seemed (thought Mr. Lewker) a trifle disconcerted.

"Anyhow," Webhouse went on quickly, "what I've got out of life I've got by being punctual and thorough. Do nothing by halves—that's my motto, whether it's a walk over Snowdon or a speech in the House. There's a lot of rubbish being talked about planning—"

"He's coming!" Tansy's excited call interrupted him. "He's running down the cliff path now!"

She sped towards them across the terrace, her golden plaits shining in the sun. She wore her "mountain clothes" and a small rucksack, and Flora frisked barking at her heels.

"Did you take that dog up the cliff path?" Webhouse demanded sharply.

"N-no, Uncle David," Tansy answered, her round happy face changing to sullenness. "She was up there and I brought her down. She doesn't go on the narrow part, though—"

"Yes, she does!" The man spoke as though his small sister-in-law was a criminal in the dock. "I've seen her smelling round the bridge up there. If I catch her going up that path again I shall thrash her—only way she'll learn."

Clare Webhouse came out of the front door in a plain blue frock that emphasized her slim beauty. Flora and Tansy galloped to her.

"Hasn't Anthony arrived yet?" she asked.

As she spoke a thin young man, dressed in shorts and jacket, came with quick strides down the path to the terrace and went straight to Clare. He was a bare inch taller than the girl and his small pointed black beard combined with his sun-darkened skin to give him a decidedly foreign appearance. The voice in which he greeted Clare and Tansy was pleasant, but high and slightly affected.

"Come on, Cattespool!" roared Webhouse impatiently. "We're waiting for you." He opened the car door. "Tansy!—Front seat, Lewker."

Anthony Cattespool caught Tansy's hand and ran with her to the car. Lewker and Feckenham climbed in, and the Daimler ground the gravel under its wheels and sped away down the drive with Tansy waving good-bye from the rear window.

Those who make the traverse of the Snowdon Horseshoe, known to mountain lovers as the finest ridge-walk south of Skye, usually start from the top of the Llanberis Pass. The Daimler bowled past the blue sparkle of Llyn Gwynant, up the long hill which Mr. Lewker had descended yesterday and where he had encountered Tansy, and swung left above it to climb the last steep mile to the Pass. A few wisps of morning cloud still hung on the flanks of the mountains, but the summits smiled assurance in a cloudless sky. It was going to be a perfect day. Even Webhouse lost some of his morning ill humor and discoursed boastfully of the bill for hydroelectric development, on the draft for which he was engaged, and Tansy chattered enthusiastically of mountains and mountain-climbing from her seat between Anthony and Feckenham.

At Pen-y-pass, the whitewashed inn that stands solitary at the crest of the Pass between great mountainsides, Webhouse parked the car and they got out. Other cars were parked there, and a few cheerful folk in climbing rig were setting off up the path that leads to the summit.

"They're going the easy way," Tansy said loftily to Mr. Lewker as, sitting side by side on the running board, they laced their climbing boots. "We're going the int'resting way, aren't we?"

"The mountaineer's way, Tough," nodded the actor-manager. "No rolling downhill today, remember."

"I don't usually roll—I told you. You've climbed the Matterhorn, haven't you? Is it very hard? It says in a book I've got the rock's very loose. Crib

Goch's a bit loose, too, 'cause Uncle Anthony's been up it and he told
me—"

"Ready, everybody?"

Webhouse, rucksack on back, came round the car. Tansy nodded and stood
up. The party clattered across the stones of the parking-place, left the well-
trodden track of the ordinary route up Snowdon, and struck up the narrow
and rocky path known—not inappropriately—as the Pig Track. This was not
wide enough for two to walk abreast, so the five proceeded in single file.
Tansy led, striding out importantly, with Feckenham behind her and Webhouse in the middle; Mr. Lewker followed, and Anthony Cattespool brought
up the rear.

"We'd no chance to introduce ourselves," Cattespool remarked, closing
up to the actor-manager as they trudged upward. "You've not met me before,
but I've seen you often—on the stage. I thought your *Lear* was perfectly
magnificent."

Mr. Lewker, who thought so too, made suitable acknowledgment. "I hear
we are to have a major work from your pen shortly," he added graciously.

"Did Clare tell you that? She's a terribly sympathetic person, isn't she?
But not a major work, I fear. Just a plain tale of the sea, with—I'm hoping—
a rather new angle."

"Indeed. With your own demolition exploits as a basis, perhaps?"

Anthony's laugh sounded embarrassed. "In a way, yes. Clare thinks one
should use a background one knows thoroughly. I rather agree. She has a
keen critical sense, you know, and her taste in fiction—"

"Best save your breath," Webhouse threw over his shoulder gruffly. "You'll
need it higher up for something more than booksy talk."

"My wind's a damn' sight better—" began Anthony angrily, and was interrupted by Mr. Lewker with pacific intent.

"A sound Alpine rule," he boomed urbanely. "Rhythm and no talk on the
path."

They went on in a silence that was broken only by the crunch of nailed
boots and a muttered comment from Anthony (which just reached Mr.
Lewker's quick ears) of "Swaggering old ass!"—referring, apparently, to the
unconscious Webhouse. Tansy, absorbed in her responsible position as guide,
was too rapt for conversation. And presently the path, steepening, set the
older members of the party breathing hard. It was mounting steadily across a
rocky shoulder, now sunlit, now shadowed by scowling crags on the left, and
the Vale of Llanberis lay far below and shimmering in heat-haze. Three-
quarters of an hour from the pass brought them to the high saddle above Llyn
Llydaw, whose glittering waters lay in the deep cwm on their left, five hundred feet below. Here, to Mr. Lewker's unspoken relief, Webhouse ordered a
halt, and they lay in the sun chatting desultorily and eating chocolate.

Mr. Lewker gazed across the cwm at the great gray precipices of Lliwedd. In a few hours they would be scrambling along the crest of those distant crags, for Lliwedd is the last "nail" in the Horseshoe of Snowdon; but it was at the sheer rock-walls under the crest that he looked, remembering more than one adventurous climb on those airy buttresses. In the back of his mind hovered a pale remembrance of yesterday's small incidents—Webhouse's unease, the airgun slug, Feckenham's cryptic remark. He recalled, too, a sound of voices raised in anger, heard just as he was dropping off to sleep in his very comfortable bed at Plas Mawr; presumably his host's interview with Sir Henry Lydiate had proved a stormy one. But these things seemed, in the vast blue amphitheater of mountains, as insignificant as the small insects that crawled aimlessly among the mountain grasses.

"Let 'em get ahead." Webhouse's voice broke in on his thoughts. "We'll have rocks coming down on us if we follow too closely."

Two men and a girl, in shorts, had passed them and started up the narrowing shoulder to the foot of Crib Goch. The Red Peak soared above the saddle, over a thousand feet of shattered reddish rock tapering to a sharp point. Tansy, who had been talking eagerly to Anthony, came and flopped down at Mr. Lewker's side. Her blue eyes were shining with excitement.

"We go straight up the rock," she told him, pointing to the peak. "There's a sort of chimney halfway, Uncle Anthony says—won't it be fun? You've done it before, haven't you? I haven't—I've always wanted to, and Auntie Clare says you persuaded Uncle David to let me, so thank you awf'ly. You must be a smasher at persuading, 'cause Mother says Uncle David's awf'ly stubborn."

"I have in my time been considered something of a smashing persuader," returned Mr. Lewker gravely. "Allow me to persuade you to a chunk of fruit-and-nut."

"All right. Have an aniseed ball—they change color when you've sucked for a bit." She sank her voice to a conspirator's whisper. "Have you done any detecting yet?"

"So far I have had small chance of exercising the deductive faculty."

"I s'pose that means 'no,' " Tansy said reprovingly. "Well, I have. I've found out what Uncle David's afraid of. Shall I tell you?"

"Pray do," replied Mr. Lewker, glancing swiftly over his shoulder to where Webhouse was pointing out distant summits to the others.

Tansy put her lips close to his ear. "It's Sir Henry Lydiate. The old gentleman I showed you when we were in your car yesterday."

"Indeed!" murmured Mr. Lewker, rubbing his ear, which tickled. "News of the strangest, lady."

"It was last night. I was excited and couldn't get to sleep, and then Auntie Clare brought someone into the study—it's under my room—and then Uncle

David came up and when they began to talk I knew it was Sir Henry. I couldn't hear words, you know, and anyhow it's rude to listen, but sometimes Uncle David shouted like he does when he gets angry, and once he shouted 'Dashed nonsense'—only not dashed, the other word. I 'spect you know the word I mean."

"Alas, I do. Continue."

"Well, after a bit the study door opened and I heard them come out, and Sir Henry said—quite loudly, not like his usual voice—'I shall fight you, Webhouse,' he said, just like that, 'and it'll be a fight to the death.' Then Uncle David gave a nasty sort of laugh and they clumped off downstairs." She sat back on her heels triumphantly. "So *I* think Uncle David's a bit scared of him, you see, 'cause Sir Henry's been to see him once or twice before and I 'spect he said the same sort of thing."

Mr. Lewker rubbed his chin.

"Ye-es," he said slowly. "But you must understand, Tough, that this talk of fighting is only a figure of—"

"Off we go!" called Anthony. "Where's the guide?"

Tansy sprang up to take her place at the head of the line and Mr. Lewker heaved himself to his feet. The party resumed the ascent of Crib Goch.

Their route was now very much steeper. Rock-strewn turf gave way to bare screes, and screes to steep rock. The backbone of the mountain narrowed and reared until its crags overhead hid the pointed summit. The rock was warm to the grasping hand and the nail-scratches of unnumbered scramblers marked the route. Mr. Lewker, remembering Clare's request that he should look after Tansy (Mrs. Pauncefoot had appeared completely unconcerned about her), had worked himself into second place, following the child closely in case she needed help. Tansy, however, was bent on demonstrating her mountaineering skill, and climbed so fast and well that he had some ado to keep up with her. The halfway chimney (fortunately for Mr. Lewker's girth it was really a slanting ledge) found her waiting at the top with hand outstretched to help him up. Far overhead faint voices sounded, fading completely as the three climbers above them passed the summit. Ten minutes of cat-walking up a gable-ridge of splintered rock, and the two pulled themselves on to the tiny platform of the top, three thousand feet above the sea. Mr. Lewker, breathless, sat down to admire the view while the insatiable Tansy pointed out the perils that lay ahead.

From the summit a knife-edged crest of rock, sheer precipice on one side and roof-like slabs on the other, sagged and rose like a tightrope stretched between the point of Crib Goch and the crumbling rock towers of the pinnacles. Above and far beyond the pinnacles, looming blue and immense, rose Snowdon summit; for the present party, reflected Mr. Lewker, an hour and a half's going away. It was almost noon, and the sun beat down upon his bald head. He knotted the four corners of his handkerchief to make a cap.

"Let's go on," suggested Tansy. "The others are miles and miles behind."

"That," boomed Mr. Lewker, "would not be good mountaineering, Tough. We have reached the hazardous part of our ascent. We collect the party and confer as to our method of assault."

"Oh yes—like Everest." Tansy lay face downwards beside him on the narrow flat slab of the summit, and peered over its edge. "They're coming up, right underneath. I could drop this bit of rock on Uncle David, easily."

"But being a mountaineer, you never drop rocks," Mr. Lewker said hastily, craning to look over her shoulder.

Webhouse, setting his big boots firmly and slowly on the steep rock, was coming up first, with Anthony close behind him and Feckenham a yard or two below. They presented the ludicrous appearance of all human beings seen from overhead. Anthony, as Mr. Lewker had already noted, showed the neat footwork of a practiced climber; but Feckenham, for all his wiry frame and apparent fitness, was clutching every projecting rock for handhold, as any novice might do on a place whence a man could roll for a thousand feet without stopping. They were less than a hundred feet below the summit, and there was room for one man to pass another. Anthony made an impatient spurt and overtook the plodding Webhouse. The words of the older man's sharp rebuke were inaudible, but Mr. Lewker caught a glimpse of Anthony's angry face as he fell back into line. There was more than anger there; the look thrown at Webhouse's broad back was of the bitterest hatred.

The three scrambled one by one to the summit, rather overcrowding the available space. When they had recovered their breath and admired the view, Webhouse announced that he had brought fifty feet of line and suggested that Tansy should rope up with Mr. Lewker. Tansy's immediate protest was supported energetically by Anthony, and—less loudly—by Mr. Lewker.

"Our guide," remarked the latter urbanely, "is as steady a climber as any of us, Webhouse. If I may suggest it, Feckenham might be glad of the rope here. 'He that stands upon a slippery place,' you know."

Feckenham shrugged. "*Ca m'est égal.* I shan't fall off."

"I should damned well think not," Webhouse said with a curl of his thick lips. "All the same," he added, masterfully, "we'll have order and care on this bit. You can go first, Tansy, and you'll go carefully. Lewker, keep close up to her. Feckenham next, then me, then Cattespool. When we get to the first pinnacle we'll go over it—safer than the loose traverse round it."

No one objected to this order, and the traverse of the knife-edge began.

A person having hands, feet, and a reasonably steady head is very unlikely to fall off the Crib Goch knife-edge. All the same, more than one scrambler has fallen to death there, as Mr. Lewker knew; and he kept within arm's length of his charge. But Tansy was on her best mountaineering behavior, and stepped neatly along the tenuous blade of rock without leaning her body into the slope, hanging her weight on her hands, or committing any other of the dangerous sins to which climbing novices are prone. For much of the passage it was possible to tread on footholds below the crest, using the crest itself as a handrail; but there were one or two places where gaps in the hand-rail necessitated a short walk along its flattened crest, and here the eye of the climber looked straight down past his booted right foot into the blue haze of Cwm Glas, while on his left the brown tile-like slabs heeled over to end in invisible crags. Loose rock had been cleared from this high-hung path across space by the passing of many parties, but Crib Goch is built of unsound material. Winter frosts prise away its rusty armor and occasional fragments clatter down its mailed sides. Mr. Lewker experienced a certain relief when Tansy reached the easier ledges under the pinnacle.

This first and tallest of the pinnacles is a massive fortress of rock perched astride the ridge, crenallated and steep-walled. By descending a little, one may pass it by shaley ledges on its western flank, a route favored by scram-blers whose nerves have been shaken by the exposed knife-edge. The climb over its top is easy and a good deal sounder, though more airy. Mr. Lewker, after a backward glance to where Feckenham's slow progress was delaying the others, followed Tansy up the thirty feet of simple hand-and-foot climb-ing to the top of the pinnacle, along its jagged crest, and easily down into the deep V-shaped gap between it and the next pinnacle. Here they sat down on the jammed boulders that bridge the gap to wait for the others.

"Well, I didn't roll, did I?" demanded Tansy proudly.

"You did most excellent well, Tough," returned Mr. Lewker. "I see you in twenty years' time, the first lady climber to stand atop of Everest."

"That'd be smashing. I'd have to be awf'ly good on snow, though, as well, wouldn't I?—Here's Mr. Feckenham, look."

Feckenham's blond head appeared on the skyline above them. His body came into view, silhouetted against the blue sky, and he climbed cautiously down into the gap. Webhouse followed him.

"I got a ciné shot of you two on the ridge," he said as he reached the bridged boulders. "Now I want one of this bit. I've told Cattespool to wait until I call him. Get one of him coming down to the gap."

He took a small ciné camera from the pocket of his rucksack. Mr. Lewker got to his feet.

"Shall I go on with Tansy?" he inquired.

"Yes. I'll have a shot of you going up the next pinnacle first, though." He squinted through the viewfinder. "Tansy, you go up a bit. Follow her, Lewker. Feckenham, I want you looking up at them from below."

The second pinnacle was a short column of rock whose wall-like face presented a ladder of large and well-worn holds. Tansy started up like a lamplighter with Mr. Lewker at her heels. Behind them the whirring of the camera mechanism began. Before it had run for five seconds a rapid succession of other sounds broke in—the crash of rock on rock, a yell from Webhouse, a thud and the metallic rattle of the falling camera. Mr. Lewker, halfway up the wall, looked down quickly.

He was in time to see a jagged rock the size of a football strike the bridged boulders of the gap and go bounding into the steep gully below. Webhouse had dropped the camera and flung himself sideways, catching his foot in the uneven rocks and pitching awkwardly on his shoulder perilously near the edge of the gap.

Feckenham hurried to him. Mr. Lewker, telling Tansy to go on to the top and sit tight there, climbed swiftly down. As he reached the bottom Anthony Cattespool's face peered down from the top of the first pinnacle.

"Ahoy, below there!" he shouted cheerfully. "What's going on? Do I come yet?"

"You had better come down," Mr. Lewker told him, and went to where Feckenham was helping Webhouse to his feet.

The big man had lost some of his color, and there was blood on his face from a rock-graze, but he was otherwise unhurt.

"That ruddy rock missed me by an inch," he gasped, and relieved his feelings with a flood of invective that made Mr. Lewker thankful that Tansy was out of earshot.

"Steady on—you're not dead," Feckenham said, somewhat sharply.

Anthony, stepping neatly down the holds, joined them.

"What happened?" he demanded lightly. "Webhouse trip over his feet or something?"

Mr. Lewker, watching Webhouse's face, expected an explosion. It did not come. Webhouse's big jaw tightened and he seemed to control himself.

"A large rock fell while I was using the camera," he said quietly enough. "If I hadn't jumped, it'd have landed on my skull. Did you dislodge it?"

"Good lord!" said Anthony perfunctorily. "No, I didn't send it down. I was well below the crest, waiting for your call."

Webhouse dabbed his grazed cheek and said nothing. There was a little pause. Feckenham stooped and rescued the ciné camera from a hole in the rocks.

"Lens smashed," he commented. "Bad luck."

"Maybe someone loosened up that rock climbing down," said Webhouse gruffly. He took the broken camera and crammed it into his rucksack. "Well, lucky it was no worse."

"It was indeed," agreed Mr. Lewker, feeling that someone should display sympathy. "Doubtless you are feeling a little shaken. I have a small flask of brandy in my—"

"I'm all right." His tone was rough, almost rude. "We'll go on."

The four men climbed in silence over the second pinnacle and rejoined the impatient Tansy.

The whole incident had not occupied more than two minutes. When, twenty-four hours later, its every detail had become of vital importance, Mr. Lewker's abnormal faculties of observation and memory—the chief weapons, he sometimes claimed, in his detective armory—were able to recall it perfectly. In the next few hours, with the sunlit spaces of the high hills all about him, he ceased to think about its possible significance altogether.

The others made no further mention of the falling rock. When they halted for lunch, halfway up the scalloped backbone of Crib y Ddisgl which joins Crib Goch to Snowdon, everyone, including David Webhouse, was in noisy good spirits. On a weathering rock-ridge, after all, the occasional dislodgment of a fragment is no very unlikely occurrence; and had it not been for what he had seen and heard earlier Mr. Lewker would not have given it a second thought. Probably Tansy's presence deterred any discussion of the matter. The child was so obviously in the seventh heaven of youthful bliss that it would have been criminal to spoil her enjoyment. She led them ecstatically over the tourist-haunted summit, down the loose shale of the upper Watkin Path, and up again to cross the triple peak of Lliwedd. Skipping goatlike on the narrow track, the deepening sunshine glinting on her golden plaits, she seemed untiring and insatiable of delight. The four elders scrambled less agilely behind her, rather (thought Mr. Lewker sentimentally) like pilgrims striving vainly to overtake their lost youth. When, after more than eight hours on the ridges, they came down the last rocky slope of the Horseshoe and struck the broad track descending from Llyn Llydaw, Tansy was still in the lead.

Mr. Lewker, dropping behind to light his pipe, was joined by Anthony, and they jogged down the track behind the others in the evening sunlight, chatting desultorily about books and plays. It was when they rounded a corner and came in sight of the Daimler parked just below them that Anthony suddenly changed the subject.

"Odd about that rock falling on the pinnacles," he said casually. "Or don't you think so?"

"Rocks do fall in such places," returned Mr. Lewker noncommittally.

"As you say. Did you see it fall?"

Something in Anthony's tone made Mr. Lewker turn to glance at him. The narrow hazel eyes that met his—and then fell quickly—held an emotion that might be curiosity or anxiety; or, perhaps, fear.

"No," he said. "None of us did, except Webhouse. I turned in time to see it hit the rock just beside him."

"Ah. Then it was a pretty near miss, as he said?"

"I imagine so."

Anthony was silent for a moment. Then:

"If I'd sent it down," he said reflectively, "I wouldn't have missed."

"Come on!" shouted Tansy as they walked up to the car. "We're late—and I'm hungry. Wasn't it a lovely climb?"

CHAPTER V

MURDERER'S NIGHT

Sir Henry Lydiate of Plas Bach, who at Mr. Lewker's first glimpse had reminded him of the White Knight in *Alice*, resembled the eccentric cavalier only in appearance. He had the bald head, long aristocratic nose, and drooping white mustachios of Tenniel's illustration; but there the similarity ended. Instead of the "large mild eyes" of the inventive warrior, Sir Henry possessed a pair of choleric blue ones, and the white mustache did not hide a jutting and obstinate lower lip. His manners were those of a vanished age. He wore a velvet jacket and a neat bow tie, and at dinner his conversation with Tansy was even statelier than Mr. Lewker's.

Tansy had been allowed to stay up to dinner as a special treat. But as she twice fell asleep during the second course she was carried off to bed by Mrs. Pauncefoot, too tired to make more than a faint protest. Sir Henry, who had been listening courteously to Anthony Cattespool's exposition of the art of novel-writing, turned to Mr. Lewker, who was seated on his left.

"Mr. Lewker," he said in his high creaky voice, "it gave me great pleasure to learn that you are to join the company of Knights Bachelor."

The actor-manager thanked him. He had not failed to notice the emphasis on the "you" and the flicker of the choleric eyes towards Webhouse, who had his head almost in his plate.

"Not," continued Sir Henry, raising a skeletal hand gracefully, "because of your theatrical labors, though those, I am sure, are admirable, but because I chance to know of your remarkable doings during the war. Personal bravery, sir, was the original fount of knighthood."

Reference to his exploits behind the enemy lines was the only form of praise that Mr. Lewker found embarrassing. He made deprecatory noises, aware that his ears were going red.

"Was it really?" said Clare, leaning forward on his other side. "That's out of date now, surely, Sir Henry."

The antique silver candelabra on the table had been lit, for dinner was later than usual and it was already dusk. The soft light lent rare charm to her beauty, and it was obvious that Anthony Cattespool thought so. Anthony had hurried up the cliff path to his cottage as soon as they returned from the climb, and had come back very spruce in dinner jacket and soft shirt. From across the table his narrow hazel eyes watched the girl as she tilted her dark head to listen to Sir Henry.

"In a sense you are right, dear lady," he was saying, "and alas that it is so, say I. Yet the title of knight is still the most ancient known to us. I am proud that I am a knight bachelor—though of all knights the most undeserving—rather than a member of one of the Orders."

"I should have thought a K.C.B. would be rather natty," said Anthony, winking surreptitiously at Clare.

"No, sir," said Sir Henry with some sternness. "Nor is a baronetcy so honorable a title. The knight bachelor, you must know, was so designated to indicate that the honor was awarded to him personally, for an act of great courage, in which his offspring could take no claim. Unhappily, it is nowadays given to persons whose services have been of a less chivalrous nature."

"Engineers and such," drawled Feckenham, toying with his wineglass.

Mrs. Pauncefoot's rasping tones forestalled Sir Henry's reply. She had returned from putting Tansy to bed, and was being loudly critical of Dilys the maid's method of bringing in the sweet. Sir Henry pulled at his mustache until she had finished, and then resumed, addressing Feckenham.

"Pray do not misunderstand me, sir. I am very far from depreciating your deserts, which I dare say may more than merit a baronetcy. What I maintain is that knight bachelorhood should be restricted—"

Mr. Lewker ceased to listen to him. He was placed facing the tall windows that looked out over the terrace to the twilit garden. The bent figure of the old gardener, Cutpursey, passed slowly across the terrace with the spaniel Flora gamboling at his heels. In the greenish radiance which was all that remained of daylight the old man looked—with his bald head and snowy fringe—like some Troll of the Northland or one of Snow White's seven dwarfs. Mr. Lewker remembered the airgun slug. Why, he wondered idly, had David Webhouse not asked Cutpursey about that slug? Did he, after all, suspect the gardener of firing it at him?

Sir Henry was finishing his oration.

"—and a knight should still hold himself bound by his ancient obligation to succor the weak, to champion the poor, to act as protector"—he made two little bows towards Clare and Mrs. Pauncefoot—"of the fair sex."

"Oh, come now, Sir Henry," Anthony laughed. "A hundred and fifty years ago Burke said the age of chivalry was gone."

"Burke, sir, was a Whig and an Irishman, and a liar on both counts. There are still, I trust, causes needing a courageous champion."

David Webhouse looked up suddenly and made a vulgar sound with his lips.

"Lost causes, eh?" he sneered. "Put on the rusty armor and go round look-ing for 'em—that's your line, ain't it, Lydiate?"

Mr. Lewker eyed Webhouse keenly. The big man gave the impression of being more than a little drunk; but Mr. Lewker was certain that he had taken only one glass of hock. His preoccupation with his food had kept him out of the conversation so far, but now he was flushed and argumentative. Sir Henry, his jutting white brows very slightly raised, turned to face him.

"No worthy cause is lost while there is a man—even an old man—left to defend it," he said with dignity, "as I am sure you will agree, Webhouse."

"Agree my Aunt Fanny," retorted the other loudly. "You're living in a democracy, if you'd try to realize it. Don't stick up your sentimental ideals and try to ram them——"

"Dai!" interrupted Clare apprehensively. "You ought to be too tired to argue," she added, trying to catch his eye.

"No more tired than you are," vociferated Webhouse. "You'll see me do-ing my evening stroll as usual before I turn in." He turned on Sir Henry again. "Just because you and a few sentimentalists like you hate change like poison, you're prepared to rob working folk of the comfort they deserve. And that's your worthy cause."

"I understood," said the old man stiffly, "that we had agreed to avoid discussion of this matter before your guests."

"Oh, run away if you like. Ever see a sentimentalist run? It's always away from the truth."

Sir Henry's thin cheek was reddening. "I have never been accused of run-ning away, sir."

"Please, Dai," said Clare anxiously.

Webhouse ignored her. He set his great hands flat on the tablecloth, jin-gling the glasses.

"No—because you fool 'em," he jeered. "You're the high and mighty St. George and we progressives are the dragon, eh? Well, hang on to your horse and your privileges—you won't have 'em long. Privileges are for the man who works for 'em, not for the mugger who plants his bottom on 'em be-cause his father owned land."

Sir Henry turned to Clare, who was looking frightened, and began to talk about the cultivation of roses. But Webhouse persisted more loudly than ever.

"I didn't swagger round with a lance to get my knighthood. I worked for it, see? And I suppose you'll say I'm not a worthy member of your precious brotherhood, eh?"

Sir Henry got slowly to his feet. He stood very straight and his lower lip jutted ominously.

"You are not a member of it, sir," he said distinctly, "and if I could prevent it you never would be." He turned to Clare. "You will graciously excuse me,

Mrs. Webhouse? I must be going."

Rather to Mr. Lewker's surprise Clare rose to the occasion admirably.

"Of course," she said in matter-of-fact tones, rising and going to the door with Sir Henry. "Did you bring a torch? It isn't really dark yet, but if you go back by the cliff path—"

The door closed behind them, leaving an awkward silence. Feckenham lounged in his chair with his faintly unpleasant grin. Anthony Cattespool was glaring angrily at Webhouse, who sat with a sneer on his thick lips as he poured hock into his glass. Anna Pauncefoot, grimly disapproving, began to collect plates with a clashing noise.

"Curse not thine enemies," she said tersely. "If I were you, David, I'd leave the room and cool my head."

David Webhouse drained his glass and stood up. He had the grace to look slightly ashamed of himself.

"Maybe I was a bit hard on the old fool," he growled. "I'll take your advice, Anna—stroll down to the lodge and back."

There was no unsteadiness in his step as he went out. Mrs. Pauncefoot rang the bell and told them that coffee would be in the lounge. Clare, looking worried, was waiting for them when they entered the drawing-room.

"I'm so sorry, everybody," she said. "They *will* argue, and they both feel so strongly about it—"

"Never mind, Clare." Anthony went across to sit beside her. "We're not worrying."

"Quite entertaining, actually," drawled Feckenham, handing round coffee as Mrs. Pauncefoot poured it out.

Clare looked apprehensively at Mr. Lewker. "But in front of our guest—"

Mr. Lewker waved a podgy hand in deprecation.

"Pray do not discompose yourself, Mrs. Webhouse," he boomed reassuringly. "I wish only to be enlightened as to the matter upon which our friends feel so strongly."

"Oh, I forgot you didn't know," Clare said. "It's Dai's hydroelectric bill. You see, the bill's to give the electricity authority powers to take any steps they like for increasing electric supply."

"That means using all the Snowdon valleys for power production," put in Anthony.

"Yes. And Sir Henry's the president of the Protest Association, Mr. Lewker. He used to own lots of land round here, and he's given most of it to the National Trust, so naturally he doesn't want power stations and things dotted all over it."

"Don't see why," said Feckenham.

Anthony put down his cup and swung round to face him.

"You don't? Good lord, man, you've seen the place—you saw Llyn Llydaw today. Imagine a whacking concrete power station stuck in that lovely valley. It'd be perfectly foul."

"Good concrete building improves any site," returned the engineer.

"Rot. And it isn't only the buildings. Pylons, pipes, wires, roads—the whole character of the place spoiled."

There was a scrabbling noise at the sill of one of the open windows, and the spaniel Flora flopped into the room and ran joyfully to her mistress. Clare picked her up and kissed her.

"That dog's been burying something again," snapped Mrs. Pauncefoot. "You'll get dirt all over you, Clare."

Flora's brown muzzle was indeed covered with clinging soil, much of which she rapidly transferred to Clare's dress.

"She's a clever, funny Flora-flora," murmured Clare. "A clever, funny Flora-flora. A clever, funny—"

"We could do with electric light here," interrupted Mrs. Pauncefoot briskly. "Oil-lamps are messy."

Charles Feckenham, subsiding still further into his armchair, nodded at Anthony.

"Voice of the people," he said lazily. "I agree with Webhouse. This country's overpopulated—no room for sentimentalists. Got to mobilize all our assets if we want to raise standards of living."

"Well, and isn't natural beauty an asset?" Anthony retorted swiftly. "Just because you can't measure it in units you seem to think it's worthless. There's not all that much of it left in this—as you say—overpopulated country. What's still unspoiled needs hanging on to if this nation's to preserve its soul."

"What about its eyesight?" murmured Feckenham. "Eyes are the windows of the soul, I'm told."

Clare put Flora down and wagged a slim finger at her cousin.

"You're just arguing for argument's sake, Charles. Dai thinks he'll get his bill through eventually," she added to Mr. Lewker, "and I believe Sir Henry's afraid he will—that's what makes him so fierce about it. I'm rather on Sir Henry's side myself."

"It is the old battle between material and spiritual values," observed the actor-manager didactically. "One can be measured, the other cannot, as Cattespool has pointed out. How then are we to weigh one against the other when a conflict arises?" The expressive voice that had thrilled so many audiences was getting into its stride; Abercrombie Lewker was enjoying himself. "Power, not truth, is the goal of modern energies. The light by which the nations live is electric light. Yet all experience shows—"

He stopped short in midsentence. The room had shaken. Immediately followed the thud of an explosion and a crashing as of masonry falling at a little distance from the house.

The other occupants of the room sat for a moment completely motionless and silent. Their eyes, which had been turned to Mr. Lewker as he was speaking, remained fixed on him—Clare's startled, Anthony's narrowed and keen, Feckenham's expressionless. Mrs. Pauncefoot's black and beady. Anthony was the first to move and speak.

"Sounds as if Cutpursey's shot at a rabbit and started an avalanche," he said lightly.

"Wasn't a gun," said Feckenham, getting to his feet. "Let's go and see."

He moved towards the door. Cattespool and Mr. Lewker followed him, the latter pausing to remark that the noise might have awakened Tansy.

"Yes," Clare said quickly. "I'll go up to her."

The three men passed through the hall and out on to the terrace. The night was as still as the previous one, but a haze of clouds was darkening the luminous sky overhead. Feckenham, who had picked up the powerful electric torch from the hall table, halted and switched on the long beam.

"Couldn't gauge where it came from," he said.

"It was behind the house, I think," said Anthony.

"Let us listen for a moment," suggested Mr. Lewker.

The night was full of small noises—the pulse of the river in the valley, the far voices of sheep, the sleepy twitter of birds. The plashing of the waterfall behind Plas Mawr sounded, to Mr. Lewker's ear, oddly muffled.

"Is there a path to the foot of the fall?" he asked.

"This way." Anthony's voice was not quite steady. "I'll have that torch, Feckenham."

He led them at a fast walk round to the back of the house and plunged up a tunnellike path through rhododendrons.

Mr. Lewker, bringing up the rear, did not consciously make any inference coupling their present quest with anything that had gone before; his normally clear mind refused to anticipate—as though it had decided to close itself to the past. He hurried on up the steepening path, stumbling now and then because Feckenham's shadowy figure in front of him obscured the flicker of the torch, feeling in his leg- white beam shone on fir boles; the sound of the waterfall was close at hand. Mr. Lewker cannoned into Feckenham, who had halted abruptly. Anthony had stopped and was swinging his torch beam to and fro through the firs on their right.

"Thought I saw someone sneaking in the wood," he said. And then— "There he goes! Hey, you! What's happened?"

There was no response. Mr. Lewker, peering and listening, saw only the boles of trees and heard only the plash of the fall.

"See him?" Feckenham demanded.

"Only for a second, a dark shape with whitish upper-works. Do we give chase?"

"I think not," said Mr. Lewker. "We have nearly reached the fall, have we not?"

"Yes." Anthony directed the torch-beam ahead. "Here's the stream—bit boggy here. And—good lord!"

They had stepped across the brook and out of the trees. A yard or two away rose the cone of scree and rubble which, twenty-four hours earlier, Mr. Lewker had looked down on from the wooden bridge on the cliff path. The light of the torch was weakened and diffused by a fine white dust which floated above the rocks. But it showed the foot of the rock-face, and the black opening that was the bottom of the ravine; it showed the runnels of water sparkling down the fan of debris, trickling now among newly fallen fragments whose pallid facets caught the beam eerily; and it showed the wooden bridge, buckled and upended, lying among the boulders below the ravine.

The beam crept downward a few feet, and stopped.

"Good—*lord*!" said Anthony again, but in a different tone; his voice, and the torch he held, wavered together.

"May I?" said Mr. Lewker, and taking the torch clambered gingerly up the boulder-slope.

He climbed a score of feet only before halting to bend over the thing that lay crumpled there between two jagged rocks. The others clambered up beside him.

"It's Webhouse?" jerked Feckenham.

"Is he—much hurt?" Anthony gulped foolishly.

Mr. Lewker, with a lack of manners unusual with him, turned the torch-beam full in each of their faces for a second before switching it off.

"Aye, past all surgery," he answered gently.

Feckenham swore, revealing jangled nerves. "Told him that bloody bridge was unsafe," he added as if in apology.

"Ah, yes," said Mr. Lewker. "But there was an explosion, you know. Look."

He switched on the torch again, directing it on the dead man, and heard Anthony swallow convulsively.

The body of David Webhouse had fallen a hundred feet on to a steep rock-slope and rolled down it for twenty more before wedging itself between the boulders; it was naturally not a pleasant sight. The face was unrecognizable, and even the head was only to be identified by a few inches of thick gray hair. It was obvious that the neck was broken. But the torch revealed other injuries. The lower part of both trouser legs had been torn away, leaving tattered ends of cloth, and it could be seen that the dead man's right foot was missing. The left foot was present, but it was shoeless and the leg below the knee was much lacerated. Mr. Lewker bent forward to look more closely at the lacerations.

"Splinters?"

Feckenham's voice was hard and controlled. Mr. Lewker straightened himself and stepped back, forgetting the instability of his foothold. A loose stone turned beneath his foot and he saved his balance by a swift clutch at Anthony's shoulder. The young man was shaking uncontrollably.

"Yes," said Mr. Lewker, switching off the torch and replying to Feckenham's question. "Splinters, deeply embedded." He glanced at the luminous dial of his watch. "One minute past ten. We may postulate five minutes to ten as the time of death. I fancy one of you had better tell me how this happened."

"What d'you mean?" Feckenham demanded sharply.

"Why, that in the matter of explosions I am no expert, and there has been an explosion. You, as an engineer, or Cattespool, with his war experience, may be able to hazard an opinion as to the cause of that explosion."

"Oh," said Feckenham, "that. Can't say. At a guess, bridge was mined in some way. Blew up as Webhouse crossed it. Blew off his foot and blew splinters into his legs. And that means—" He checked himself. "What's your opinion, Cattespool?"

"Oh, hell—what's it matter?" Anthony said shrilly. "Do we have to stand here chatting? Can't we—can't we get him down to the house? Or get a—a doctor, or something?"

"Or the police," Feckenham suggested harshly.

"Shall we return to the path?" said Mr. Lewker, shining the torch down the slope.

They stumbled down to the edge of the firs again. A small wind whispered and muttered in the feathery branches, adding its voice to the ceaseless chatter of the waterfall. The three men halted on more level ground.

"We have two things to do," Mr. Lewker said, almost briskly. "The news of this has to be broken—and as you, Feckenham, are Mrs. Webhouse's cousin—"

"I'll tell Clare," said Anthony quickly.

"Very well. And Mrs. Pauncefoot also. It would be well to ensure that Tansy knows nothing of what has happened until tomorrow, when she will have to be told. The second and more urgent duty is to inform the police. Plas Mawr is on the telephone, I think?"

"Yes," said Anthony dully. "The county police at Caernarvon, I suppose. That's fifteen miles by road from here."

"Feckenham, will you ring them at once? Tell them exactly what has happened, that the death may or may not have been caused accidentally, that the body is not being touched until their arrival."

"Right."

"After that, you had better seek out the gardener and the maid and warn them not to leave the premises. You do not mind my taking charge, I trust?"

"Course not. You're pretty thick with the arm of the law, according to the papers." There was a suspicion of a sneer in Feckenham's voice. "What are you going to do?"

"I shall remain in the neighborhood of the body," said Mr. Lewker. "I will retain the torch."

"Look out for the bloke Cattespool saw," advised Feckenham. "Come on, Cattespool."

The two hurried away down the path. The sound of their footsteps and the rustle of bushes diminished and ceased altogether, leaving only the impersonal conversation of the rising wind and the waterfall.

Mr. Lewker, left alone, tucked the torch under his arm and filled and lit his pipe. As the match flared, making a temporary haven of light in the uneasy darkness, he reflected that the sneaking figure in the wood, whom Anthony (and Anthony alone) had seen, might be watching him. The thought did not greatly worry him. Mr. Lewker was feeling already the promptings of those instincts which urged him to find out, to get to the bottom of things, to strip away the layers of human idiosyncrasy and concealment until the naked truth lay revealed.

That Webhouse had—in a fashion—sought to enlist his protection did little to add to this urging. He had not liked the man, nor did he regard himself as in any way responsible for his death. It occurred to him now that no one at the dinner table that evening had liked Webhouse—except, presumably, his wife. How would Clare take the news which Anthony must now be breaking to her, he wondered? Strange that the word murder had not been uttered by any of the three who had found the body. Yet murder it must be, for an accident resulting in the blowing-up of the footbridge just as Webhouse was crossing it was scarcely conceivable. And if Webhouse had been murdered, then a number of other incidents pointed—

Mr. Lewker collected his wandering thoughts resolutely. The time for weighing evidence was not yet, still less was it in order to speculate. The night wind smelt of rain, and rain might obliterate vital evidence. He tapped out his pipe and, switching on the torch, proceeded to make what examination he could of the scene of the crime.

First he climbed back up the rubble slope to the body. A second and more careful examination—without touching it—yielded no new fact, and he went slowly on, sweeping the debris with his torch beam, to where the bridge lay drunkenly a dozen feet higher. The wooden handrail was smashed and one of its supports missing; the two heavy planks that formed the footing were both buckled in the center, and the ends that had rested on the path ascending from Plas Mawr were torn and splintered. Mr. Lewker spent a little time in examining those ends, before turning his attention to the handrail. It told him nothing of interest. He began to look for the missing handrail support, casting to left and right of the fallen bridge with the probe of his torch beam, and came—with a start, for he had forgotten it—upon David Webhouse's right foot. He built a hurried cairn of stones to mark its position and continued his search. He found the handrail support almost at the top of the rubble slope, in the mouth of the ravine. The spray from the little waterfall spattered on his cheek as he bent over the four-foot wooden stanchion. The support had been torn from rail and plank but was otherwise intact; judging from the lashing of greenish cord bound tightly round its base with seven or eight turns, a split in the wood had been suspected and roughly repaired at some past time. About nine inches of the cord hung from the lashing and its end was frayed. Peering closely at it, Mr. Lewker saw that it was a woven nylon line of the type used for parachute cord. He picked his way slowly down the slope again, still searching the dark pockets between the rocks but finding nothing more. The white pencil of light passed quickly over the broken and tattered thing that had been David Webhouse, knight bachelor designate, and left it to the darkness.

Down on the path once more, Mr. Lewker behaved rather oddly. He coughed loudly, struck a match, and held it to a tobaccoless pipe. Then he walked somewhat noisily down the path between the rhododendrons with the torch beam swinging carelessly before him. He reached and turned the corner of the house, marked time with diminishing heaviness of tread, and switched off the torch. Two minutes later he was squatting motionless at the foot of the rubble slope, having retraced his steps with the absolute noiselessness of a prowling cat.

For twenty minutes he remained there, a mere patch of blacker darkness under the fringe of firs; but the visitor he had invited did not come. Whoever had slunk away through the wood at their approach either had nothing to return for or was too wary to risk return. Mr. Lewker sighed and struck a match, this time applying it to a full pipe.

It was exactly eleven o'clock by his watch when the sound of cars coming up the Plas Mawr drive fell on his ear. He stood up stiffly, feeling suddenly very tired. He had, after all, taken his thirteen stone to the summit of the highest mountain in England and Wales that day, and by no easy route; mind and body demanded rest. He greeted the advent of Inspector Evans and his four men with relief.

Inspector Evans, as his quick response to Feckenham's phone call proved, was no time waster. He was a small bright-eyed Welshman, chary of words but brisk in action. For the next hour he acted with decision and rapidity, while Mr. Lewker remained a passive and approving spectator. Flashlight photographs of the body … all yours now, doctor … broken neck, yes indeed … marks of explosion … bring that stretcher … statements from all members of the household …

Mr. Lewker caught a brief glimpse of Clare Webhouse as she went into the small library where Inspector Evans and his sergeant were taking the statements. Clare's face was pale and drawn, but she seemed composed. In the drawing roomAnthony Cattespool and Charles Feckenham sat glumly, turning the pages of back numbers of *Punch* without a smile. Feckenham spoke only once, to Mr. Lewker sitting like a pipe-smoking Buddha in an armchair.

"Can't find Cutpursey. Lodge's empty and no one's seen him."

The big clock in the hall struck midnight. A few minutes later Inspector Evans put his head into the drawing roomand beckoned Mr. Lewker to come out.

"I've been on the phone to the Chief Constable, sir," he said when they were both out in the hall. He appeared a trifle crestfallen. "The C.C. insists on calling in the Yard. He'll be telephoning now, indeed. He tells me, sir, that you're known at the Yard."

"That is true, Inspector."

"Well, sir. I'm leaving a constable here and reporting back to Caernarvon now. The corpse and the—um—fragment have been removed. If this man Cutpursey should turn up, sir, I'd be obliged if you'd phone me at Caernarvon."

He departed briskly. Before the sound of the police car and the ambulance had died away Mr. Lewker was busy at the telephone. His business took him twenty minutes and involved the rousing from sleep of Assistant Commissioner Sir Frederick Claybury, but he got what he wanted. Five minutes afterwards he was in bed and composing himself to slumber with the aid of a favourite book; and sleep, that deep sleep that makes the night seem no more than a fleeting moment, came quickly.

It was nearly nine o'clock of a dull morning when he stirred, awakened by the sound of a car pulling up on the terrace. He was at the window in time to see Detective-Inspector George Grimmett climb stiffly out of the rear seat.

CHAPTER VI

GRIMMETT TAKES OVER

"Well now, sir," said Detective-Inspector Grimmett, wiping his sandy mustache, "this is very snug, so it is."

He was sitting with Mr. Lewker at the small table in the library, whither Dilys the maid had brought breakfast for two. This arrangement was by Mr. Lewker's request, for he had known and worked with George Grimmett in those dark days at the beginning of the war when the alliance of the Fifth

Column in Britain with the criminal gangs was threatening the heart of the country. They had met again, by chance, in the affair that had been called by the newspapers The Youth Hostel Murders, and it was Mr. Lewker's doing that his old friend was at Plas Mawr now. The actor-manager watched him with affection as he poured himself a fourth cup of coffee.

Grimmett was not unlike Mr. Lewker in shape. He was stocky and broad-shouldered, and almost exactly the same height as Mr. Lewker. But in every other point of appearance he was different—fresh-colored instead of pale, blue-eyed instead of black, and angular at the places where Mr. Lewker curved. His bristle of sandy hair and his red mustache, which was horizontally short but vertically rather long, gave him the look of an old-fashioned drill sergeant. The countrified simplicity of his face concealed, as Mr. Lewker had reason to know, a capacity for dogged hard work and an exceptional shrewdness.

"Very snug indeed," he repeated, beaming round him at the bookshelves that lined the little room.

"And in what sense, Grimm," boomed Mr. Lewker, "do you find this affair snug?"

"Why, sir, here we are, so to speak." The inspector raised his hand and held up stubby fingers one by one. "There's a first-class murder—victim in the public eye. There's no fiddlefaddle about time of death and alibis—seemingly, anyhow. There's a nice fresh method of killing which they don't work down in London. And there's you here on the spot to tell me all about the suspect or suspects."

"You do me too much credit, good my lord. Grimm, I arrived at Plas Mawr just forty hours ago. Except for Webhouse, whom I met twelve years ago, I knew no one."

Grimmett nodded. "But I know you, sir. You've noticed a thing or two, I'll wager. What made the county police bring in the Yard so early, now?"

"Pass the marmalade, if you please, and if you have left any. Thank you. I fancy one reason may be that three of the persons concerned are in the Birthday Honors List."

"Aye, I'd thought of that," said Grimmett. "This case will tickle the press lads, not a doubt of it. Three oncoming Sirs in the house and one of 'em murdered. You'd be due up at the Palace in a day or two, I reckon?"

"In three days from now," agreed Mr. Lewker. "Or rather, let us say, in forty-eight hours I leave for the capital. That is our limit, Grimmett—pray forgive the imperfect rhyme—since the appointment is one I do not care to miss."

Grimmett's china-blue eyes opened wide. Then he chuckled and pushed back his chair.

"Solution in two days," he said, standing up. "Well, I hope we can make it, so I do. Best get started."

"Did you contrive to sleep on the way here?"

"Aye, a bit. Sergeant Pitt's a wonder at the wheel—two hundred and forty miles in seven and a half hours, and smooth as silk all the way."

"Does Sergeant Pitt know anything about explosives?" inquired Mr. Lewker.

"He does. The A.C. detailed him, as you asked." The inspector grinned widely. "Sir Frederick's language was a mite flowery, so to speak, when he rang my office. Caught me just as I was leaving and told me you'd pulled him out of bed to blackmail him. Was that so, sir?"

"Nothing of the kind, Grimm. I merely said I would tell the Lord Chamberlain that one of his new K.C.B.'s kept a scrapbook of low limericks, unless he put you on this case. And now, what is our program?"

Grimmett passed a hand over his square chin.

"A shave first," he said. "Evans told me on the phone he'd be here at tenthirty with the statements. When I've seen those I'll get you to show me round, sir, and then we'll get down to brass tacks, if that suits you. By the by, I understand there's one of the household missing. Any sign of him?"

"You mean Cutpursey, the gardener. He inhabits the lodge at the drive gates. The constable Inspector Evans left here tells me there is no one at the lodge this morning, and Dilys—she is the maid—has seen nothing of him near the house."

"Aha. Is there any reason to—but that can wait until my whiskers are off. I like to start clean on dirty business."

Having shown Detective-Inspector Grimmett the way to the bathroom, Mr. Lewker returned to the hall. He was not anxious to meet the Plas Mawr folk at the moment. Clare had not come down from her room, Mrs. Pauncefoot was in the kitchen, and Feckenham was in the drawing roomwith Anthony Cattespool, who had slept at Plas Mawr. Mr. Lewker went out of the front door into the gray still morning and paused to fill his pipe and sniff the air, which was cool and fresh after the light rain of the night. The hills across the valley were hidden beneath low-hanging mists. From somewhere down by the river came the halting song of a cuckoo.

"Hallo," said a small and sober voice behind him.

He turned to find Tansy, hands behind back and heels together like a modern Alice, regarding him with very round blue eyes.

"Hallo," he returned cautiously.

There was a short pause. Mr. Lewker, for once at a loss, cudgeled his brains for a suitable opening. What attitude ought a middle-aged guest to adopt towards the eleven-year-old child of a household whose head has just been murdered? He had rejected in turn the Heavily Sympathetic, the Chin-Uppish, and the Talk-As-If-Nothing-Has-Happened, when Tansy came to his aid.

"Does it hurt when you break your neck?" she asked earnestly.

Mr. Lewker hastily rallied his conversational forces.

"No, Tough, no," he replied, relief lending emphasis to his words. "You feel no pain at all. Why do you ask?"

Tansy sighed satisfaction. "Well, you see, I asked Dilys, and she said it was breaking his neck killed Uncle David, and if he didn't feel it it's not so bad, is it? Mr. Cutpursey says rabbits don't feel it when he breaks their necks, so if Uncle David didn't I shan't mind so much."

"Oh!" Mr. Lewker was a trifle shocked. "But you are sorry he was killed, are you not?"

"Let's walk up and down, shall we?" suggested Tansy. "I don't like standing—it makes thinking harder."

They began to walk along the terrace, Mr. Lewker with his hands clasped behind his back and Tansy beside him in an exactly similar posture, rather like Dr. Johnson and Boswell.

"I'm sort of sorry, but not *very* sorry," Tansy continued, frowning intensely; she was clearly laboring to be honest with herself. "I'm sorry it had to be such a nasty sort of dying, but I don't feel I want to cry, or anything. I told Mother, and she was angry and said I ought to pretend to be sorry anyhow. Ought I?"

"Well—I think, Tough, you must consider other people a little. Your aunt will be very sad, for instance, and when she is with you it would be best to show that you are sorry, too."

"Oh, I don't think Auntie Clare will be very sad," returned Tansy with confidence. "He was awfully nasty to her sometimes, you see—same as he was to Hilda. I 'spect she'll soon marry Uncle Anthony, anyhow," she added reassuringly.

Mr. Lewker found nothing to say to this blunt realism.

"Mother says Uncle David won't go to heaven," Tansy went on meditatively, "and I *am* sorry about that. Still, if they did send him there, it'd be awf'ly awkward really—because of all the swear words he'd use. So perhaps it's all for the best."

"I see what you mean," said Mr. Lewker gravely.

They turned at the end of the terrace and began to pace back again. Tansy kept silence for a few steps. Then:

"Uncle David was murdered, wasn't he?" she said suddenly.

"Now who told you that?" wondered Mr. Lewker.

"Oh, no one, only I heard them saying they'd better keep it from me, so I got it out of Dilys—she can't keep secrets, and the policeman told her. I saw that gingery-colored man come in the car this morning. Dilys says he's a detective, but he wasn't chewing anything and he took his hat off when he came into the house and he smiled at me and said 'Good morning, miss'—so I wondered."

Mr. Lewker began to perceive that he need not have worried about his companion's youthful vulnerability. Films and radio had made Tansy familiar with the externals at least of homicide and its resultant routine. He explained why Inspector Grimmett had come to Plas Mawr and why he failed to conform to the habits of American detectives as portrayed on the screen. As he was finishing, a car came up the drive. The arrival of Inspector Evans of the county police, with his Chief Constable, prevented further conversation. Mr. Lewker escorted the new arrivals into the hall (where Feckenham, coming out of the drawing-room, eyed them as if they were tourists from a leper colony) and seated them in the small library. A moment later Inspector Grimmett, new-shaven and glowing like a health food advertisement, joined them.

The Welsh inspector performed introductions with his customary briskness, and handed the typed copies of the statements he had taken the previous evening to Grimmett. The Chief Constable, a florid gentleman with a shrewd eye and an urbane manner, leaned across the table to speak to Mr. Lewker.

"We hope you'll lend a hand, of course," he murmured. "Heard of your activities, naturally. A nasty business this—may be a simple solution, may not. Count it as fortunate that you happen to be here."

The actor-manager said he would lend what assistance he could. "It is more fortunate still," he added, "that Scotland Yard was able to spare Inspector Grimmett. I know him for one of their best men."

"Excellent, excellent." The Chief Constable turned to Grimmett, who had been glancing quickly through the statements. "Well, Inspector, I trust you're satisfied. You fellows always complain we send for you too late."

"No complaints this time, sir," returned Grimmett pleasantly. "Inspector Evans here's made a very neat start, so he has."

The Chief Constable nodded at the papers in Grimmett's hand. "Can you get a line from those?"

"Nothing to speak of, sir. This case won't depend on folks' whereabouts at time of crime, far as I can see. The statements agree pretty well, such as they are. Time explosion was heard tallies. All those who were in the dining room when Webhouse went out say he stated his intention of walking down to the lodge and back, 'stead of which he seems to have gone up what they call the cliff path. Nobody knows anyone who might have wanted him dead— they never do in these first statements." He looked at Mr. Lewker. "Not even in yours, sir."

"I hope I am as wise as my fellows," boomed Mr. Lewker. "You will observe, however, that in my statement I record that David Webhouse left the room to take his stroll about one minute after a warm argument had ended in Sir Henry Lydiate's leaving the dinner table somewhat abruptly.

May I ask whether anyone else mentioned that fact?"

"Only Mr. Feckenham," said Grimmett, "and he puts it rather stronger. We shall need to have a chat with Sir Henry, I fancy."

"I've known Lydiate for thirty years," interposed the Chief Constable. "He's a fine old boy, stubborn as a mule but very popular in this valley. He'd nothing to do with this business, you'll find."

"Quite so, sir," said Grimmett noncommittally. He took a paper from among those given him by Evans. "Your police surgeon's report confirms time of death nicely, I see. Cause of death—well, I reckon this means broken neck. Injuries—um—'compatible with results of explosive detonated beneath victim's feet.' "

The Chief Constable made a noise indicative of profound disgust.

"That's what I find so sickening about this business," he declared. "Bombs—explosives—it's so damned un-British."

Mr. Lewker suppressed a chuckle. "Murder," he remarked, "is itself hardly a British habit."

"No, no. Quite. Murder most foul, even when at its best, as Shakespeare says—"

" 'As in the best it is,' " groaned Mr. Lewker.

"Eh? Oh, yes. Well, what I say is this isn't the best by a long chalk. I want to see the perpetrator caught and hanged."

Inspector Evans, who had been shifting his feet uneasily during this politico-literary chat, leaned forward.

"There's the man Cutpursey to catch, sir," he suggested.

"He's been missing since yesterday evening, and that's very suggestive. We have advised all county stations and sent a description, but there is no news this morning. Should we try a wider search, now?"

"That's a point," said the Chief Constable, looking at Grimmett. "Had we better put out the big net, Inspector?"

"Might try the ports—Holyhead, for instance—and the railway stations, sir. I'd like a quick look round here, then I'll phone you if we want a nationwide search."

"Quite. Call on me for any help you require. Naturally. By the way, you've only a sergeant with you, I gather. Want any more men?"

Grimmett considered. "No-o. If you'll leave that fat constable of yours, the chap Inspector Evans put on duty last night, I reckon we can manage nicely. Seems his name's Jones, same as the maid's here, and they're first cousins twice removed, or maybe second cousins once removed, so all's nice and snug, so to speak."

"Is that quite wise?" frowned the Chief Constable.

"Thinking of Dilys, sir? Have you seen her? If she turns out to be a murderess I'll go back on the beat without a murmur."

"Very well, Inspector."

The Chief Constable got up and took his hat and stick from a chair with an air of relief. Inspector Evans jumped to the door and whisked it open.

"What about the press, sir?" asked Grimmett as they passed through into the hall and out on to the terrace. "The papers'll be on to this soon, so they will."

"They're on to it now, my boy," chuckled the Chief Constable as he got into his car. "Jones was holding the gate against a pair of journalists when we came through."

"Can I leave them to you, then?"

"You can. I'll give 'em the usual bare facts, hint at possible accident, police taking charge and so forth—All right, Inspector—Good-bye!"

The big black car slid away between the glistening rhododendron bushes. Grimmett scratched his bristly head as he watched it out of sight.

"Seem mighty happy to get clear of this case, so they do," he commented.

" 'Hint at possible accident,' " Mr. Lewker repeated, frowning. "You know, Grimm, it could just possibly have been an accident."

"You don't believe that, sir," returned Grimmett placidly. "Ah," he added as they turned, "there's Pitt by the coach-house. Got the chuck from his best girl last week, so he's a bit broody-like—Sergeant!"

Sergeant Pitt, a hatchet-faced young man with a dark mustache, came up to the terrace with the racing stride of a trained harrier. His double-breasted dark suit made him look even thinner and taller than he was.

"Tag along, Sergeant," Grimmett told him. "Mr. Lewker's showing us round the grounds."

"Yessir," said Sergeant Pitt. "And very nice too."

"The cliff path first, I think, sir," said the inspector. "I fancy you didn't examine that?"

"No. I thought it better to leave it for daylight and the experts."

Mr. Lewker led the way up the path above the rock garden, the path to the cliff and the now unbridged ravine. A few yards beyond the point where it entered the belt of rhododendrons they came round a corner to see Tansy sitting on a damp-looking rock beside the path. She held one end of a piece of string while the spaniel Flora tugged ecstatically at the other. As the three men approached she got up, loosing the string and allowing Flora to bolt with it down the path.

"Hallo," she said. "I thought you'd come up here soon, so I waited, 'cause Mother said I was on *no* account to go up to see where the bridge blew up, and if you said I could that wouldn't be no account, would it?"

Mr. Lewker, disentangling this un-Shakespearean passage with some difficulty, wagged his head slowly at her.

"I am afraid it will not do, Tough," he boomed. "We are on weighty business bent. But allow me to present an old friend—Detective-Inspector George Grimmett. And Sergeant Pitt."

"How do you do?" Tansy returned politely. "I've seen *you* before," she added to the inspector.

"So you have, Miss Tansy." Grimmett beamed at her. "And I reckon we'll be meeting again soon. Just now I'd prefer you not to come along with us, because we've got a bit of private work to do, and we're not allowed—"

"You and Mr. Lewker's going to find out who murdered Uncle David, aren't you?"

The inspector gulped and shot an appealing glance at Mr. Lewker, who grinned and ignored it.

"Well, miss," he stammered, "you've hit it, so to speak That is, we hope—"

"So you'll prob'ly want some help," nodded Tansy. "And I'd like to help, 'cause I'm sorry he was killed in that sort of way, and I know I'm not very old yet but I got ninety-three per cent in Maths and Miss Palliser wrote 'Shows remarkable intelligence for her age' on my report. So perhaps I could look for clues, or something," she finished hopefully.

Grimmett, who had recovered himself, nodded gravely.

"Now I take that very kindly of you, Miss Tansy," he said. "If and when occasion offers, myself and Mr. Lewker will surely avail ourselves of your help."

"All right," said Tansy, looking disappointed. She turned and began to walk slowly away. "But if it turns out to be someone I like," she added over her shoulder, "I shan't help at all."

With which declaration she broke into a gallop and vanished among the rhododendrons.

"That's a particularly outspoken young lady," remarked Grimmett as they recommenced their ascent of the path.

"Trample a few pore blokes' hearts under her feet when she's ten years older, I'll warrant," said Sergeant Pitt with some bitterness.

"Don't judge by your own experience, young Pitt," Grimmett told him severely. "Blue eyes and golden locks aren't always cruel and heartless, as maybe you'll find out some day. How does she fit into the family, sir?"

Mr. Lewker explained Tansy's relationship. "Doubtless she inherits her plain speaking from her mother."

"Ah, Mrs. Pauncefoot—she as good as told me I was a nuisance, interfering with the Lord's judgment. Nice clean little bedroom she's put me in, though—By gum, sir, what's this? Scenic railway?"

They had passed through the fir wood and plodded up the zigzag where the path climbed above the heathery glacis. Now the hewn ledge of the cliff path slanted up in front of them, clinging across the bare gray wall of rock.

This morning the place looked more impressive by reason of the low-hanging mist, which dropped its trailing fringes below the crest of the bluff overhead. The precipice above the path rose into obscurity, so that to all appearance the cliff was topless.

Mr. Lewker halted his party at the commencement of this passage.

"Grimm," he said, "it is upon my conscience that I have so far behaved very carelessly in this affair. I have made assumptions."

"Have you, now, sir? Might I ask what assumptions?"

"I have assumed that Webhouse was killed by absent treatment, as it were. Ignoring any other possibility, I jumped to the conclusion that some sort of trap was laid, that Webhouse inadvertently set off this trap, as he was intended to do, that the murderer—I assumed him as well—was not present when the crime was committed."

The inspector passed a hand over his mustache, concealing a grin. "Seems a pretty sound assumption to me," he declared. "What's wrong with it?"

"I failed to consider the other possibilities," said Mr. Lewker deprecatingly. "Setting aside that of accident, the explosion might have been caused by a bomb flung from above. Again, if the bridge were mined, what more likely than that the mine should be exploded by the murderer from some concealment whence he could gauge the right moment for action?"

"Trying to make it harder, aren't you, sir? The police surgeon's report talked of injuries caused by explosive detonated under the victim's feet. I reckon that wipes out your first alternative. As for the second, who's going to wait about on the spot, when he's got a method of killing that can be fixed so's he's somewhere else when it happens?"

"Anthony Cattespool saw someone making off into the wood just after it happened," Mr. Lewker pointed out.

Sergeant Pitt, who had been listening with impatience, pushed forward.

"If you'll let the dawg see the rabbit, sir, we'll save time," he said. "Let's have a dekko at where the bridge was."

Mr. Lewker nodded. "Very well. I suggest, however, that we examine the path carefully as we go."

They went on again, more slowly now, eyes on the solid rock on which they trod. Small fragments had trickled down from the rock wall on the right to the path, but there was no place where the imprint of a foot would show. Half a dozen match stalks and a rotting cigar end, besides one or two evidences of Flora's visits, were all they had discovered by the time the ravine was reached.

Here there was no lack of signs. The nearer edge of the gap was hacked away as with a giant chisel. Where the end of the wooden bridge had rested was a ragged and newly split edge of rock, showing plainly that a foot or more of the path had come away. One or two jagged lumps lay about near the verge.

"There you are, Sergeant," said Grimmett. "That's not quite fourteen hours old. See what you can get."

Pitt had already taken a bulky leather wallet from his pocket and was peering concentratedly at the broken path. He got down on hands and knees and craned cautiously over the edge. Then he lowered his beaky nose and began to sniff like a dog at the rock.

"That's the bridge down there on the scree, I take it," said Grimmett, calling Mr. Lewker's attention from Pitt's Holmesian activities, "Whereabouts was the body lying, sir?"

"A little below the position of the bridge. And one foot—human, not linear—some distance to the right."

"Ah! We'll have a look down there afterwards," nodded the inspector. "Seems to me," he added, "there's going to be no help from fingerprints in this case. Not a hope here, for instance—even if our man was fool enough to leave any."

He tapped the iron railing on which he was leaning. Its surface was knobbed and roughened with the rust of years.

"This wood where Mr. Cattespool saw the man," he continued, "just before you found the body. Those fir trees, was it?"

"Yes. But remember, Grimm, that only Cattespool saw and heard this person, and he described what he saw as 'a dark shape with whitish upperworks.' He can have had no more than a glimpse of it."

"And you and Mr. Feckenham heard nothing. Odd, that. Anyway, this person or thing would be clearing off into those trees?"

"Yes. The firs on the left of the scree as we look down from here."

"So it was moving towards the bottom of the path we've just come up." Grimmett turned to look at the yawning gap of the ravine. "Seven feet and more. Wouldn't like to jump it myself, but it could be done. Well, Sergeant, anything to give us?"

Pitt, with his trousers well smudged with rock dust, was sealing three small envelopes in which he had placed the results of his labors. He stood up from his squatting position, replacing a steel scraping tool with a fine curled-up edge in his wallet.

"Got a bit of good deposit," he announced, looking more cheerful than he had done all morning. "Residue, that is. All mixed up with dust, o'course—I'll have to get to work on it before I can give you the gen."

"What he means, sir," said Grimmett, turning to Mr. Lewker, "is that the blast of the explosion left slight traces from which he may be able to get a line on what sort of explosive was used."

"Not 'blast,' please," Pitt said in pained tones. "It's the expanding gases as leaves the residue. Some of 'em don't expand quite quick enough to get clear. But as to the way this job was worked, I'll tell you what it looks like to me."

"Get on, then," said Grimmett as he paused.

"Okay, Inspector. This is how I see it." Pitt went to the inner side of the path and laid his hand on the wall of rock. "There's the start of a crack here, see. Rhyolite, this rock is, with lines of cleavage running in pretty well at ninety degrees to the face. You'll find the strike runs northeast to southwest, and if I'd a compass we could take the dip—"

"All right, all right," broke in his superior impatiently. "We'll come to the lecture later, Professor. What about this explosion?"

"I'm coming to it," retorted the sergeant resentfully. "This crack goes right down, see, not so deep but getting a bit wider, and crosses the path. Leastways, it did cross the path, side to side, 'bout eleven inches from the edge. Before the bust-up happened, that was. Would you say, Mr. Lewker, that the end of the bridge used to cover that crack?"

"I would say so," replied that gentlemen, his little eyes narrowed intently.

"Well, then. Here's a crack running under the bridge-end very convenient. I want to place a charge to bring the bridge down. I heaves up the bridge-end, shoves it aside, and plants my charge in that crack. It'll be quite a small affair that charge—maybe a four-ounce, 'bout the size of my middle finger, see, with a hole in the top for a detonator. We'll leave the detonator for a minute. I put the bridge back and in doo course I detonate the charge. What happens? She fires mainly upwards, because I haven't tamped her, and chucks the bridge up and out. And she fires a bit outwards, because there's only eleven inches between the crack and the edge of this ravine. On the other side of the crack there's good solid rock, so I won't expect to find that shifted, with an untamped charge. I'll expect to find the rock split away from the outer edge of the crack to the ravine, and the bridge sent to glory. And that," finished Sergeant Pitt triumphantly, "is what I do find, see?"

"Then the upshot of all that rigmarole," said Grimmett, "is that a packet of explosive was put in a crack under this end of the bridge and touched off. Right?"

"That's what I said, didn't I?" retorted Sergeant Pitt aggrievedly.

Mr. Lewker was rubbing his chin, slowly and reflectively.

"Let us suppose, Sergeant," he said, "that you wished this charge to be detonated by someone stepping on the bridge. How would you arrange that?"

Pitt considered for a moment. "I'd have to use a fulminate detonator— little tube 'bout an inch and a half long and three-eighths diameter. That slips into the hole in the charge. I might arrange to fire that electrically."

"That would mean batteries and wires and so on, I presume. Could it not be detonated in the same way as a rifle cartridge is fired?"

"By percussion—well, yes, it could." Pitt screwed up his hatchet face. "Easy enough to fit a firing-cap to a detonator. I'd need a striker—nail in the underside of the plank would do it—and some sort of spring to hold it clear."

Mr. Lewker remembered something. "When I came up here with Mr. Webhouse I stepped on to the bridge. It was made of two broad planks, and I trod first on the inner plank. It gave under my foot, and Webhouse said it was slightly split."

"That'd do!" Pitt exclaimed. "Have your charge there, your nail-point just clear of the detonator cap, and your spring between plank and rock. Step on the plank, down goes the nail—*ker-whop*! You're flying through the air with the greatest of ease."

Mr. Lewker shivered slightly. The inspector blew through his red mustache and stepped forward to the broken edge.

"Can you give us an idea, sir, where this bridge rested?" he asked.

"Within an inch or two, I think. It was about three feet wide and the end rested here." He pointed. "The inner plank, the one that gave under pressure, would lie roughly across that darker-colored rock."

Pitt was down on his knees again and peering over the edge. When he looked up at them his eyes were bright with excitement.

"That tapes it, sir!" he announced. "You can see where the charge was centered. It'd be right under the middle of that loose plank o' yours."

He got to his feet and faced them, hands on hips.

"I'll tell you another thing," he went on. "I won't know for certain till I've made tests on this residue I've got samples of, but I had a good sniff—my scent's as keen as anyone's—and I'll lay a quid there was dinitrobenzole in that charge."

"Meaning?" jerked Grimmett.

"Meaning the stuff used was rackarock, like as not."

"And what may rackarock be?"

"Patent explosive—Sprengel's patent," Pitt explained; "79 parts chlorate of potash, 21 parts dinitrobenzole. Old-fashioned blasting cartridge, but they still use it in some quarries. Better look for a quarryman, sir."

"And," said Mr. Lewker quietly, "David Webhouse brought Cutpursey here from a local quarry."

CHAPTER VII

EVIDENCE

CLARE WEBHOUSE, with Anthony Cattespool at her elbow, was waiting on the terrace when the three investigators came down to the house. She wore a dark green housecoat and her face, though extremely pale, was composed, only the eyes showing any sign of strain. Pallor did not detract from her beauty; and Mr. Lewker observed that both Inspector Grimmett and Sergeant Pitt were impressed, the latter noticeably.

"I'm so sorry, Inspector," Clare said when formalities were over. "I should have—have welcomed you when you arrived. But I expect you'll under-stand—"

"Don't you worry, ma'am," interrupted Grimmett paternally. "It's a bad time for you, so it is, and I won't intrude more than I can help."

"You've got to find who—" She stopped, unable to say the word. "You've got to do your duty, I know," she substituted haltingly, "and—and—"

Anthony came to her assistance.

"Mrs. Webhouse was waiting to tell you that lunch is ready," he said coldly; his glance, shifting uneasily from face to face, belied the indifference of his tone. "It's laid in the library for the two—ah—officers."

"I'm afraid I don't know the proper etiquette on these occasions," said Clare with a pathetic attempt at lightness. "Sergeant Pitt, I hope you don't mind sleeping in the coach-house loft with the constable?"

"More than comfortable, Mrs. Webhouse," Pitt said earnestly. "It's a very nice little setup there."

"I'm so glad. It *is* rather nice—Dai had it done up for Cutpursey and a chauffeur when we—oh, *Flora!*"

The spaniel raced out of the front door and past the group. She had a slipper in her mouth, and made off with it in the direction of the rock-garden. Clare took a step after her, stopped with a hand to her eyes, and then ran hurriedly into the house. Anthony, checking an obvious impulse to follow her, turned to the inspector.

"Well," he said a little defiantly, "am I allowed to know what's going on?"

"Is there a reason why you should, sir?" returned Grimmett mildly.

Anthony flushed. "I'm Mrs. Webhouse's friend and neighbor. She's suf-fered a terrible blow and I don't want her badgered and worried. If you've anything to ask her or tell her you can do it through me."

"I'll try not to badger anybody," said the inspector gently. "But I shall want to see her, and each member of the household in turn, this afternoon. Perhaps you'd give them all that message, sir—from three o'clock onwards, if that will suit."

Anthony looked as though he was about to protest but thought better of it.

"I suppose we've got to go through it," he said sulkily. "That means Web-house was definitely—murdered, I take it? You know Cutpursey's cleared out?"

"I do, sir."

"You'll find he's the man you want. Look here, Inspector, I'm keen to help. Webhouse was a friend of mine, you know. I know a bit about explo-sives, and if as I suppose he was killed by some sort of mine—a perfectly foul bit of work—I might be able to fish up a clue or so."

"Is that so, sir? I'll certainly bear it in mind, and thank you." Grimmett smiled, nodded, and turned to Pitt. "Well, Sergeant, I reckon we'd better get our lunch."

They went into the house. Anthony scowled after them.

"Not giving anything away, your inspector pal. And I don't care for that spiv type he's got with him." He faced the actor-manager. "What's the position, Lewker? We're all suspects—or have you set the bloodhounds on Cutpursey?"

"The evidence found so far," said Mr. Lewker carefully, "points to no particular person."

"Oh, I forgot," Anthony said with a touch of bitterness. "You're well in with the coppers and I'm with the thieves. What's it like to hunt a man down?"

Mr. Lewker forbore to show resentment.

"My dear sir," he boomed equably, "murder makes hunters of us all, and rightly. Let me remind you that you yourself volunteered assistance but a moment ago. In a matter such as this the police and all good citizens seek the justice that Shakespeare phrased: 'Where the offense is, let the great axe fall.' "

"Oh, come and have lunch," said Anthony irritably.

Lunch, as was to be expected, was hardly a cheerful meal. Clare was absent from the table (Mr. Lewker gathered that she had retired to her room again) and Tansy, who was present and plainly anxious to discuss untimely subjects, had all her attempts at conversation firmly foiled by her mother. Mrs. Pauncefoot, grim and composed as ever, displayed no other sign that anything untoward had happened at Plas Mawr; indeed, Mr. Lewker fancied that her bony face was being restrained from showing any feeling at all. Feckenham, unexpectedly, seemed to be in a conversational mood, and engaged Mr. Lewker in a jerky discussion on police organization.

The meal dragged through its dull progress. At the end of it Anthony, breaking gloomy silence, announced the inspector's desire to interview everyone during the afternoon; the news pleased no one except Tansy, whose face fell when Mr. Lewker remarked gently that she would be exempt.

As soon as he could get away, Mr. Lewker went in search of Grimmett. He found the inspector coming out of the cloakroom in the hall, where the telephone was located.

"Pitt's 'busy' with his chemistry in the coach-house," Grimmett said. "Tells me he'll have a report ready in an hour. I've been on the phone to Sir Henry Lydiate. He'd heard the news—funny how it travels, eh, sir?—and he's coming round at three. I've been through to Caernarvon, too."

"About Cutpursey?"

"Yes. They've got nothing so far, but it's a bit early to expect anything. We'll go to where the body was found, sir, if you're ready. The maid, Jones, says Cutpursey's hat and raincoat's gone from the lodge, likewise an old canvas bag and some other things. The net'll be out in an hour or two and we'll pull him in—though mind you, sir, from your description of him I wouldn't say he'd rig a booby-trap as neat as this was."

They rounded the corner of the house and climbed the narrow path to the scree slope. Mr. Lewker pointed out the spot where Webhouse's body had lain, and they climbed up to the broken bridge. Grimmett got out his notebook and made a rough sketch of the area, and with Mr. Lewker's assistance ran his fifty-foot tape over the distance between bridge, ravine, and resting place of body.

"Not," he said resignedly, "that it'll be any use, but take what ye can and glower for mair, as my old mother used to say."

A sketch of the bridge went into his notebook also, and he spent five minutes examining the splintered wood.

"We may note," remarked Mr. Lewker, "that all the signs confirm Sergeant Pitt's hypothesis."

Grimmett nodded. "This rail was on the outside, so these smashed ends of the footplanks were on the right-hand edge of the gap, looking up from here. The explosion that blew them off blew off Webhouse's foot as he stepped on 'em. Where's the stanchion from the other end?"

Mr. Lewker showed him where it lay. The inspector bent to finger the frayed end of cord that dangled from the lashing.

"Bit of a gimcrack affair, this bridge," he commented; "nothing but its own weight to hold it in place and one of the handrail supports mended with string."

"It was a temporary structure only. Webhouse told me he had ordered a steel bridge and was expecting its early arrival. Incidentally, Grimm, can you see any reason for that cord lashing?"

Grimmett looked more closely at the wooden post.

"No," he admitted at last. "Someone may have suspected it was sprung a bit."

"What do you make of the lashing itself?"

"Neat bit of work, sir, put on naval whipping style. Be neater if this long end had been cut off. Nylon cord, woven—parachute cord, don't they call it?"

"It is a not very common sort of nylon cord," said Mr. Lewker. "I saw something of it in the war days. Mark III parachute cord is its proper description. The stanchion to which it is attached," he added casually, "was of course at that end of the bridge nearer to the upper path, the path leading to Anthony Cattespool's cottage."

Inspector Grimmett stood up, placed his hands on his hips, blew through his mustache, and fixed his companion with a twinkling blue stare.

"Now, sir," he said severely, "you've got something up your sleeve, as usual. I reckoned you had, when you were giving me the dope on the circumstances of death, at breakfast time."

"We agreed then, Grimm, to deal with the material evidence first. I have one more item in that category to show you. Have we finished here?"

Grimmett cast a final look round the rubble slope.

"I'd like to find the nail that struck the detonator cap, so I would," he said longingly, "but it'd take a year to go over this stuff. Right, sir—lead on."

They descended the slope and walked past the house to the commencement of the cliff path. Mr. Lewker led the way through the rhododendrons and the fir wood to the outlying tree under the bluff, and pointed to the embedded slug. Concisely, but repeating Webhouse's words with accuracy, he described his late host's manner of calling attention to the slug. Grimmett took out his tape measure and laid it against the trunk.

"Three foot eleven," he announced, frowning sideways at the actor-manager. "And he thought Cutpursey might have fired at him from the wood, you say?"

"Yes. Well, Grimm?"

"Well to you, sir. Let's hear your views this time."

Mr. Lewker nodded and pursed his lips, looking like a benevolent china mandarin.

"In the first place," he said in measured tones, "Webhouse twice declared that the slug passed his head—'zipped past my ear,' to use his exact words. Webhouse was at least six feet in height. If he was standing, as he said he was, on the path at this spot, the shot must have passed his head on a steep downward trajectory to have struck the tree where it did. It is, moreover, in the side of the tree facing the bluff. We may therefore reason that the shot was fired from the bluff above."

"Right you are, sir. From the beginning of the cliff path up there, in fact."

"If Webhouse's statement was accurate, yes."

Grimmett gazed up at the heathery steeps above them. The mists were slowly lifting, but the day was no less gray and windless. The bluff was clear of cloud, but the bulge of heather and turf hid its summit from them.

"A man could get away along that path without being seen from down here," he reflected aloud. "Looks as though he could scramble off to the right, down into the wood here, or—on up the path towards Mr. Cattespool's cottage, to the left. Anything else, sir?"

"That is the last of the material evidence known to me. But we should remove the slug, I think. Will Sergeant Pitt be able to tell us anything about it?"

"He might." Grimmett took out his pocketknife and dug the morsel of lead from the tree-trunk, taking care not to scratch or bend it. "He's done his firearms course."

He slipped the slug into his waistcoat pocket and glanced at his watch.

"Just nice time, sir. Pitt ought to have his report on the residue ready, and then you can pull the nonmaterial evidence out of your sleeve before we start the interviews."

"Forslow no longer, make we hence amain!" boomed Mr. Lewker cheerfully, starting down the path. The hunt was gathering impetus, and he felt the old thrill of the hunter.

The coach-house of Plas Mawr, where Sergeant Pitt and Constable Jones had their temporary quarters, was a sizeable two-storied building at the side of the drive fifty yards below the terrace. Three-quarters of its lower story formed the garage where the Daimler and Mr. Lewker's Wolseley were lodged together with Feckenham's battered sports Bentley; the remaining portion of the ground floor was occupied by a small workshop (its door was locked) and a separate staircase leading to the floor above. Here there were two neat and well-furnished bedrooms and a bathroom. Constable Jones was absent on duty at the gate. Sergeant Pitt, in shirtsleeves and wiping his hands on a towel, greeted Mr. Lewker and the inspector as they came up the stairs.

"Just cleaning up, sir." He led them into the bedroom, where a faint smell of chemicals lingered, and pointed to the dressing table. "Got what you want, all right."

A newspaper had been spread on the table and a large black case stood open beside it. On the newspaper were arrayed a small balance, a spirit lamp, and several test-tubes.

"That charge was rackarock," Pitt announced with satisfaction. "Thought it would be—I'm not often wrong."

" 'Cept in the matter of females, eh?" said Grimmett. "All right, Sergeant—nice work. This rackarock, now. Is it easy to get hold of?"

"Not easy, no. You can't buy it at any old ironmonger's. They have to have a police license to supply. Easiest way of getting it'd be to slip ten bob to one of the poppers at a quarry."

"Poppers?"

"That's what they call the blokes that lay and fire the charges."

"There are several large slate-quarries in this neighborhood," remarked Mr. Lewker.

"More likely to be from a granite quarry, sir," Pitt corrected. "They use more of this type of thing. Even then, it wouldn't be a modern quarry—rackarock's out-of-date stuff, as I said before."

Grimmett looked at Mr. Lewker. "There's a good line there, worth trying. Find a local quarry, old-fashioned methods, slack management. Get hold of a—um—popper who's got spare charges to flog. The official approach won't do—looks like a little job for you, Sergeant."

"Suits me," grunted Pitt, wriggling into his jacket. "I'd like to see the chap swing that fired that charge. That pore girl—she's hard hit, she is. Bit like Vivien Leigh, too."

"Now then, my lad!" said the inspector reprovingly. "I thought blue-eyed blondes were your speciality, so I did. Know anything about air guns?"

"I might do, sir. Why?"

Grimmett handed the flattened slug to him and turned to Mr. Lewker. "Can we get at the weapon, sir?"

"Webhouse said he had locked it up. I fancy it may be in the locked room below."

"We'll try it. I've got the keys—Mrs. Pauncefoot handed them over—Well, Sergeant?"

"Child's play, sir," returned Pitt, who had been examining the slug with a pocket lens. "Air-rifle fired this, not airgun. You can see what's left of the rifling marks. There's traces of wood here——"

"We know all about those," Grimmett interrupted. "Can you—or a fire-arms expert, identify the particular gun that was fired from?"

"What—with the proj. flattened out like that?" Pitt's tone was scornful. "Lord 'elp you, Inspector, I'm enough of an expert to tell you not a hope. Tell you this though, it's come from an ordinary type of air rifle—might be a 'Diana' number one bore—and it's a waisted slug."

"Right. Let's go below."

They went down the stairs to the door of Webhouse's workshop, which Grimmett unlocked with a key from a large bunch taken from his pocket. The workshop was well lighted and fitted with a bench, vises of wood and steel, and neat racks of tools for woodwork and metalwork. On the walls hung shelves of pigeonholes filled with oddments; beside these, suspended from two hooks, was an air rifle with wooden butt and shining blue-metal stock and barrel.

"Prints!" warned the inspector sharply as Pitt stepped over to the gun.

The sergeant ostentatiously clasped his hands behind his back without deigning to reply.

"Diana number one bore," he reported. "And there's your box of waisted slugs, in the pigeonhole alongside."

Grimmett cast a somewhat uncertain glance at Mr. Lewker, who had been (for him) unusually silent.

"Well, sir," he remarked diffidently, "seems Webhouse's gun is the sort that could have fired that slug, and probably did fire it, and unless we can get any significant prints off it that's about as far as we can go. If he didn't keep it locked up before, anyone could have got at it. Anything more?"

"Yes," said Mr. Lewker. "I would like Sergeant Pitt to tell us whether this air rifle could kill a man at a distance of about one hundred and fifty feet, from a point at an angle of roughly thirty degrees above the target."

Pitt considered. "Effective range would be thirty-five yards, and a bit more at that angle. Might just do the job, sir—*if* you got him in the eye."

"Not otherwise?"

"Very unlikely, sir."

"Thank you."

"That all, Mr. Lewker?—Right, Sergeant." Grimmett frowned at his watch. "You've got just thirteen minutes. I want that gun tested for prints, photos if you find any. One minute to three, report to me in the library ready for short-hand notes."

Leaving Sergeant Pitt to dash up the staircase two steps at a time, they went up to the house.

"Versatile officer, our friend Pitt," remarked Mr. Lewker as they gained the terrace.

"He's a good lad, is Albert Pitt," agreed the inspector. "Pity he doesn't get married—he always seems to be breaking off an engagement, and it inter-feres with his work. That black bag of his is a joke at the Yard. Got all manner of detective gadgets in it, and knows how to use 'em. That's why I like him along—don't care for an ontoorage when I'm on a case."

Anthony Cattespool came out of the drawing roomas they entered the hall.

"Sir Henry Lydiate's arrived," he said shortly. He paused, and then added, "We're all awaiting the ordeal in here. Make it snappy, will you?"

"In ten minutes' time, sir. I'll let you know."

"You might see Mrs. Webhouse first. She'd like to get it over."

"Very natural, sir," nodded Grimmett pleasantly. "I'll certainly see Mrs. Webhouse first."

"Kind of you," said Anthony, not without irony, and returned to the draw-ing room.

"Tansy is not required for this interview, I take it?" said Mr. Lewker.

"I reckon not, sir," Grimmett replied, opening the door of the library. "I'd like to talk with her, but informal like."

He closed the door behind them and locked it. The library and the room used by David Webhouse as his study were small rooms next door to each other, leading off the passage connecting the hall with the kitchen. An inner door had been made in the wall between the rooms, and Grimmett passed through this into the study, which was furnished with a central table and a roll-top desk, with three or four comfortable chairs.

"All very convenient," beamed the inspector, setting a chair for Mr. Lewker and sitting down himself. "And now, sir, shoot, as they say. The story of your life, so to speak, at Plas Mawr, and—"

" 'And the particular accidents gone by since I came to this isle,' " boomed Mr. Lewker.

With which introduction he set himself to detail, with that conciseness of which he was master, all the incidents, conversations, and impressions that had befallen him from the day of his arrival to the evening of Webhouse's death. Grimmett's notebook was open on the table and from time to time he scrawled memoranda in it. Once, at the mention of the falling rock on the Crib Goch pinnacles, he blew very loudly through his mustache. At the end of the five minutes which the exposition occupied he sat back in his chair and stared hard at Mr. Lewker.

"By gum, sir," he said seriously, "but this is sharpening matters up, with a vengeance."

"And so grows to a point, Grimm. Yes."

"Look at this." He turned the pages of his notebook. "Webhouse is afraid of someone. He as good as tells you so. He's a well-to-do man with a pretty wife half his age. He's been shot at from a path that leads to a neighbor's cottage. Neighbor's a youngish man, some might call him presentable. On this mountain climb a rock falls and nearly gets him—only person who could have started it falling is this same neighbor. Webhouse is killed, that same night, by an explosive booby-trap. Neighbor, again, won his war decoration for daring use of explosives."

He slapped his notebook shut and once again stared hard at Mr. Lewker, who rubbed his chin and scowled.

"You in here, sir?" Pitt opened the study door and came in. "Library's locked."

Grimmett looked at his watch. "Nice work, Sergeant. What about the prints?"

"Didn't even get the camera out—there aren't any. Theair rifle's been wiped off thoroughly and rubbed over with oil."

"As you'd expect. All right, then—got your notebook? In here with you." He opened the door leading into the library. "I want you out of sight. You'll hear all right if we leave the door ajar."

Pitt disappeared into the room. Grimmett glanced round the study.

"They seem a pretty quiet bunch," he explained, "and I want 'em at their ease, far as possible. Friendly like. Hope you agree, sir?"

"It is your party, Grimm, and I agree that a pacific atmosphere should promote the flow of soul."

"Cigarettes'd help, but I don't smoke and I reckon you only smoke a pipe, sir."

"David Webhouse may have kept some in here," Mr. Lewker suggested, going to the roll-top desk. The drawers on the right of the kneehole were unlocked, and in the second one he found what he wanted. "A half-used fifty packet," he announced.

"That'll do nicely. We'll have 'em handy on the table."

As Mr. Lewker passed the cigarettes to Grimmett a slip of paper, which he had inadvertently picked up with them, fluttered from his fingers. He caught it, examined it, and passed it to the inspector in silence.

"Um," grunted Grimmett. "Local paper, probably, and several years old. Poor photograph, showing group of men in front of corrugated iron shack. Caption: 'David Webhouse, M.P., chatting with old friends at Llanerch Quarry.' Anything notable about it, sir?"

"Only that the little man who is standing on Webhouse's left is undoubtedly Cutpursey."

"Employed at Llanerch Quarry, maybe. Well, might be a useful tip." He returned the cutting and placed the cigarettes on the table. "And now, sir, if you don't mind acting callboy for once, we'll have Mrs. Webhouse in."

CHAPTER VIII

THE WIDOW AND THE WAR HERO

Clare Webhouse had changed her green housecoat for a coat and skirt of dark tweed. She looked small and apprehensive as she came into the study, but only for a moment. Flora the spaniel, creeping through the narrowing opening of the door after her, got herself nipped and emitted an ear-piercing shriek, and the effusion of apologies and endearments that followed seemed to restore her mistress's equanimity. Mr. Lewker, indeed, fancied he detected a new air of freedom and self-reliance in Clare's bearing as she sat in the chair opposite Detective-Inspector Grimmett with Flora on her lap. Her voice as she declined Grimmett's offer of a cigarette was firm, if subdued.

"I'll start with an apology and get it over, Mrs. Webhouse," Grimmett began with disarming awkwardness. "I'm sorry to trouble you at a time like this. To interrogate you in your own house, and in such—um—tragic circumstances—well, it's downright unmannerly, so it is."

Clare caressed the spaniel and smiled faintly.

"Please don't consider it, Inspector," she said. "It's got to be done, and that's that."

Mr. Lewker, sitting a little withdrawn from the table and admiring his friend's approach, considered that Grimmett's sigh of relief was overacted.

"That's mighty good of you, ma'am," he said. "It makes things easier. We want all the help we can get in matters like this, and I'm sure you're as anxious to help as anyone. Mr. Lewker here has kindly agreed to assist with the investigation, so between us we ought to get to the bottom of this business without much trouble."

After this exordium, the inspector took Clare gently through her statement of the previous night, to which she had nothing to add. He made a note or two and then sat back in his chair.

"Well now, ma'am," he said pleasantly, "that's all plain sailing. I take it Mr. Webhouse and Sir Henry Lydiate were strongly opposed to each other over this hydroelectric business. They'd had arguments about it before last night?"

"Oh yes." Clare appeared quite at her ease. "Sir Henry had called several times to talk to him about it—I think he hoped eventually to persuade Dai to change his views. I'm afraid my husband was always rather—brutal to him, poor old man."

"Brutal?"

"Well—rude, you know. It was Dai's usual manner."

"But you asked Sir Henry to dinner, all the same?"

"Yes. Sir Henry's a neighbor, and a sort of local lord of the manor, and I wanted him to meet our guest." She glanced briefly at Mr. Lewker. "I had no idea Dai would behave as he did."

"Your husband was—um—ruder than usual, then?"

"Much ruder. I'm sure he's never spoken to Sir Henry like that before. After all, sir Henry's an influential person."

Inspector Grimmett consulted his notes, and there was a short pause.

"I'm a naughty, wicked little bitch," said Clare suddenly.

Grimmett's pencil clattered to the floor. He goggled. Mr. Lewker choked slightly.

"I'm a *destructive* little bitch," added Clare, tapping Flora's nose. "Pulling at people's buttons until they come off. Stop it, darling, and lie still."

Grimmett picked up his pencil, coughed loudly, and resumed his questioning with a slightly heightened color.

"Now, Mrs. Webhouse. I understand that your husband, in the course of his argument, mentioned his impending knighthood, to which Sir Henry replied that if it was in his power to prevent it that knighthood would not be bestowed?"

Clare nodded. "Something like that. Sir Henry left the table after saying it—he was very angry."

"I see. And now, if you don't mind, a few particulars of your household here. Mrs. Pauncefoot is the mother of Mr. Webhouse's first wife, I gather."

"Yes. Hilda Webhouse died two years ago, and I—Dai and I got married a year later. It didn't seem nice to turn Mrs. Pauncefoot out—and she's an awfully good manager, you know."

Grimmett nodded. "And you have only the one maid, Dilys Jones, who lives in?"

"There's Mrs. Price, who comes in twice a week to clean—and of course there's the gardener." Clare leaned forward suddenly. "Inspector, I'm worried about Cutpursey. Where do you think he can have gone?"

"Well, ma'am, I thought maybe you could give us a bit of help there. Mrs. Pauncefoot tells me he'd no family or relatives. Did he ever clear out like this before?"

"Yes, he did. Several times since he's been with Dai he's gone off for a night—up in the hills watching animals and birds, he told Tansy. We never found out where he went. He turned up next morning quite unconcerned. He's a funny old chap in some ways."

"Funny time to choose for disappearing, just now," remarked Grimmett dryly.

Clare twined her fingers nervously in Flora's coat; her big dark eyes were anxious.

"You mustn't think Cutpursey had anything to do with—with my husband's death," she said earnestly. "He was absolutely devoted to Dai, you know."

"So Mr. Webhouse gave me to understand," interposed Mr. Lewker from the background, and received a grateful glance from the girl.

"Hum," grunted the inspector. "No doubt there's some good reason for his absence. Mr. Feckenham, now. He's your cousin?"

"Yes—my father's brother's son. Charles and I have been very friendly ever since I was a tiny girl. He's been abroad a long time—in Ceylon, I expect you know all about that—and when he came home to have his knighthood, you see, we asked him to stay here so that he and Dai could go up to London together."

"Very natural, ma'am. And how long has Mr. Feckenham been staying here?"

"Just over a fortnight."

"But he was away for two or three days during that time, perhaps—to go to the Derby?"

Clare looked surprised. "He was, yes. How did you know?"

"I thought a gentleman who's so keen on racing as Mr. Feckenham is reputed to be wouldn't stay away," said Grimmett, pretending not to see Mr. Lewker's sidelong glance. "Did he have good luck or bad?"

"I can't tell you," replied Clare rather coldly. "You had better ask Charles."

"Quite so, ma'am. Well, that—with the addition of Mr. Lewker here—is all those who were staying in the house at the time of death. Mr. Anthony Cattespool was dining here that night. He's a pretty frequent visitor, I understand."

At the mention of Anthony's name a subtle change appeared in the girl's demeanor. She was no less calm and self-possessed, but there was a wariness in her eyes and a new carefulness in her answers. She looked down, toying with Flora's ears.

"Yes," she said. "He's our nearest neighbor—in fact, his cottage is on Plas Mawr land."

"Ah, yes—on the hill above." Grimmett turned a page of his notebook. "Does he often go shooting with that air rifle of your husband's?" he added.

Clare was startled. She took a little time before answering.

"Why—he has borrowed it once or twice, I think, to do some practice. He can't shoot for nuts, though. Why?"

"I just wondered. Now, Mrs. Webhouse, I want you to think carefully. Have you noticed, in the last few weeks, any sign that your husband was unduly nervous—afraid of something, shall we say?"

Again Clare paused before replying. "No," she said at last, with decision. "Dai was always rather jumpy and irritable, but he was the last man to be afraid of anything. He had nothing to be afraid of."

The inspector refrained from direct comment.

"Can you suggest anyone—anyone, Mrs. Webhouse—who bore your husband sufficient enmity to desire his death?" he asked urgently.

"No, Inspector, I can't—that's just what's so awful about this dreadful business."

She was twisting and untwisting her hands now, and her face was no longer calm; but Mr. Lewker, his little eyes intent upon her, thought of certain ladies from provincial dramatic societies who had demonstrated their art before him, and was sorry for her. Grimmett fussed with his papers, obviously giving her time to control her emotion.

"Well, ma'am," he said after a moment. "I've just one more question to bother you with, and that's to ask if, to your knowledge, your husband left a will."

"I know he made one, just after our marriage."

"Do you happen to know where it is?"

"With his solicitors, I think—I've got their address somewhere." Clare pushed Flora from her lap and picked up the handbag she had brought in with her; as she took out a small black address book Mr. Lewker caught a momentary glimpse of a small coil of greenish nylon cord, unmistakable against the crimson lining of the bag. "Here you are," she added, consulting the book. "Lloyd and John, 51 High Street, Llanerch. That's the little town just south of Portmadoc, near the coast."

Grimmett thanked her and turned to Mr. Lewker. "That's all from me, sir. Maybe you've something to ask Mrs. Webhouse?"

"One small point, if she will allow me." The actor-manager leaned forward. "Mrs. Webhouse, when you took Sir Henry Lydiate to the front door last night, did you notice in which direction he went?"

Clare wrinkled her brow. "You know, I scarcely noticed," she confessed. "I just said good night and hurried back into the house—I was so worried about what you and the others would think. But he wouldn't go by the cliff path, if that's what you're thinking."

"There is a short cut to his house by using the cliff path and descending on the other side of the hill, is there not?"

"Yes—but he told me he wasn't going that way. I offered to lend him our torch, but he wouldn't take it."

Mr. Lewker bent his head. The inspector, smiling genially, half rose to his feet and then sat down hurriedly with a grunt.

"Oh," cried Clare, getting up, "she's got your shoelace, I expect. That's *very* naughty, Flora! I'm so sorry Inspector."

"Not at all, ma'am." Grimmett kicked himself free. "And thank you kindly. I wonder if you'd mind asking Mr. Cattespool to come along in here."

"All right," said Clare. "Flora! *Naughty* thing!"

She pushed the dog out through the door, which Mr. Lewker had opened for her. As it closed behind her Grimmett went quickly to the half-open door leading to the library.

"How's it going, Sergeant?" he demanded.

"Okay for sound," said the invisible Pitt.

The inspector returned to the table. "Not much sorrow wasted for her husband, sir. What d'you say?"

"She is frightened on Cattespool's behalf, I fancy. Perhaps for herself also. She lied, of course, about not noticing her husband's recent uneasiness—even Tansy noticed that. Grimm, what is this about Feckenham's racing proclivities?"

The inspector looked smug.

"When Sir Frederick rang up," he said rapidly, "he told me who I'd find here—you told him, I reckon. I took the opportunity to ask him if he knew any of 'em, and he said Charles Feckenham was a member of his club and the buzz was he'd dropped a real packet on some Derby horse. Rumor, of course, but——"

The study door opened and Anthony Cattespool came in. He stood for a moment looking round him, his black beard jutting defiantly.

"Just like those perfectly foul visits to the Head's room at school," he said, with a lightness that did not ring true. "Except, of course, our friend Lewker present and our other friend, as I suppose, in there"—he jerked his head at the library door—"taking all this down."

"Take a seat, sir," said Grimmett imperturbably. "And a cigarette. Match?"

"I've a lighter, thanks." Anthony lit his cigarette and lounged in his chair, hands in pockets. "Bring your sergeant in here, why don't you? I shan't mind. By the way, oughtn't I to ask for a solicitor or something?"

"Sergeant Pitt's quite comfortable, sir, and we find conversation goes smoother if the shorthand man's out of sight. As for the solicitor, you're perfectly at liberty to refuse to answer questions, or to demand that no record shall be taken. But if you feel a solicitor is desirable in your interests at this stage—"

"Good lord, no," said Anthony hastily. "Carry on, Inspector. Only my fun."

"Very well, sir."

Mr. Lewker, who knew his friend, knew that Grimmett was annoyed. The inspector had a sense of humor, as all men must have who deal professionally with the darker side of human relationships; but he disliked flippancy in those who were personally concerned in a murder case. The brisk manner in which he took Anthony through his statement, however, held no trace of animosity. As he laid the statement aside he beamed and nodded as though the man before him was a favorite son.

"Now, sir," he said, "you offered to help us, I fancy. Well, the best help you can give is to be absolutely plain and frank in answering a few questions. You'd known David Webhouse some time, hadn't you?"

"Depends what you call some time. I'd never met him until I came round here last February looking for a cottage."

"You rented your cottage from him, I gather, and became a frequent visitor here. Were you close friends?"

Anthony glanced quickly from the inspector to Mr. Lewker and back again.

"No," he said, with the air of a man being devastatingly honest, "we were not. The man was a fearful blighter. We didn't hit it off at all."

"He disliked you and you disliked him. May I ask what made you dislike him, Mr. Cattespool?"

Anthony flung the ash from his cigarette with an angry gesture and sat up. "You didn't know him, did you, Inspector? The man was a brute in every sense. His manners were appalling. You should have seen him eating soup— both elbows spread, napkin in his collar, head well down below shoulder-blades, eyes shut. Six inches between his nose and the plate and no stopping until he'd scoffed the lot. And all the time a noise like a herd of cows walking through a succulent bog. It had to be seen and heard to be believed."

Mr. Lewker found the description cruel but vivid; Anthony Cattespool's novel, he thought, might be worth reading. Grimmett did not seem impressed.

"Table manners," he remarked, "aren't much of a ground for strong dislike, sir."

"No? If you'd seen Clare—Mrs. Webhouse—sitting there looking apologetic for him, knowing that if she ventured a word of criticism he'd blast her head off—well, in any case I was only giving a sort of sample, Inspector." Anthony seemed to be regretting his heat. "I suppose Webhouse was a good enough fellow in his way, but I don't like domestic bullies."

"Very understandable, sir," nodded Grimmett. "And since it wasn't friendship for Mr. Webhouse that brought you here so frequently, I presume your relations with Mrs. Webhouse were more amiable, so to speak."

The cigarette in Anthony's fingers required a certain amount of attention before he answered.

"I rather think you do presume, Inspector," he said, blowing a thin cloud of smoke. "But you are perfectly correct. Mrs. Webhouse has been most hospitable and sympathetic. Shall we leave it at that?"

"If you wish it, sir. Now, in these past four months you must have seen Mr. Webhouse pretty often, even though you weren't friendly. Would you say there's been any change in his general manner recently—within the past few weeks?"

Again Anthony examined his cigarette with care. "Now you mention it, I did notice he seemed a bit nervy. I thought it might be something to do with this knighthood of his—he was pretty excited about that, you know."

"It didn't strike you he was afraid of something?"

"Well—I don't know. Could have been." Anthony's narrow eyes turned to Mr. Lewker. "When that rock came down, on the pinnacles yesterday, he seemed devilish upset, don't you think?"

"My impression," boomed the actor-manager, "was that he took it remarkably calmly."

"Well," said Grimmett, making a note, "we'll leave that. You were in the Navy during the war, sir, I'm told."

"Correct. Torpedo branch."

"That's to do with explosive?"

"Right again. I gave you a hint about that before lunch."

"So you did, sir. And I gather you're a bit of a marksman, too."

Anthony's stare suggested both surprise and amusement. "I don't know where you gathered it, Inspector," he said, "but you've culled the wrong blossom there. I'm the world's worst shot."

"Then you were trying to improve your shooting when you borrowed Mr. Webhouse'sair rifle seven days ago?"

Amusement faded from the narrow hazel eyes; they became keen and wary.

"I dare say I've had a pot with the gun once or twice," said Anthony lightly. "It's Tansy's really. I gave it her for her birthday in March, but that old—but Webhouse wouldn't let her use it. Tansy's a better shot than I am, as she'll tell you if you ask her."

Mr. Lewker sat forward, cocking an eyebrow at Grimmett, who nodded.

"Mr. Cattespool," said the actor-manager, "were you by any chance using theair rifle seven days ago?"

Anthony looked puzzled. "Blessed if I know. I borrowed the thing once, just before Webhouse locked it up. When was seven days ago?"

"I will be more exact, and ask if you were using theair rifle at any time on the evening of June the fourth."

"Look here, what's all this about the damned gun, anyway?" The black beard was tilted angrily. "Am I supposed to have shot someone?"

Grimmett raised a deprecating hand. "If you'd just answer Mr. Lewker's question, sir—"

"All right, all right. June fourth—wait a bit. No, I didn't use the gun any time that day. I went down to Portmadoc in the afternoon to see a friend of mine—chap who's giving me a few details for my book. I was at his house until after ten o'clock. The last bus back had gone then, so I rang up the garage at Beddgelert and got a taxi to come for me. That took time and it was half-past eleven when the taximan dropped me at Plas Mawr lodge. Is that an alibi?"

"Thank you, sir," said the inspector, ignoring the resentment in Anthony's tone. "Perhaps, while we're at it, you wouldn't mind telling us the name of this friend you visited, and the name of the taxi driver."

"Can't I hear what I need an alibi for?" demanded Anthony bitterly. He crushed his cigarette into the ashtray petulantly. "Oh, well—one supposes you know your job. Will Evans is the chap I went to see in Portmadoc. He was a tiffy—artificer—in a ship I was in one time. He works in the Llanerch Quarry now."

Grimmett's fountain pen stopped suddenly in its traverse of the page.

"Llanerch Quarry, sir," he repeated.

"Yes. He's what they call a popper there. Address 152 Madoc Street, if you want it. Taxi, Dewi Roberts. That's the little garage on the right as you go into Beddgelert. It's on the phone, if you'd like to find out whether I'm a liar or not."

Grimmett finished noting these particulars without replying. Anthony reached irritably for another cigarette and lit it.

"Now, sir," said Grimmett after a rather obviously deliberate pause, "we'll come to the night of Mr. Webhouse's death, if you don't mind. The moun-taineering party got back to Plas Mawr about a quarter to eight, Mr. Lewker tells me. You then went up to your cottage to change. By the cliff path, that'd be?"

"It would."

"And you'd come down it again when you had changed. About what time would that be?"

"I was just in time for dinner, if that's good enough. It was due to begin at eight-thirty—an hour later than usual."

"Then at eight-twenty-five, let's say, you crossed the wooden bridge on the cliff path. Did you—looking back now, sir, very carefully—did you no-tice anything particular about the bridge when you crossed it coming down?"

"Such as a land mine hanging on the rail, or a long fuse burning? I did not, Inspector."

Grimmett tapped meditatively with the butt of his pen on the table.

"Mr. Cattespool," he said, but as though to himself, "David Webhouse was probably killed by the explosion of a booby-trap, set to go off when he—or anyone else—trod on the bridge. You didn't set it off when you crossed the bridge at eight-twenty-five. At nine-fifty-five, an hour and a half later, David Webhouse tried to cross the bridge and the trap went off. So that—if we accept those facts—someone must have gone up to the bridge between your crossing and Webhouse's death. We know of no one, so far, who—"

"It's escaped your notice, I suppose, that Cutpursey's missing—and that I saw someone who could have been Cutpursey in the wood just before we found the body?"

There was something more than sarcasm in Anthony's tone. The long thin hand that held the cigarette to his lips was shaking slightly.

"Ah yes, sir," said the inspector. "This person in the wood, now. You're certain you saw someone?"

"I got the merest glimpse of a human figure. Seemed to have a whitish head. That's all."

"Would you say it was a man or a woman?"

"I don't know, I tell you! Better get after Cutpursey, and ask him."

"You consider Cutpursey may have murdered his master, then?"

"He's done a bunk, hasn't he?"

"So he has, sir. But as far as we know, Cutpursey had no reason to want Mr. Webhouse dead."

Anthony hurled his cigarette into the fireplace and stood up abruptly. His thin swarthy face was dark red and his beard seemed literally to bristle.

"And I had—that's it, isn't it?" he said between his teeth. "You don't have to play ring-o'-roses with me, Inspector. I had reason—I didn't like Webhouse's manners and I did like his wife. So I first try to brain him with a rock and then blow him up. No doubt my success with the latter method was due to the practice I had on Jerry. It all fits in, doesn't it? All right—go ahead and prove it!"

The study door banged behind him before the inspector's protest could find expression.

"Exit," murmured Mr. Lewker, "in high dudgeon. A weasel hath not such a deal of spleen, as Lady Percy said of her fiery spouse."

"Ah, Harry Hotspur, you mean," said Grimmett, who read Shakespeare as lesser men read detective novels. "Do you reckon Cattespool's a hothead, now?"

"Hotspur was an exceedingly courageous man, Grimm. His fault was over-confidence, perhaps not too bad a fault when one is setting out to blow up a harbor wall under fire."

Grimmett sat up, his blue eyes agleam.

"As Mr. Anthony Cattespool did. Impudence, too, that sort of thing takes."

"Called daring in such cases. Did you notice, Grimm, that although the falling rock on Crib Goch had not been mentioned he brought it up himself as a possible attempt at murder?"

"I did, sir—brought it up and chucked it at us, so he did. I've known 'em play that game before now, and it's usually been the fake-innocent giveaway of evidence we can't help but find later. Look what we've got against him now, sir." The inspector flipped open his notebook. "He hated Webhouse and there's no doubt he wanted his wife. He was the last to go near that bridge before Webhouse was killed. He was in cahoots with a popper at the Llanerch Quarry—"

"He presented us with that information himself," interposed Mr. Lewker.

"Knowing we were bound to find out, sir—and not knowing we could identify the type of explosive used for the murder. As for theair rifle, anyone can show himself a bad shot. By your own account, no one but Cattespool could have made that rock fall. By gum, sir," Grimmett ended, "a bit more taping-up, and we'll have enough circumstantial evidence for a case!"

"And the alibi for the time Webhouse was fired at?"

"Alibis can be faked, sir."

Grimmett shut his notebook with a slap. Mr. Lewker looked thoughtful.

"The hypothesis, then," he boomed, "is that Anthony Cattespool, having murdered David Webhouse in this extraordinary way, is so confident of our inability to prove his guilt that he is prepared tacitly to admit motive, opportunity, and means."

"If you put it like that," said the inspector less confidently, "it does look a bit extra audacious."

Mr. Lewker nodded.

"And I have no doubt," he said, "that the deed for which Anthony Cattespool received the Distinguished Service Order was likewise extra audacious."

CHAPTER IX

THE KNIGHT AND THE MOTHER

As Mr. Lewker, fulfilling his office of callboy, entered the hall and crossed it towards the drawing-roomdoor, he saw Tansy. She was sitting on the step of the open front door with her thin brown arms curled tightly round the spaniel Flora. Her back was towards him, but something forlorn in her attitude touched him. Mountains, murders, and melodrama might draw Mr. Lewker as with steel wires; but if anything could break the bond of his amateur or professional enthusiasms it was the sight of a child in trouble. Postponing his mission to bring Sir Henry Lydiate to the study, he walked to the front door.

"Greeting, Titania," he boomed cheerfully. " 'The female ivy so enrings the barky fingers of the elm.' "

Tansy looked round and smiled up at him briefly.

"Flora's not feeling very barky just now," she said, "and I'm not either. I'm worried."

Mr. Lewker sat down on the step beside her. Flora thrust her muzzle into his lap, and presently, having received the expected fondling, withdrew and began to tug at his shoelace.

"Worried?" he repeated. "With myself and Inspector Grimmett here, Tough, there is no need for you to worry. All will come right in the end, as it did with those people in the wood near Athens."

"That was a dream and this is real," said Tansy unanswerably. "It's Mr. Cutpursey I'm worried about," she added.

"I expect he has gone off into the hills to watch beasties, Tough. That was what he did before, was it not?"

Tansy nodded. But there was no smile on her small face and the blue eyes were troubled.

"I heard Uncle Anthony saying it must have been Mr. Cutpursey who—who did it," she said miserably, "because he wouldn't have run away if he hadn't. You don't think so, do you? I like Mr. Cutpursey awf'ly, you see, so he *can't* have done it. He told me all sorts of things about rabbits and squirrels and foxes, and I know he was cross and funny to some people but he wasn't really cross and funny when you got to know him like I did—so please don't go thinking that, will you?"

Mr. Lewker patted her hand. "It is in Cutpursey's favor that Tansy Pauncefoot stands up for him," he said gravely. "But it would be a very good thing if he came back to Plas Mawr."

"Would it?" she said eagerly. "Why?"

"Because, Tough, I think he could help us to find out the real criminal."

"Oh." Tansy was silent for a moment. Then she said slowly, "I don't think I want to find out the real criminal. I don't want anyone to have done it."

"I know," said Mr. Lewker gently. "But someone did, and they will have to be punished." He regarded her golden head meditatively. "I suppose Cutpursey did not tell you where he went to watch beasties?"

Tansy bent to slap Flora. "Up in the hills somewhere," she replied. "Flora, you *are* naughty! Look, she's pulled your shoelace untied."

Mr. Lewker retied his lace and stood up.

"Enough! Hold, or cut bowstrings," he said. "You remember Bottom the weaver, Tough? 'I will sing, that they shall hear I am not afraid.' Take Flora for a walk down to the lodge—you might introduce her to Constable Jones—and try singing on the way. For my part, I have work to do."

"All right," said Tansy more cheerfully.

Mr. Lewker went to the drawing room. He found Anthony and Clare sitting on the sofa in earnest talk; Clare's hand was in Anthony's and they scarcely looked up at his entrance. Feckenham was reading and Mrs. Pauncefoot was knitting grimly. Sir Henry Lydiate, who had been sitting near the window, rose stiffly at the actor-manager's summons and followed him to the study.

Grimmett, after a brief glance of mild inquiry at Mr. Lewker, became the deferential official.

"It's most kind of you, sir," he said gravely, when the old man was settled in his chair, "to come along and help us. This is a very unfortunate business."

"Shocking," said Sir Henry, raising a thin hand and letting it fall. "Quite shocking. When my housekeeper told me of it this morning I refused to believe her."

"It's true, unhappily, sir."

"Yes, yes—quite. Unhappily, as you say. Most unhappily. That poor little woman—but she is bearing up bravely, bravely. Yes, Charles Feckenham has given me the gist of the dreadful affair. It could not have been an accident, I understand?"

"We feel pretty certain it was murder, sir."

"T'chk!" Sir Henry wagged his head and tugged at his white mustache. "Quite incredibly shocking. And you have no clue to the identity of the ruffian who did the deed?"

"It's there, sir, that we hope you may help us," said Grimmett evasively. "You left the house about fifteen minutes before the explosion occurred. If you went up the cliff path—"

"Ah, but I didn't," said Sir Henry quickly. "I walked down to the lodge and along the road."

"That's a longer way round to your house, isn't it?"

"True, Inspector. But the cliff path is steep, and I am an old man. Furthermore, the evening was darker than the evenings have been of late, and I preferred to take the easier footing of the highway." He turned courteously to the actor-manager, who was as usual seated a little away from the table. "I was saying only the other day, Lewker, that the brilliant weather of the past week was unusual for North Wales, even in June. I fear it has broken—indeed, I would say, from long experience of Welsh weather, that we shall have a heavy storm within the next day or two."

"The glass is certainly falling steadily," agreed Mr. Lewker.

"Ah, that is the thing to watch," nodded the old man. "A sudden fall, and it will soon rise again. A slow and steady fall, and there will be bad weather, depend upon it. These wireless forecasts are quite unreliable in our mountain valleys."

Inspector Grimmett, who had listened to this meteorological discourse with commendable patience, opened his notebook.

"Would you mind, Sir Henry, answering a few questions?" he asked. "We are trying to fill in the details. In a case like this, you'll understand we're in duty bound to get a clear idea of all the circumstances, both before and after the crime."

Sir Henry nodded his bald head vigorously. "Of course, of course. Duty must be done, Inspector. Pray ask me what you will."

Mr. Lewker, watching from the background the lined and bony face, the high-bridged nose and heavy-lidded eyes wondered if there was not a shade too much of the innocent dotard in Sir Henry's manner. He could not be more than seventy-one or two, and his speech and spirit at the dinner table of last night had suggested a mind active and keen. Perhaps, though, this was his courteous way of attempting to make things easier for Grimmett.

"Thank you, sir," Grimmett was saying. "A few general ones first. The late Mr. Webhouse, I gather, has been a neighbor of yours for the past three years. Is that so?"

"That is so, Inspector. Until the present year, however, we had hardly met. Webhouse was in London a good deal. He bought this place from Lord Capel's executors, as I expect you know, when he married."

"That would be his first marriage, of course."

"Yes. To Hilda Pauncefoot, the daughter of Mrs. Pauncefoot, whom you have doubtless met. She was an actress, I believe."

Sir Henry's tone implied that he preferred his last statement to remain a belief rather than a faintly unpleasant fact. Mr. Lewker, remembering something, ventured to put a question of his own.

"Did you ever meet the first Mrs. Webhouse, Sir Henry? I will say frankly," he added, "that I have heard rumors—and though rumors are always unpleasant these may have some slight bearing on the case—that Hilda Webhouse died of drink, her husband's ill-treatment of her being the root cause."

"Scandal, sir," returned Sir Henry with severity, "I detest and avoid as I would the plague. I advise you to do the same."

"And yet," countered Mr. Lewker, unabashed, "even the plague has its cause. And some of those who detest it are not allowed to avoid it."

Sir Henry fingered his mustache (Cavalry? wondered Mr. Lewker) and unbent slightly.

"True, Lewker, true. None the less, hearsay is not a thing I care to deal with. I will, however, give you my own impression, if you think it would be of any use, Inspector?"

"Pray con—please go ahead, sir," amended Grimmett hurriedly; he found Sir Henry's nineteenth-century manner contagious.

"I thank you. I met Hilda Webhouse only twice. She was a pretty little thing, far too young for Webhouse. I received the impression that she was an unhappy woman. And," said Sir Henry more warmly, "with reason, I should imagine. *De mortuis nil nisi bonum*, gentlemen, but David Webhouse was a boor. It passes my comprehension how any gently nurtured gel could marry the fellow. A coarse, half-educated demagogue—but my tongue runs away with me."

"You think he ill-treated his first wife, sir?" pressed the inspector.

Sir Henry raised his hand, palm outwards. "Ill-treatment, Inspector, may mean many things. I say no more, except to admit that I was profoundly shocked, on my second meeting with the first Mrs. Webhouse, to observe that she was undoubtedly slightly—ah—tipsy."

Grimmett, after a rapid glance at Mr. Lewker, who remained impassive as a stone Buddha, resumed his questioning.

"You told us, sir, that until the present year you and Mr. Webhouse hardly met at all. This year, I take it, you've visited here more often."

"Half a dozen times, perhaps, in all. Twice to dine—the present Mrs. Webhouse, poor little woman, was charmingly hospitable—and on other occasions on business."

"The business being this hydroelectric bill of Mr. Webhouse's?"

"Yes." Sir Henry seemed disinclined to speak about it.

"You are the president of the protest association against this bill?" Grimmett persisted.

"I am."

"And Mr. Webhouse, as I understood, was the leader of the party in the House of Commons who will try to push the bill through Parliament?"

"He was."

Grimmett blew gently through his mustache, shuffled papers, affected to make a note. Then he resumed as patiently as before.

"Your visits here, sir—to Mr. Webhouse, that is—were for the purpose of discussing the bill?"

"Yes."

"You were trying to persuade him to drop it?"

"Yes." Sir Henry stopped, then continued as though unable to hold in the words. "I was trying to prevent the maturing of a dastardly crime, sir."

Grimmett looked startled.

"The enslaving of this land of Snowdonia to the hydroelectric engineers," went on the old man, growing more vehement as he proceeded, "would be a crime against society, against posterity. Who was Webhouse that he should rob our children of their heritage, for the sake of a futile experiment? Experiment it would be, gentlemen, for the engineers themselves are not certain that the fluctuating waterpower of these hills can be harnessed economically—and one cannot doubt, with past examples plain before us, that electricity as a source of power will be outdated before the end of this century.

And for this temporary expedient the fellow was willing to ruin a country-side, to filch from the nation of its few and dwindling areas of unspoiled beauty!" He gestured with trembling fingers. "Inspector—Lewker—I contend without fear of contradiction that theft on such a scale would be a crime. Yes, a crime blacker than any in the calendar."

His high voice cracked a little on the last word and he sat back heavily in his chair. Mr. Lewker was impressed. No sign of the failing, repetitive dotard here. Sir Henry's normal phraseology might be archaic, but he knew how to condense his arguments into pithy and striking form when he wished; knew, too, how to use his voice, which was no longer creaky and affected when he spoke with feeling. The old man was no unworthy opponent for David Webhouse, M.P. Grimmett, however, went placidly on with his questions.

"Did your arguments make any impression on Mr. Webhouse, sir?"

"None." The monosyllable had the inflection of finality.

"He felt as strongly on the other side as you feel on yours, I take it. With Mr. Webhouse's temperament, that doubtless led to heated arguments."

"The arguments, Inspector, generally ended in Webhouse's being insufferably rude. It was his way."

"You came to see him on the night before the murder took place. May I ask why that particular night was chosen, Sir Henry?"

"I had that afternoon received a telephone call from Belmont-Jones. Edward Belmont-Jones is a member of the protest committee and we are on the same board of directors of a small company. He informed me that he had heard, in connection with his business, that Webhouse had been round to certain local quarries addressing the quarrymen in support of his bill. You will think it odd, perhaps, Inspector, but I felt I must go without delay to remonstrate with the fellow."

"I see, sir," nodded Grimmett. "And I take it the resulting argument was as heated as usual. Mr. Webhouse would end up in a temper, and you'd assure him you intended to continue the fight." His wide blue eyes looked up suddenly, gazing unwinking at Sir Henry. "Did you, perhaps, say it'd be a fight to the death?"

The quick glance the old man threw at him from beneath his white brows was angry and suspicious.

"I may very well have used some such phrase," he said irritably. "God bless me, Inspector, you're not fool enough to imagine I threatened the man?"

"No, sir, of course not," Grimmett said hastily. "I only wanted to—"

"Do you suggest that I—*I*—had any hand in Webhouse's death, sir?" Sir Henry appeared to be working himself into a passion. "Gracious heaven, man, use your brain, not your imagination! Why in the name of goodness should the fact—yes, I grant it you—that I would joyfully have seen Webhouse defeated, discredited, ruined if you like—why, I say, should that fact lead you to suppose that I would commit murder? Do I look like an assassin? Confound it, sir, even that pompous ass Sherlock Holmes would know better!" He stood up, caught Mr. Lewker's faintly amused eye, and coughed loudly. "Pray forgive me if I grow impatient, Inspector. Do you wish to ask me anything further."

"Thank you, sir—no."

Sir Henry made a very slight, very stiff little bow and went out. Grimmett sat back in his chair and sent a small gale whistling through his mustache.

"Your error, I think, Grimm," commented Mr. Lewker, wagging his head. "You should not have tried to frighten the last of the Lydiates."

Sergeant Pitt came in from the library.

"Fiery old cock, that," he remarked, helping himself to a cigarette. "All right, sir? I've run out of fags. Struck me, though, he was a bit too good to be true. Stamp the fellow into the mud? Ho, yes—but kill him? What, me? Ho, no! That's his line, and it sounded phony to me. He's the sort that'd think killing a bloke a sight more gentlemanly than ruining him like he said. If you ask me—"

"We don't ask you," snapped Inspector Grimmett with unusual venom. "Get back in there and keep your ears open."

"Yessir," said the sergeant, retreating smartly. "Not," he muttered as he disappeared, "that there's been much worth hearing so far."

Grimmett sighed and turned to Mr. Lewker.

"Maybe you're right, sir," he said. "But there was no reason for him to fly off the handle like that. He must know we haven't found the murderer yet and that there was a possibility we might consider him. Yet the first jolt I give him, he sees for the very first time that we're looking round Webhouse's enemies for possibles. That's what he wanted us to think, I reckon."

"Yes," returned Mr. Lewker meditatively. "But Sir Henry Lydiate, Grimm, dates from a time when people were very sharply divided into classes and grades. If you were a gently nurtured gel, it was incredible that you could marry a half-educated boor. If you were an actress, you were indubitably immoral and hardly mentionable. Crimes were committed by the criminal classes. It is not impossible that Sir Henry believes himself to be incapable of murder merely because of his position in society, and therefore finds it strange and shocking that we should so much as think of him as a possible murderer."

"I don't know about that," said the inspector dubiously. "But I do know he had a nasty row with Webhouse a quarter of an hour before the murder and that he could have gone up the cliff path and set the booby-trap."

Mr. Lewker sat up. "Yes, Grimm. The trap had to be set. That is something we must concentrate on. Assuming for the moment that Cattespool did not set it when he came down the cliff path before dinner, we may—"

He was not allowed to develop this thesis. A knock at the study door was followed immediately by the entry of Dilys the maid with a tray. Behind her entered Mrs. Pauncefoot, knitting in hand.

"Put it on the table, girl," she rapped. "Not there—in the middle. Now get on with you and clear the things from the drawing room."

Dilys obeyed and retired, breathing heavily. Mrs. Pauncefoot seated herself in the chair opposite the inspector and nodded at the tray, which bore teapot, jugs, and three cups.

"You'll be ready for a cup," she said shortly. "They've had some in the drawing room."

"That's very thoughtful of you, ma'am, I'm sure," said Grimmett, who had intended to question Charles Feckenham next. "But I wonder if you'd mind—"

"You can pour out yourself, I expect," said Mrs. Pauncefoot. "The other one's in the library, is he? Don't stint the sugar. There's plenty."

She flicked her knitting into position (it appeared to be the groundwork of a red woolen vest) and began to knit. Grimmett rubbed his cranium and glanced helplessly at Mr. Lewker, who grinned shamelessly.

"I've got five minutes," announced the lady significantly. "Then I'm going to start getting dinner. What do you want to know?"

"Well," muttered Grimmett, "I'd prefer it, ma'am, if Mr. Feckenham could come here—"

"The tea 'll get cold," said Mrs. Pauncefoot, knitting rapidly. "Pour it out, take a cup to your man next door, and we can start. You can sup it while I'm talking."

Grimmett gave in. When the unseen Pitt had received his cup he resumed his seat and his official dignity and looked somewhat sternly at the grim face in front of him.

"We'll start, ma'am," he said, "with your statement of last night. You say here—"

"What I said then," said Mrs. Pauncefoot, "I abide by. I'm not one of those here today and gone tomorrow. Let thy word be thy bond. No flightiness. I'm not flighty, Inspector."

"No, ma'am," said Grimmett with conviction. "All the same, it would—"

"I'm not the talking kind," said Mrs. Pauncefoot, her needles flying. "Never did believe in it. But I've come here to talk and talk I will. You want to get after the man who killed David Webhouse and not waste time. I can't tell you who killed him, but I'll tell you this. He was a well-hated man, was David Webhouse, and reason behind it. Sinful he was, and a blasphemer, as Mr. Lewker's heard from his own lips. There'll be no weeping and wailing and gnashing of teeth at David's death, unless it's from that Cutpursey."

"Ah, yes." Grimmett succeeded in butting his way in. "Cutpursey was what you might call devoted to Mr. Webhouse, so I hear."

Mrs. Pauncefoot made a short contemptuous sound in her throat.

"Some might call it that," she said. "I call it two of a kind. Both of 'em surly, ill-mannered men and godless too. Typical quarrymen, my late husband would have said, and he knew quarrymen."

"Was your husband a quarryman, then?" Grimmett thrust in sharply. "I should say, was—"

"He was not, Inspector. But it's David Webhouse I'm talking about, so don't interrupt, if you please. Ill of the dead isn't what I'd speak if I had my choice, but according to books the police want to know everything when it comes to murders. David was a bully. He enjoyed bullying, and he bullied his wife, my Hilda that was. What she saw in him I never could think, though going on the stage—and against my wishes and her father's, as you well may fancy—gave her queer ideas. He made her life as wretched as a man can make a woman's, Inspector. She took to drink for comfort and it killed her. And that, if you want to know, is why *I'm* shedding no tears."

Her rasping voice, as she fired off her sentences, scarcely altered a semitone. Mr. Lewker, watching that grim unchanging face, the wide thin-lipped mouth set like a trap, the eyes turned always downward to her knitting, reflected that tragicomedy, though shunned by successful playwrights, was the real stuff of life. A playwright might have made a good comedy character-part out of Mrs. Pauncefoot, but he could never have given her that last speech.

"You must have disliked David Webhouse intensely," he said, seizing his opportunity as she paused. "Yet you stayed in his house after your daughter died. Why did you stay?"

"I had to live somewhere, and there was Tansy to think of." There was a momentary softening of the hard features as she spoke the child's name. "David wasn't averse to having his house looked after while he was away in London, either. Then when he got married again he'd have turned me out lock, stock, and barrel, if Clare hadn't persuaded him. That girl's flighty, but she's got a good heart. There was another reason for my staying on. Maybe you won't understand it."

"You wished to help Clare, perhaps," suggested Mr. Lewker gently.

Mrs. Pauncefoot spared him one sharp glance.

"You're no fool," she returned. "Yes, there was that, I'd no wish to see another girl go the way of mine. But there was this, too. I believe in the Scriptures. Vengeance is mine, saith the Lord, I will repay. I waited for that. It came. I knew it would. I'm satisfied."

"Well, I'm sure that's understandable, ma'am," said Grimmett, not without embarrassment, "but you'll understand we've got our duty. Whoever did this—"

"Very well, Inspector. Thou shalt not kill—that's Scripture. But you won't find the killer here. David Webhouse made enemies wherever he went. It was his nature. You'll find one of them did this."

"Someone outside this household altogether, you mean?"

Mrs. Pauncefoot nodded. "That's what I mean. Cast thy net wide. No need to stare at me, Inspector. I can't tell you more than that."

"But there is something you must have noticed, Mrs. Pauncefoot," said Mr. Lewker. "Had not Mr. Webhouse shown unusual signs of nervousness lately?"

"He had." The knitting needles flew faster. "The man was afraid. He felt vengeance upon him."

"For instance," continued the actor-manager, "he complained about his food?"

She looked up at him quickly and keenly, and for a moment did not reply. Then she resumed her knitting, eyes cast down.

"I wondered how you knew. The milk he gave to the dog, wasn't it?"

"Yes. The glass of milk and soda you brought to his study. He poured some of it into a saucer for the spaniel."

"He'd talked of queer tastes in the food before," said Mrs. Pauncefoot. "Good food it was, as he well knew. It's my opinion he was afraid of being poisoned. That was part of his punishment."

She stopped knitting and gathered up the half-finished garment. Outside the study window the afternoon was darkening, and the room was gloomy. As she folded the dark red wool Mr. Lewker had the unpleasant illusion that her hands were dipped in blood.

"I've got to get the dinner," she said, standing up. "Is that all?"

"One thing, Mrs. Pauncefoot," Mr. Lewker said. "Your late husband had some contact with quarrymen, it seems. How was that?"

"My husband was a traveler for Ball's Explosives Limited of Caernarvon," said Mrs. Pauncefoot, going to the door. "They make quarry blasting charges. And," she added, with a touch of pride, "he was a personal friend of Mr. Edward Belmont-Jones, one of the directors."

The door closed behind her.

CHAPTER X

THE MAID AND THE BRIDGE-BUILDER

Mrs. Pauncefoot's exit was followed by a long-drawn whistle from the invisible sergeant in the library, a grunt from Mr. Lewker, and a windy fantasia on Inspector Grimmett's mustache.

"By gum, sir, the field's opening up a bit!" exclaimed the inspector, flopping back in his chair and staring at the actor-manager. "If it's connections with explosives we're after, the whole boiling of 'em seems to be in it."

"You will probably find the maid's father is a quarryman and Mrs. Price who comes in to clean uses blasting powder for scouring."

"All very well to joke, sir," said Grimmett, reproachfully, "but here's Mrs. P., who on her own showing hated Webhouse like poison—more or less praises the Lord he's been killed—and her husband knew all about blasting charges. It's a safe bet she knows what rackarock is and how to use it."

"She gave us the information about her husband quite freely, Grimm."

"All right, sir. That's more than Sir Henry did about his company. If he's a fellow director of this Ball's Explosives firm with what's-his-name—Belmont-Jones—the odds are he knows a bit about rackarock. That is, if they make it, as I presume. Sir Henry had means and opportunity, as well as motive of a sort. But—going back to Mrs. P., sir—what's all this about poison?"

Mr. Lewker relit his pipe. The short regular stabs of flame as he held the match to it emphasized the gloom of the study and showed his brow deeply furrowed.

"Webhouse disliked the spaniel and the fuss made of her," he said slowly. "Yet he poured half his glass of milk and soda into a saucer for her. That came out in conversation on my first evening here, and I thought it odd. I think it odder still now."

Grimmett massaged his scalp furiously. "The whole setup's odd, so it is," he said irritably. "Everything points to Cattespool but we can't lay a finger on a good solid clue. Now everyone turns out to be an explosives expert. It's a bit odd, that is."

"Not at all," Mr. Lewker returned. "Webhouse began life in a quarry and married the daughter of a traveler visiting quarries. He took on an old quarryman as gardener. There is nothing odd, therefore, about his mother-in-law and his gardener being acquainted possibly—with quarry explosives. As for Sir Henry Lydiate, a firm of explosive manufacturers is a natural product in a country where stone and slate are quarried, and a man like Lydiate, whose father in all probability started the firm, is naturally a director. No, Grimm. There is no oddness here. But elsewhere there is."

"Where, then, sir?"

Mr. Lewker, by subtlety of voice and gesture, became Alonzo, King of Naples. " 'These are not natural events.' " he boomed in Alonzo's words. " 'They strengthen From strange to stranger.' By which, Grimm, I mean that the events we already know of grow more strange with each added morsel of information bearing on them."

Grimmett eyed him suspiciously for a moment.

"Sounds to me as if you're on to something," he growled.

"Who—I? Far from it, Grimm, I do assure you. But this I feel." He raised an impressive finger aloft. "Someone is manipulating evidence. Someone is being clever. And that, in my peevish way, I begin to resent."

Someone knocked timidly on the door. The inspector roared a somewhat testy *Come in*! The maid Dilys opened the door and shuffled apprehensively into the room with one eye on the tea things and the other on Grimmett, who hastily substituted his beaming smile for the scowl he had been wearing.

"A very nice cup of tea, Miss Jones," he said ingratiatingly. "Very nice indeed. No—don't take the tray out just yet. While you're here we may as well run through one or two small details. Take a chair, will you?"

Dilys lowered her plump form on to the very edge of the chair, without taking her large brown eyes from the inspector, and by means of two spasmodic wriggles occupied a small part of the seat. She was short and fat and fair, and her round pale face wore an expression of mingled awe and excitement. She pushed back an untidy wisp of hair from her forehead without moving her gaze from Grimmett's face. He read aloud her brief statement, made to Inspector Evans, which amounted to little more than that she had heard a loud bang sometime after dinner when she was in the kitchen washing up.

"Very clear, Miss Jones," Grimmett said pleasantly, laying down the paper. "A sad business this, I'm afraid. You know we think someone killed Mr. Webhouse, I suppose?"

"Well, I do, sir, yes."

"We are here to find out who it was, and we want your help. Was Mr. Webhouse a good master?"

Dilys looked surprised. "Well, now, sir, I didn't see that much of him, like. Mrs. Pauncefoot, she tells me what to do, isn't it?"

"Ah, of course. And Mrs. Webhouse as well, eh?"

"Well, not her, much. Seldom she comes into the kitchen." Dilys came near to tossing her head. "Too busy with her own affairs, I dare say."

A denser person than Inspector Grimmett could have seen that Dilys had something to impart and would impart it or burst.

"Her own affairs?" he prompted.

"Well, it's not for me to tell tales, isn't it?"

"I think it is," said Grimmett, having disentangled the grammar of this. "But," he added gravely, "only if the tales are true, Miss Jones."

Dilys drew in her breath and wriggled further back in her chair.

"Well," she said rapidly, "if a certain lady goes walking with a certain gentleman when her husband's away, and meets him in secret, like, when her husband's at home, it's not for me to say good or bad but I can't help noticing, isn't it?"

"How do you mean, now—in secret, Miss Jones?"

"Well, sliding out into the back shrubbery at night, when Mr. Webhouse might be working in the study or snoozing after his dinner, like."

"You mean you've seen this?"

"Well, yes, indeed—just outside my scullery window, kissing and that, I couldn't help seeing, isn't it? And," added Dilys, with unctuous satisfaction, "Mr. Webhouse, he's seen it too, he has."

"How do you know that?"

Dilys looked away and shuffled her feet.

"Well, now, sir, it was by accident, like. I went out for a stroll in the garden, it being a fine moonlight night, not going near where Mrs. Web—I mean where this certain lady and gentleman was, and——"

"Just a moment, Miss Jones. When was this, please?"

"Well, it would be about three weeks ago. I'd done the dinner washing-up and my time was my own, like, so out I went in the garden, round by the little paths. Dark it was, too." Dilys's voice had lost its nervousness, and its singsong Welsh accent made the commonplace story sound strangely dramatic. "They two was whispering in the rosydendrums up the hill a bit—not that I went near to them, but it was a still quiet night. And then I happened to look up at the house, like, and there at the window, the bathroom window it was, and not a light in it, was a white face looking down at them two, white with the moonlight on it. Mr. Webhouse it was, sir—looking down at them two."

She paused theatrically. Mr. Lewker, though he did not much admire Dilys, admired her delivery and her effective use of repetition.

"Tell me, Miss Jones," he said. "Do you think the—um—two persons knew that Mr. Webhouse saw them?"

"Well, sir, I was just coming to that," Dilys said, not without a touch of reproachfulness. "The moment after I saw him looking down, they stopped whispering and came sliding through the bushes to the path where I was. Quick I was to hide away in the rosydendrums then, and they passed me by very close. And I heard him say, panting, like, 'This can't go on,' he says. Then they was past and gone and I saw them no more."

She finished on a "dying fall" that delighted Mr. Lewker. Grimmett rubbed his nose with his pen.

"And the name of this gentleman?" he demanded.

Dilys fidgeted and looked askance at him.

"I never did like him," she said.

"No? And his name?"

"Well, it was that Mr. Cattespool," said Dilys defiantly.

"Ah, yes. And now, Miss Jones, I wonder if you can tell us anything about

James Cutpursey. As you know, he has left Plas Mawr without saying where he was going."

Dilys seemed disconcerted by the lack of effect produced by her story. She took some time before responding to the inspector's new line of inquiry.

"Well," she said rather sulkily, at length, "he was a funny old sort, isn't it?"

"So he was. A bit surly, perhaps?"

"Well, that. But I meant always fussing after birds and animals, like. Buzzards and crows and such."

"You told me his old coat and his canvas bag were missing from the lodge. Might that mean he's gone off to look at buzzards somewhere?"

Dilys considered. "Yes, it might, then. Before now he's gone off all night— and he keeps odds and ends of food in the lodge."

Mr. Lewker leaned forward. "I would like you to think very carefully, Miss Jones, and tell us if Cutpursey ever said anything to indicate where he had been when he spent those nights out in the hills."

"Well, sir, I did ask him," she replied, "but never a word could you get out of him, isn't it?"

"He brought nothing back with him?" Mr. Lewker persisted.

She shook her head; and then put a finger to her plump chin.

"Well, now, he might, now you mention it. The next day it was I did out the lodge, and there on the mantelpiece was some old bits of rock, put there new, like. They had shiny bits in like gold."

"Are they there now?"

"No, sir. But—" She hesitated. "But if it's important, like—"

"It may be," said Mr. Lewker gravely.

"Well, then, sir, there was lots of them, so not meaning anything wrong and thinking he wouldn't miss one bit, I borrowed one, isn't it?"

"Can you show it us?"

"Well, I can then, sir," said Dilys, looking from Mr. Lewker to the inspector in evident puzzlement.

"We'd be obliged if you'd fetch it for us, Miss Jones," said Grimmett.

He turned to frown at Mr. Lewker as the girl went out.

"What's this, sir?" he demanded. "Is there a gold mine in the plot now?"

"A mine, possibly," returned the actor-manager, "though not—this time— an explosive one. Incidentally, Grimm, if I had that girl for a couple of months I could train her voice to perfection. She has natural inflection and tone depth. As Lady Macbeth she would be magnificent."

"What—with that face and figure?"

"Figure, my dear Grimm," boomed Mr. Lewker with dignity, "is far less important, on the Shakespearean stage, than voice. A truth," he added, "of which I am, perhaps, no unworthy example."

"As you say, sir. But I reckon in this case the tale was more than the voice.

That's a neat bit of confirmation she gave us, so it is. Cattespool was carrying on with Mrs. Webhouse—we could have guessed that but we've got it plain now—and he knew three weeks ago, if he didn't before, that Webhouse knew what was going on. I've said it before and I'll say it again. Everything points to Cattespool. All this other stuff is leading nowhere, and we'll find—"

Dilys knocked at the door and came in. She held out an irregularly shaped piece of gray rock about two inches square and an inch thick. Mr. Lewker took it from her and held it so that Grimmett could see the little cubes of bright yellow metal embedded in it.

"Copper pyrites," he observed. "Sometimes called fool's gold." He turned the piece of rock over, revealing a rough black metallic surface. "And here we have a little manganese—used, I believe, in making explosives."

"Tcha!" said Grimmett exasperatedly.

His bland smile as he returned the piece of rock to Dilys was less natural than usual.

"Thank you, Miss Jones. Perhaps you'll take the tray out with you? And if you'd kindly ask Mr. Feckenham to step in here for a moment I'd be obliged."

Dilys, plainly disappointed at so tame an end to her interview, picked up the tea-things and went to the door.

"One more question, Miss Jones," said Mr. Lewker suddenly.

She turned eagerly. "Yes, sir?"

"What kind of lighting is there at the lodge?"

"Oh, the lodge, sir?" Dilys's face fell again. "Well, it's candles. That old Cutpursey, he won't use the oil lamp. At some poor place in Derbyshire he came from, they always used candles, he says."

"Yes. Thank you, Miss Jones. That is all."

Grimmett waited until the door had closed behind her and then faced the actor-manager.

"And what may be the case against Cutpursey, now?" he demanded sarcastically. "Made explosives, did he, out of manganese he got in the hills? Used a candle as a time fuse?"

"I think not, Grimm," returned Mr. Lewker seriously. "For one thing Sergeant Pitt tells us that rackarock was the compound used, and for another I very much doubt whether manganese dioxide could readily be used by the maker of explosives in the home."

"It couldn't, sir," confirmed Pitt's voice from the library.

"Then," grumbled the inspector, "what's so noteworthy in Cutpursey having the stuff on his mantelpiece?"

Mr. Lewker twinkled at him. "Why, manganese is nearly always mined by driving tunnels into the rock, Grimm. What does that suggest to you?"

"Not a damned thing," snorted Grimmett, sounding rather like a mild explosive himself.

The door opened and Charles Feckenham came into the study.

"Just answered the phone," he said. "In order I hope? For you, Inspector—from Caernarvon."

Grimmett thanked him and went out hastily, leaving Feckenham to lower himself into a chair and light the cigarette Mr. Lewker offered him. He drew at it for some time in silence. Mr. Lewker, filling his pipe, glanced speculatively at the brown immobile face. There was character to be read there, in spite of its lack of expression: active mind, impulsive nature, a strong will allied to recklessness; the mask of languid indifference could not conceal the signs. Feckenham's bridges in Ceylon, he thought, were probably miracles of engineering. Here was a man to whom every obstacle would be a challenge; who would meet opposition with daring and ingenuity.

"Is there a murderer here?" Feckenham said unexpectedly, breaking into his thoughts. "Shakespeare quotation," he added with a wry grin. "What you were wondering, though."

"I am wondering," said Mr. Lewker, holding a match to his pipe and puffing spasmodically, "what you meant when you said that David Webhouse was afraid of theft."

"Obvious, surely. Cattespool was after his wife."

"I see."

There was another silence. Feckenham sighed, rose lazily from his chair, and going to the library door put his head inside.

"Afternoon, Sergeant," he observed affably, and returned to his seat. "Oughtn't I to be warned or something?" he added to Mr. Lewker.

"Not at this juncture. I fancy you are at liberty to protest against your words being taken down, or to refuse to speak, if you wish."

"Ah." He lay back and blew a long jet of smoke at the ceiling. "Clare says my Derby flop has cropped up. That so?"

Mr. Lewker nodded, watching him.

"Looks as if I'd better come clean," drawled Feckenham. "If there's anything against you tell the tale yourself. Sound maxim. Or isn't it?"

Inspector Grimmett came in frowning and took his seat at the table. He rustled papers and coughed officially.

"Well, Inspector, have they got Cutpursey?" Feckenham asked with a curl of his thin lips.

Grimmett scowled at him. "Cutpursey's been seen in three places at once," he said shortly. "Getting into a train at Denbigh, getting off a boat at Holyhead, and being thrown out of a pub in Blaenau Ffestiniog, wherever that may be." He cleared his throat gruffly. "Now, sir. This statement of yours."

He dealt briskly with the statement and proceeded, more affably, with interrogation.

"I believe Mrs. Webhouse is your cousin, sir?"

"Right. Kids together and so forth."

"And you've been staying at Plas Mawr for the last fortnight—a bit more than that?"

"Sixteen days. Away for three days at Epsom. The Derby."

"The Derby, yes. During your stay here, sir, have you noticed anything at all odd? Mr. Webhouse's behavior, for instance?"

Feckenham considered. "Webhouse was damn' bad tempered and false genial by turns," he said. "Didn't like him. Didn't like the way he treated Clare."

"You didn't think he was at all—apprehensive, shall we say?"

"Jumpy's the word. Complaining about his food. Kicking the dog. Reason—Clare and Anthony Cattespool hitting it off too well for his liking."

"That's your opinion, sir. Yes. Well, we'll leave it for the moment. To come to another small matter, your visit to the Derby, sir. I understand—"

"Half a jiffy, Inspector."

Feckenham leaned forward to put his cigarette end in the ashtray. His gaze met and held the inspector's.

"Don't know what you've heard," he said evenly, "but here's the straight story. I went down to Epsom—left here early on the fourth, Friday, and got back for dinner on Monday. I was damn' tight for money when I went. When I came back I was worse than broke. Shoved everything I could borrow on Sunny Day—you know what happened."

"Yes, sir?" prompted Grimmett as he paused.

Feckenham's stare seemed to be trying to reach the mind behind the inspector's china-blue eyes. Then he relaxed and helped himself to another cigarette.

"Expect the maid overheard us, or something," he said resignedly. "If she told you she probably got it wrong. In fact, I was in here on Monday night, trying to get a loan out of Webhouse. I needed the money like hell, and still do. Webhouse refused. Refused with a sneer—he would. I was rude in return. He bellowed at me. Short but noisy row. And that's all."

The inspector's fresh-colored features did not move a muscle. One would have said that he had heard all this before. He jotted briefly in his notebook and nodded.

"Very well, sir. Have you any objection to telling us what sum you asked Mr. Webhouse to lend you?"

"Four thousand. Just enough to save my bacon. He could afford it, you know. He was rich, as rich goes these days."

"Yes. I reckon, sir, this urgent need would have something to do with—um—your impending knighthood?"

The other's twisted smile flickered for a moment. "Right. Wouldn't do for prospective knight bachelor to be had up for debt. Bankruptcy Court to Buckingham Palace. Not so good."

"As bad as that, sir, was it?" Grimmett commented.

"Yes. And still is."

"I'm sorry, sir." Grimmett glanced at Mr. Lewker, who shook his head. "Then for the present that's all—and I appreciate your frankness, sir."

Feckenham got slowly to his feet.

"I didn't kill Webhouse, you know," he said, and went out.

Grimmett drew a long breath and swung his chair round to face Mr. Lewker.

"Well, that's the lot," he grunted. "And a rare tricky lot, so it is. What d'you reckon made Feckenham give us all that about his row with Webhouse, sir?"

"Frank," said Sergeant Pitt, coming in from the library, "is our Mr. Feckenham's middle name."

"Frank and explicit is the line to take," murmured Mr. Lewker, "when you wish to conceal your own mind and to confuse the minds of others—No, Grimm, not Shakespeare this time. Benjamin Disraeli said that."

"Proper Tory misruler, he was," Pitt interjected disgustedly.

"But I fancy the reason for Charles Feckenham's disclosure might have been this," Mr. Lewker continued thoughtfully. "Clare Webhouse told him that we knew of his visit to the Derby and seemed interested in it. Feckenham thought it likely that his row with Webhouse had been overheard—by Dilys, possibly—and jumped to the conclusion that we knew of his betting losses and his attempt to borrow from Webhouse. He therefore decided to come clean, as he put it."

Grimmett nodded. "Conjecture, sir, but not unlikely. Anyhow, I reckon he wouldn't have told us if he could have counted on keeping it quiet. What's Ceylon like, sir—difficult country?"

Mr. Lewker wagged his head reprovingly at the inspector.

"The central part of the south, where—as I gather from the newspapers—Charles Feckenham's bridges have been built, is exceedingly mountainous," he replied. "No doubt a great deal of blasting had to be done. But, Grimm, a civil engineer like Feckenham is chiefly concerned with plans and calculations. He does not detonate explosives."

"Maybe not, sir," persisted Grimmett, "but he'd know all about 'em, so he would. The thing is, with Feckenham, that he'd get nothing by killing Webhouse—except revenge, and I can't see him blowing Webhouse up for refusing to lend him money."

"Wait a bit, sir," Pitt said quickly. "Have a go at this. Mrs. Webhouse and her cousin seem pretty friendly, eh? Kids together—both of 'em mentioned it. She wouldn't refuse him four thousand if she'd got it, and if he's in as tight a place as he says. Well, then, if Webhouse has left———"

"By gum, Sergeant," interrupted Grimmett, smacking his thigh, "that'd do it, so it would. I ought to have thought of it myself—reckon I'm getting old. If Webhouse left his money to his wife, and Feckenham knew that, we've got a motive there, right enough. But it's conjecture so far. We must get after that will, first thing tomorrow."

Faintly through the closed door came the measured tones of the grandfather clock in the hall.

"Six o'clock!" ejaculated the inspector. He began to gather his papers together. "Here—we'll have dinner time on us before we're ready."

"What is your next move, Grimm?" inquired the actor-manager, tapping out his pipe.

"Well, we want to sort out what we've got, of course, but that'll do after dinner. Tomorrow I want to get straight after the rackarock business—Llanerch Quarry first call—and we'll call on Webhouse's solicitors on the same trip. Immediate action, to put through a phone call or two, regarding Messrs. Cattespool and Feckenham. After that, might have time to check Cattespool's alibis for theair rifle evening and call in at Plas Bach. What time's dinner?"

"Half-past seven," Mr. Lewker informed him. "Grimm," he added, "will you need Sergeant Pitt for your immediate action?"

"No—I reckon not." Grimmett eyed him sharply. "What's your idea, sir? Something I've left out?"

"Hardly that. But I doubt, Grimm, I doubt. 'Honest doubt is called the beacon of the wise,' you know."

"No use doubting evidence," declared the inspector.

"Nevertheless I do," boomed Mr. Lewker, rubbing his chin. "I doubt all the evidence in this case. None of it is proof."

"Well, then, sir," Grimmett said patiently, "where do you propose to get your proof?"

"There are two things I need. One is Cutpursey. The other is knowledge of the exact method used in setting the trap for Webhouse."

Grimmett shook his head and began to push papers into his briefcase with the air of a man who has no more to contribute.

"I thought we'd got a good enough idea of how the charge was set off," he said, "and as for Cutpursey, I reckon he'll turn up in time and prove to have nothing to give us. He'd no motive anyway."

Pitt, who had been rapidly running through his shorthand notes, looked up suddenly. "You don't think we ought to get a posse from the county and comb the woods round here, sir?"

"Why should we?"

"Well, suppose whoever killed Webhouse thought Cutpursey knew too much. Suppose he bumped him off neat and tidy and hid the body in the thickets."

"After Cutpursey had taken his coat and bag from the lodge, ready to clear out?" retorted Grimmett.

"Might have been a blind," countered the sergeant.

"Or might not." Grimmett picked up his case. "Come on—we've had enough talk to go on with. Hallo, who's this?"

A knock on the door preceded the appearance of Dilys.

"There's another cup, please," she said.

"Mine," said Pitt. "I'll get it." He went into the library.

Mr. Lewker addressed the girl. "Mr. Cattespool stayed here last night, I gather," he said. "Has he been to his cottage since then—to obtain clothing, for instance?"

"Well, no, sir. Mr. Feckenham lent him a spare pair of pajamas, and clothes, like. He hasn't been out at all."

"Thank you."

Pitt returned with his cup and handed it to Dilys, who departed reluctantly.

"And now," said Mr. Lewker, "I presume I may have the pleasure of Sergeant Pitt's company for an hour?"

"You're welcome, sir." The inspector stared at him suspiciously. "I'd like to know what you're up to, so I would."

"I think it would be better if you did not. You shall have a full report afterwards, I promise you."

"Too kind, I'm sure," growled Grimmett, going to the door.

"I am kind as I am fair, like Sylvia. But there is one thing you should know, Grimm."

"And what may that be, sir?"

"There was a piece of Mark III nylon parachute cord in Clare Webhouse's handbag."

CHAPTER XI

BITS AND PIECES

As Sir Henry Lydiate had observed, the glass was falling steadily. The barometer in the hall (a ship's barometer by Bailey of Bennett's Hill, Mr. Lewker noted) had moved back its slender pointer almost to the curly-tailed "9" of twenty-nine degrees; and when he drummed gently on the glass with his fingertips the pointer moved another fraction of an inch towards the left. So gloomy was the early evening that the figures on the barometer dial were hard to decipher in the dark hall. The atmosphere was heavy, ominous of coming storm.

Inspector Grimmett made for the cloakroom where the telephone was located, and locked himself in. Mr. Lewker and Sergeant Pitt went out into the garden. They met no one in hall or garden; Plas Mawr was as silent as the overcast day itself, and might have been deserted by all its inhabitants. Only a distant yelp, suggesting that Flora had incurred the displeasure of someone in the kitchen, signalized the existence of life within its walls.

Mr. Lewker led the way to the spot where Webhouse's body had been found. The rhododendrons hung their big leaves slackly and not a leaf stirred in the shrubbery. The two men came through the narrow fringe of firs to the foot of the slope of debris. Above it rose the rock wall with its unbridged cleft, its top clear now of mist but dark and lowering under the darkening sky.

"I want you to look at the bridge, Sergeant," said Mr. Lewker. "In particular, one of the uprights of the handrail."

He started up the scree towards the splintered skeleton of wood.

"Correct me if I'm wrong, sir," Pitt said as he followed, "but it's the setting of the trap you're after, isn't it?"

"I want to know if it could be set, and if so how." He reached the bridge and halted. "Inspector Grimmett, I fear, has a prepossession towards Anthony Cattespool as the murderer. He cannot free his mind from the idea that Cattespool set the trap as he came down the path to dinner."

"Well, sir, it's a likely idea right enough," said the sergeant loyally. "Stand back and look at the case, and he's the only one as sticks out."

"True. But I want, for the moment, to forget Cattespool as a suspect. Let us assume that he did not set this trap. One of two things must have happened, in that case. Either the detonator and charge were not in place when Cattespool crossed the bridge at eight-twenty-five last night—which means that the murderer went up the cliff path and put them in place some time in the succeeding hour and a half—or they were in place but prevented from exploding until the murderer released some trigger or mechanism."

Pitt took off the soft hat he invariably donned when going out of doors and wiped his brow with a handkerchief.

"Feels like a steam laundry out here," he remarked in parentheses. "There's surely a possibility Cattespool happened not to tread on the end of the plank, though?"

"Is there?" Mr. Lewker shook his head. "This bridge consisted of two planks, not particularly wide. What man would set his feet one behind the other on the outside plank?"

"All right, sir. Rule that out, then. But—just supposing for a moment that Cattespool had set the trap already—he could have done just that, purposely, and got over without detonating the charge."

"Yes. Dismiss the possibility, Sergeant, if you please. Examine the bridge, or what is left of it, and then, if you will, plan for me 'the deep damnation of his taking off.' "

"Eh?" Pitt looked sideways at the actor-manager.

"Describe to me in detail how you yourself would have arranged the trap."

"I'd have done it different. For instance—"

"No, no—using the method we have postulated."

"Ah. Righto, sir."

Pitt frowned at the broken bridge, then stared up at the gap in the path a hundred feet above.

"I'm a bloody-minded murderer," he said, as if to himself. "I'm going to shove a charge in a crack under the bridge-end and fix it to detonate when a nail in the plank's pushed down. Well, I'm a careful chap—am I, sir?"

"Yes, I think you are."

"Good. Then I'll certainly test the doings proper. I'll have a mock-up—"

"A—mock-up?" interrupted Mr. Lewker.

"Yessir. Service slang for a dummy trial."

"Thank you, Sergeant. The word is new to me, though I should have guessed its meaning. A good English verb meaning to mimic, strengthened—as our common tongue so often strengthens and salts its verbs—with a preposition. But pray forgive me for mounting my hobby."

"That's all right, sir," said Pitt tolerantly. "Mine's carpentry. Now for this mock-up," he went on. "I'd want a detonator case, empty, and a chunk of wood or something the size of the rackarock charge. I drill the dummy charge so's I can push the detonator case in, put a filling of plastic wood to represent the firing cap—the nail's got to strike that—and place the dummy in the crack. Oh, and I'd want a short coilspring to support the plank."

"You would first have to move the bridge aside," Mr. Lewker pointed out.

"S'pose I would. Well, then I move the bridge back—bit of a weight, but looks as if I could heft it—so that the split plank was over the charge. Let's have a go."

He bent and took hold of the broken framework. On the loose footing of the scree he had some trouble in lifting it, but he succeeded in raising one end and moving it aside.

"Can be done, but needs muscle," he commented, breathing hard. "Unlikely to get shifted again by accident. Well, now I take out my folding steel rule and measure off the spot where I want to drive my screw."

"Not a nail?"

"Long screw, sir—the wood'll hold it more rigid. I drive my screw, bend it a fraction with a pair of strong pliers if it don't go true to the detonator, and there we are. Back I go, walk up the bridge and step on it natural. Then I look to see what's happened to my mock-up. Ah, all tiggity-boo."

"Tiggity—? Never mind, Sergeant. Go on."

"Everything's jake, sir. The plug of plastic wood has taken the imprint of the screw point. That means the detonator 'll be well and truly plonked."

Mr. Lewker nodded. His little eyes were gleaming.

"And now you have to place the real charge."

"All right, sir. Can do, but needs care. Shift the bridge—no, first I mark its exact position. A scratch on the flat rock'd do that. I put in the live charge just as I did the dummy. Now comes the ticklish bit, shifting the bridge back. But there's no real danger, because I've made certain the screw's clear of the detonator until the plank's depressed. I can test for readiness by lying down and squinting under the plank and pressing it down until the screw point's nearly touching. And—well, she's sitting pretty, sir."

"How long has all this taken you?" inquired Mr. Lewker.

Pitt closed his eyes and considered. "From the time I arrive at the bridge with my dummies all ready, I'd say a good ten minutes. But I could have tried out the mock-up beforehand. Then all I'd have to do would be to roll up with the real stuff, shift the bridge, substitute live ammo for dummy, replace bridge, test for readiness, and scram."

"Could you do this—the ticklish bit, as you described it—in the dark?"

"I wouldn't fancy it, sir," Pitt replied, "and that's a fact. If I did, I'd have a good torch handy, if only to make dead sure the screw point was going to strike true."

"And that," said Mr. Lewker with satisfaction, "would mean showing a light which might be seen by anyone on the terrace. Thank you, Sergeant. Your description was admirable. I feel it is a good thing you have an alibi for the time of this murder."

Pitt chuckled. "If I was planning murder," he said, "I'd find a better way than this. It may be self-acting, but there's too many pointers about it. I see what you're driving at, though. Trying to rule out the murderer rigging the trap after Cattespool crossed the bridge, aren't you?"

"Would you say that we have done so?"

"Shown it to be unlikely, sir, anyway. But if Cattespool rigged the trap as he came down, it wouldn't be dark, not to speak of, and—"

"Beshrew me your Cattespool, Sergeant! I come to my second alternative, which is that the trap was fully prepared with a live charge some time before Cattespool crossed the bridge last night, and that the murderer had arranged a safety catch, as it were, which could be quickly released. Let us proceed a little farther."

He went up the scree to the detached upright, the sergeant following, and halted by the broken post.

"Inspector Grimmett saw nothing very remarkable here," he said. "Well, Sergeant?"

Pitt bent and fingered the lashing of green cord with its frayed end dangling.

"Nylon parachute," he commented. "Don't know why the lashing—post's not sprung." He straightened himself suddenly. "Crikey, sir, was this the stuff you spotted in Mrs. Webhouse's handbag? You don't reckon it's got anything to do with the—why, that girl wouldn't hurt a fly, sir, take it from me!"

Mr. Lewker shook a sorrowful head at him.

"I fear you are too susceptible for a detective officer," he said. "And as to hurting flies, Crippen, as you will remember, was a most humane man."

"But—"

"Has it not occurred before, and recently, that when a husband stood in the way of wife and lover it was the wife who took the initiative?"

Sergeant Pitt removed his hat again, and again mopped his brow. He said nothing.

"Now," said Mr. Lewker cheerfully, "for a trifle of crime."

He began to cross the scree slope obliquely towards the fir woods on its left.

"Crime, sir?" echoed Pitt, scrambling in the rear.

"Breaking and entering, possibly. I understand the path leading from the road climbs to Cattespool's cottage up the hill beyond this wood. We should be able to find a shortcut."

Mr. Lewker's shortcut turned out to have the characteristics of its kind. A prickly progress through thick-growing firs brought them to a wall of rhodo-dendron bushes, through whose twisted branches they squirmed like explor-ers in some mangrove jungle of the Amazon. Pitt, whose skin and bone were better adapted to threading arboreal tangles than was the actor-manager's rotund figure, was the first to arrive at the boundary fence of the Plas Mawr demense. It was barbed wire, well concealed in the thickets, and it was at once apparent that he had discovered its presence by painful contact.

"For shame, Sergeant!" boomed Mr. Lewker severely, coming up in time to hear the tail end of his execrations. "Remember these unfortunates in Plas Mawr, doomed to silent anxiety while we enjoy ourselves!"

Pitt, spluttering, bundled through between the strands and landed knee-deep in a boggy stream. He drew some comfort from the fact that Mr. Lewker found an even deeper and wetter landing, and waited with interest for his remarks. Mr. Lewker, who maintained that Shakespeare provided a *mot juste* for every occasion, was not at a loss.

"May the devil damn thee black!" he gasped, and added, drawing on two other plays: "Thou scurvy patch! Ay, kennel, puddle, sink, whose filth and dirt Troubles the silver stream where England drinks!"

"Looks like a bit of solid up this way," said Pitt, hiding a grin and floun-dering towards a patch of green.

When he had sunk well into the patch of green and crawled out again, scratched his face in a bramble-smothered marsh, and fallen flat on some slippery boulders, he announced to his panting companion that he had found a stone wall. The indefatigable Mr. Lewker urged him over it on to the steeps of bracken beyond. Hordes of midges rose from the bracken to settle happily on their streaming faces. They ploughed through the forest of six-foot stems, slipping and stumbling on the slope, and having climbed another stone wall (on which Pitt barked both shins thoroughly) emerged upon a hillside of cropped grass. Below on the left the vale of Gwynant lay dark beneath the heavy skies. A winding track climbed the hillside towards the cottage whose chimney was just visible over the brow above.

"Angels and ministers of grace defend us!" puffed Mr. Lewker piously, slapping his midge-infested dome with energy. "But at least, Sergeant, we have arrived."

Pitt stooped to wring out the bottoms of his trouser legs. "If that's your shortcut, sir," he said, "I vote for the long cut back."

"I agree. However, we have established that the cottage, and the upper end of the cliff path, can be reached from Plas Mawr without going past the lodge, even when the bridge is down."

"And is that going to help us, sir?"

"Probably not," said Mr. Lewker blandly. "Shall we proceed?"

A few sheep rose lethargically and trotted from the path as they mounted it towards the cottage. On their right the heathery summit of the bluff was close at hand, and the gate in the wall at the top of the cliff path appeared. The cottage stood a hundred yards above, with the rock-strewn mountain-side rolling up behind it to merge in the gray haze.

Anthony Cattespool's temporary residence was a typical Welsh *hafod* or sheiling. Small and low-built, its massive stones whitewashed and uneven, it showed a door and two windows under its slated roof. Its front wall was protected by a small enclosure paved with huge flat rocks. The wooden gate leading into this enclosure had been newly painted with green paint, as had the door and the deep-sunk window-frames.

Mr. Lewker opened the gate and tried the door. It was locked. With Pitt at his shoulder, he peered through each window in turn. One of the tiny rooms was obviously a kitchen-cum-sitting-room; the table near the window held books and a portable typewriter. The other was a bedroom. Both were plainly furnished. The sash windows were tightly shut and secured.

"We will take the fortress in rear," announced the actor-manager, leading the way round to the back of the cottage. "Ah, this looks more promising."

The building was set in the slope of the hillside, and a space had been cleared behind it by hewing away the ground. A wooden hut, plainly of much more recent construction than the cottage, occupied most of this space. Its corrugated-iron roof slanted up to meet the cottage wall, against which it was built. The door was fastened with padlock and staple, and the small window in the side of the hut was not made to open. Mr. Lewker looked in through the window and then returned to the door.

"You may turn your back if you wish, Sergeant," he remarked, producing from his pocket a penknife which boasted a screwdriver among its other gadgets. "We have no warrant, you know."

"I reckon I can take a chance," Pitt said, a little doubtfully. "What are we looking for, sir?"

Mr. Lewker, who was already at work unscrewing the staple, finished removing one screw before replying.

"Tangible evidence," he said briefly, and started on the second screw.

In three minutes the staple was dangling from the padlock bar and the door was open. Pitt followed his leader into the hut, which was exceedingly hot and stuffy and smelt of creosote. It seemed to be a miscellaneous store-room and was not particularly tidy; old paint pots and bottles, broken oil lamps and odds and ends of paper and string, jostled each other on the narrow shelves that lined its walls. One or two stout ash sticks stood with a shepherd's long hazel staff in a corner, and a hand axe and a saw in good condition hung from nails near the door. Below the window stood a carpenter's narrow bench with a small steel vise fitted at one end.

Sergeant Pitt, forgetting his uneasiness, began to poke about in the cobwebby space under the bench.

"Thought these Navy types were supposed to be fussy about neatness," he grumbled. "Here's a couple of chisels, rusty—fair make any carpenter weep, that would."

"There must be some good tools somewhere," Mr. Lewker remarked, without turning round from his methodical examination of the shelves. "Did you not observe, on the floor beneath the vise, both metal dust and wood filings?"

Pitt muttered an exclamation and continued his rummaging with increased enthusiasm. He pulled out a paraffin can and an old biscuit tin full of shavings, presumably saved for fire lighting. Behind them was a small wooden chest, painted service gray and bearing on the lid, in neat white lettering, the legend:

ANTHONY V. CATTESPOOL

LT/CDR. R.N.V.R.

It was locked, but when Pitt shook it there was a rattle of metal objects inside.

"Got 'em, sir!" exclaimed the sergeant. "These are his tools, I'll swear. Can't get it open with a screwdriver this time, though."

"Just a moment," came Mr. Lewker's muffled tones.

He had reached the end of the shelves and was engaged in sorting through a pile of old sacks that lay in a corner. A cloud of dust enveloped him, but he persisted until he had cleared the last from the floor. As he picked up the final sack some small object rolled from beneath it. With a grunt he rescued it and dropped it into his pocket before turning to examine Pitt's find, which now stood on the bench.

"I want that chest open, Sergeant," he said at once. "As we have already committed burglary perhaps I may proceed."

"Not burglary, sir." Pitt sounded shocked. "Housebreaking, at this time o' day—and seems to me we're clear of that, too. This hut hasn't got no direct or enclosed communication with the dwelling, so we won't get more than seven days."

"Thou art as wise as thou art beautiful, Sergeant. Can you reach the piece of stiff wire that dangles from yonder beam? Thank you."

He took the wire and with the aid of the steel vise bent its end into key shape. He inserted it into the keyhole of the chest, twiddled it expertly, withdrew it, bent it in a different manner and inserted it again.

"When I was in Vichy in 'forty-two, disguised as an electrician's mate," he said as he delicately felt for the wards, "I had to open the Foreign Minister's dispatch case with a hairpin in one and a half minutes. Since then, I fear, my sense of touch has not improved. No—this is a simple lock, fortunately, but we shall need to try again."

The wire needed four more adjustments before the lock turned. Mr. Lewker lifted the hinged lid of the chest. An upper tray, much shallower than the space underneath it, held a shining row of tools ingeniously secured on a layer of felt.

"That's more like it," said Pitt admiringly. "There's four nice chisels and a pair of gouges, all in the pink of condition, besides three bits for a small brace—half-inch, quarter-inch, and three-sixteenths. Brace is underneath, I expect. Do we want fingerprints, sir?"

"Not just at the moment. We may lift the tray, I think."

The body of the chest held screwdriver, small hammer, and various other implements in neat leather sockets on the sides. A brace and a hacksaw, with wood files and metal files, lay in the bottom beside some rolls of sandpaper and emery paper.

"If those are lifted out by their extremities," said Mr. Lewker, "we shall do no harm. Place them on this sheet of newspaper."

"Right." Pitt began to lift the tools out one by one, using his handkerchief round thumb and forefinger. "By the way, sir," he added, without looking up from this task, "don't think I'm inquisitive—but what are we after? Anything to do with that bit of something you found under the sacks?"

"Sergeant, you anticipate my dramatic revelation. Tell me, first, what size and shape the rackarock charge for the murderer's purpose would be. I believe you mentioned it this morning."

Pitt nodded. "Almost certainly a four-ounce cartridge. That'd be four and a half inches long and three-quarters diameter."

"With a hole for the detonator in one end?"

"Yessir. Three-eighths diameter—I've seen 'em."

Mr. Lewker took from his pocket the object he had found and held it out on the palm of his hand. It was a piece of wood, cylindrical in shape, with a hole drilled in one end.

Sergeant Pitt sucked in his breath sharply as he stared at it.

"Well—slap me with a wet lettuce!" he ejaculated. "You know what that is, sir?"

"I think so. A dummy rackarock charge. That was a good guess of yours, Sergeant."

"Guess nothing," retorted Pitt. "He was bound to test his contraption somehow if he wanted to make sure it'd work, and a dummy was the safe way. Bit careless of him to leave it about, though."

"He may have lost it and been unable to destroy it."

"Silly thing to do. Still, murderers do 'em. They're that casual, you wouldn't believe." Pitt took the wooden cylinder and examined it. "I'll just run a rule over this," he added. "Too rough for prints. There's a steel rule here—no, I'll use my own."

He took out a thin metal folding rule and took the measurements of the cylinder.

"Bang-on," he announced with satisfaction. "Exact, they are. Careful craftsmen here, sir, even if he was a careless murderer."

Mr. Lewker's pouchy face was screwed into an expression of intense thought. He rubbed his chin slowly with his hand and his little eyes were very bright.

"I wonder," he said. "I wonder. The affliction of my mind amends, Sergeant. That detonator hole is three-eighths of an inch in diameter, I think you said?"

"That's so, sir."

"It was drilled with a three-eighths bit?"

"Course it was. Nothing else would have done it."

"Of course."

Pitt frowned at him for a long moment. Then he turned and began hastily to take the rest of the tools from the chest. When he had spread them all on the newspaper he put his hands on his hips, straddled his legs, and pursed his lips.

"No three-eighths bit in this chest, sir, nor a place for one," he declared. "I get you. But what's it prove, I ask you?"

"Nothing," replied Mr. Lewker mildly. "Can you see a tube of plastic wood anywhere?"

The sergeant peered into nooks and corners before his eye fell on the roll of emery paper, which was secured, like the roll of sandpaper, with a stout rubber band. He picked it up and slipped the band off. There was a partly used tube of plastic wood in the roll.

"Well, it all seems to be here, right enough," he commented, "But you'd expect to find plastic wood in any outfit like this."

"I wonder what else we might expect to find," Mr. Lewker murmured.

He picked up the roll of sandpaper and placed it to his eye like a telescope.

"Has it ever occurred to you, Sergeant," he asked, "that even a fairly wide tube restricts the vision to a quite extraordinary extent? Through this cylinder I can see no more than a circle of nine inches diameter at the other end of the hut. I find it symbolic of this case."

"That so, sir?"

"You find the idea a little fantastic, I perceive." He had removed the rubber band and was unrolling the two or three sheets of sandpaper. "Yet I have so far, in this case, been restricting my vision in a somewhat similar—ah. I believe, Sergeant, I have out-Holmesed Holmes this time."

He held out a soiled piece of paper which had been rolled between the stiff sheets. It was a page torn from a cash-ruled notebook of cheap pattern, and on it in pencil was a drawing, apparently a carpenter's rough plan of work. Pitt took it eagerly, holding it by its extreme edge as Mr. Lewker had done, and frowned at it concentratedly.

"Sort of open box with one end missing, this'd be," he said, looking up. "Strip of brass on the bottom, seemingly—don't know why—and a hole in the end. Drawn upside-down, for some reason. Look here, sir, what is this? Did you know it'd be here?"

"I had a hunch," boomed Mr. Lewker, in high good humor. "An excellent colloquialism, Sergeant—that word 'hunch.' Its second dictionary meaning is a push or jerk, and a jerk is exactly what my too, too inflexible mind experienced a little earlier."

"Were you looking for this?" demanded Pitt suspiciously.

"Shall we say that I thought it not improbable that a paper would be found? Always hide a paper, if you wish to hide it, with other papers, Sergeant. The classic example, of course, is Poe's *Purloined Letter*. I put myself in the murderer's place, as all the best amateurs do, and considered it to be at least possible that a paper had been hidden. Thus I look for other papers, let them be newspapers, emery papers, or—"

"But what *is* the blasted paper?" The sergeant's patience was being too sorely tried. "Sorry, sir," he added at once. "I s'pose I ought to spot what it is myself."

"I think you ought," agreed Mr. Lewker, beaming at him. "So we will reserve the revelation until Inspector Grimmett has had his chance. Now," he went on briskly, "to tidy up. We will take with us, neatly wrapped, the brace and the steel rule from Mr. Cattespool's toolchest. I myself will take charge of this paper and the dummy charge. I will likewise re-lock chest and door." He glanced at his watch. "Quickly, now, Sergeant, if you please, or we shall be late for dinner."

Five minutes later they were on their way down the hillside path to the road. The evening was heavier and more ominous of storm than ever. The mists had cleared, but so thick was the haze that not a summit was visible across the valley where Snowdon rose above the deep cwm that twisted through the mountain walls to the very foot of its peak. Mr. Lewker slapped continually at the persistent midges as they came down through a wood of scrub oak to the lane not far from Plas Mawr lodge; but Sergeant Pitt was sunk so deeply in frowning thought that he appeared not to feel any physical irritation.

Constable Jones, prowling in the vicinity of the gate, greeted them with a smart salute and the information that there had been "a proper welter of towrists come a-peeping, but was now gone off for their suppers." On the terrace Clare Webhouse was walking up and down, a cigarette in her fingers and the spaniel at her side.

"Dinner is just ready," she said as they came up to her. "Mrs. Pauncefoot says you asked for yours to be served in the library," she added, turning to Mr. Lewker. "Do you really want it there? Because please don't think—"

"I think it would be best, if you will allow it," Mr. Lewker said gently. He took his pipe from his pocket. "I wonder if you can lend me a match? My box is empty."

"I've—" began Pitt.

"And the sergeant has none," added the actor-manager quickly.

"Of course." Clare opened the handbag that hung on her arm. "You'd better take the box—I've got some more in the house."

"Thank you. And—forgive my curiosity—but is not that a piece of nylon parachute cord in your bag? I remember seeing it often in the war days, but it is quite rare now."

Clare's swift glance showed that this somewhat unsubtle question had made her suspicious. However, Mr. Lewker's bland countenance was turned away from her as he struck a match for his pipe, and she answered without hesitation:

"I don't know, really. It's nylon, I think, and I was going to use it for edging a small cushion—it's just the right shade."

A gong boomed in the house and they began to walk towards the door.

"You had a brother in the parachute corps, perhaps?" Mr. Lewker said casually.

"Oh, no. I happened to find this in Anthony's little workshop, when I was up there with him a few days ago."

CHAPTER XII

SIX-PART TRIO

"And now, Grimm," said Mr. Lewker, "let us concoct an interim report."

The two policemen and the actor-manager were seated in the small library after dinner. By general consent, no discussion of the case had taken place during the meal, which had been served to them in the study by Dilys. Now, with an old-fashioned oil lamp shedding its soft light from the center of a round table, the conference was about to begin. The library window was partly open to admit the night air, but so warm and still was the atmosphere that the room seemed stuffy. The gray-blue smoke from Mr. Lewker's pipe hung in scarcely moving layers under the ceiling.

"Well, sir," the inspector said, sighing heavily as he laid his notebook on the table and opened it, "I reckon I'd better open the ball. And the first item is, Anthony Cattespool's alibis for theair rifle evening are pretty well watertight."

"Never trust a watertight alibi," remarked Sergeant Pitt with the air of an epigrammatist.

"I don't, my lad," Grimmett retorted. "But judges and juries do. On June fourth, Robert's garage in Beddgelert got a phone call to send a taxi to Portmadoc to pick up Cattespool at 152 Madoc Street. Time of call, ten-five— saw it in the garage book. Taxi put Cattespool down at the lodge here about eleven-twenty. That—"

"Half a mo'," Pitt interrupted. "Voice on phone's no alibi. Someone else— this Will Evans he went to see—could 've rung up, disguising his voice. Cattespool could 've been here at nine-thirty, say, and beat it down to Portmadoc getting there in time to be at Evan's house when the taxi arrived."

"Sprinting eleven miles, I suppose. There's no bike here or in Cattespool's cottage and he hasn't got a car."

"Well, all the same," Pitt said defiantly, "we've got no definite time for thisair rifle shooting—have we, sir?"

Mr. Lewker, thus appealed to, recalled David Webhouse's words. "Webhouse said he was admiring the last of the sunset. But in clear June evenings the sunset colors linger in the sky for a considerable time after the actual sunset, which on June the fourth would have been about ten past nine British Summer Time."

"Anyhow, I maintain the alibi could 've been faked," Pitt insisted.

Mr. Lewker gently shook his head.

"Consider, Sergeant," he said. "Webhouse was taking his usual stroll, which it was his custom to take before turning in, as he expressed it. That was probably at ten o'clock or after. Take that in conjunction with his admiring the last of the sunset, and we may say with fair certainty that theair rifle incident occurred between nine-thirty and ten-thirty. Cattespool had to replace theair rifle, and cover eleven miles without transport, in an hour."

"Well, let's get on," said Grimmett, referring to his notebook. "I went round to Plas Bach, Sir Henry Lydiate's place, and managed to get a word with the old dame who keeps house for him, Mrs. Tuke. She says he came in just after twenty past ten last night—noticed the time because he was earlier than she expected—and got him a hot drink, he looking a bit tired and shaken." He glanced up at Mr. Lewker. "Plas Bach's only about a mile from the lodge, and he left here round about twenty to ten."

"An old man, walking in the dark, might take forty minutes to walk a mile," Mr. Lewker pointed out.

"He might. It don't give us much. I phoned the Yard and put them on to Cattespool's records as a marksman in the Navy and Feckenham's financial affairs. county police haven't got anything more about Cutpursey." Grimmett shut his notebook. "Now, sir, I'd like to hear what you've been up to, so I would."

Mr. Lewker drew an envelope and a small parcel from his pockets. From the first he very carefully took the drawing found in Anthony Cattespool's toolchest, and from the second the dummy rackarock charge.

"Definitively thus I answer you," he boomed, laying them on the table in front of Grimmett. "I found these in a small workshop attached to Anthony Cattespool's cottage. An attempt had been made to hide them, especially the sketch. The latter, I think, should be tested for fingerprints, as should a small brace and a steel rule taken from the same place and now in Sergeant Pitt's possession."

The inspector, after a perfunctory shake of his head over this breach of the law, frowned closely at the two exhibits. Pitt was looking smug.

"Leaps to the eye what they are, eh, sir?" he remarked.

Grimmett glanced askance at him. "Suppose you tell us, Sergeant."

"Righto. That bit of wood's the exact shape and size of a four-ounce rackarock charge. Must 've been made special to test the explosive trap. And the drawing—"

He paused, with a triumphant look at Mr. Lewker; the meaning of the drawing had dawned upon him during dinner. Inspector Grimmett spoke before he could continue.

"Leaps to the eye, Sergeant," he said grinning. "I'd say this contraption was to fit under the end of the split plank and hold the nail clear of the detonator. How's that?"

"Clean bowled," Pitt acknowledged, with a surprised glance at his superior. "It took me best part of an hour to get round to that."

Grimmett beamed at him. "You're young yet, Pitt. Another ten years in the force and your wits'll sharpen up nicely, so they will. Now, I was trying to follow Mr. Lewker's line of investigation, you see, and I reckoned he was after something like this—something as'd delay the action of the trap. But I'll admit I can do with a bit more explanation. I can see this is a stoutly built kind of shield, as you might say to keep the striker from the charge. Strip of brass to make certain it didn't stick in the wood. But what's the hole at the back?"

Mr. Lewker took his pipe from his mouth. "I fancy," he said, "that a long piece of cord was attached there, threaded through the hole and secured with a stopper knot, probably a figure-of-eight."

"Cord?" repeated Grimmett sharply.

"Yes, Grimm. For example, Mark III parachute cord of the sort that is lashed round the broken upright. The same sort of cord that Clare Webhouse, as she says, found in a small coil in Cattespool's workshop a few days ago and popped into her handbag."

The silence which followed was broken after a moment by the mustache-blowing of Inspector Grimmett as he sat back heavily in his chair.

"Piling up against Cattespool, it is," he said, staring at Mr. Lewker. "But I can see you aren't satisfied, sir. Think this is a frame-up? Someone planted all this for us?"

"It could have been," returned Mr. Lewker reflectively "I want you to note one other thing, Grimm. The hole in the dummy charge was drilled, so Sergeant Pitt asserts, with a three-eighths bit. There is no such bit in Cattespool's outfit of tools."

"He might have chucked it away," Grimmett said. "Though why, if he did, he didn't destroy this paper and the dummy beats me. I don't quite follow how this cord business worked by the way."

Pitt hastened to recover his lost prestige.

"My guess is, the nylon cord was fastened to the wooden shield at one end and the other lashed to the upright—disguised as a strengthening lashing. The shield 'd be pushed under the loose plank. There was flat rock for it to rest on and it's made so as to fit over the charge like a shallow box. The cord 'd run under the bridge out of sight."

"Then all the murderer had to do to set the trap was to pull the shield away?"

"That's it."

"And," said Grimmett, suddenly intent, "the other end of the cord was fastened to the upright at the bridge end nearest Cattespool's cottage. Seems to mean he was going to pull the shield away as he crossed going back to his place, knowing Webhouse was bound to come that way for his evening stroll. But it didn't work out like that. I wonder why."

Mr. Lewker, who had been watching his friend's face with a kind of smiling expectancy, turned to Sergeant Pitt.

"Do you see your way, Sergeant?" he inquired.

Pitt frowned and drummed on the table with his bony fingers. "Webhouse went up that cliff path before his usual time," he said slowly. "Cattespool couldn't know he'd do that—or could he? And in any case—"

He stopped abruptly and jerked his head up. Mr. Lewker nodded at him.

"I know, Sergeant," he said sympathetically. "You are going to ask the question we should all of us have asked much earlier. Why, in any case, did David Webhouse go up the cliff path at that time? Who or what made him alter—"

"He told the folk at dinner," Pitt said eagerly, plainly unaware that he was interrupting, "that he'd stroll down to the lodge and back to cool his head. Instead he went up the cliff path. See here—old Lydiate had gone out only a minute or so earlier. Suppose they met, suppose he and Lydiate went up that path for some reason." He stopped and scratched his head. "But Lydiate hadn't set the trap, unless evidence counts for nowt. He might have spotted it, though, if he happened to come over the path a day or two before."

"Opening it up, aren't you?" Grimmett grumbled. "As I see it, you're starting three or four hares at once. A, the intending murderer, sets the trap for Webhouse with the shield in position, B, another person who wants Webhouse killed, spots the trap and removes the shield, thus being the actual killer. But why shouldn't B let A's little scheme go ahead, instead of meddling and rising suspicion? It won't wash, Sergeant."

Mr. Lewker, leaning forward, tapped out his pipe on the edge of the large plastic ashtray with the rhythm of a chairman calling a meeting to order.

"Conjecture," he said reprovingly, "will not help us at this juncture. Our need, as Inspector Grimmett will doubtless agree, is to summarize our findings on the evidence to date."

"That's so," agreed Grimmett. "But there's some big gaps yet, sir."

"True. Cutpursey's absence is the biggest gap of all. We still lack the evidence of the will and the evidence of whoever supplied the rackarock charge, if he can be found. We may, however, deal with the actual circumstances of the murder and the evidence affecting the six persons who may be listed as suspects."

Grimmett nodded and opened his notebook at a fresh page.

"So we may, sir. List 'em under means, motive, and opportunity, as per usual?"

"I wonder, Grimm, if we might vary the method to advantage," suggested Mr. Lewker. "This afternoon Sergeant Pitt gave an admirable performance as the murderer by putting himself in the murderer's place. Doubtless each of us three has in his mind a predilection for one or other of our suspects as the most likely murderer, and possibly a second person as first reserve, so to speak. Let each man put himself in the place of his murderer and build the case against himself."

"I'm no actor, sir," said the inspector dubiously. "And what's more I reckon you're the only one that's got any doubt about Anthony Cattespool as the likeliest suspect."

"Hold on," begged Pitt. "The more I think of him, the more I fancy old man Lydiate."

"There you are, Grimm," remarked Mr. Lewker. "You shall take Cattespool. You remember how Richard the Third opens the tragedy in soliloquy?—'I am determined to prove a villain.' Take that line and prove yourself a murderer."

"Very well, sir," Grimmett said uncertainly.

He was silent for a moment, with knitted brows. Then he began, warming to the work as he perceived its value.

"I'm Anthony Cattespool, then. I came here four months ago to rent the cottage up above and write books. I disliked Webhouse from the start—hated him, you might say, especially after I'd met his wife. I fell in love with her and she with me. It was—"

"No evidence Mrs. Webhouse fell in love with Cattespool," interjected Pitt.

"I'm Cattespool, and I say she did," retorted Grimmett. "Well, it was plain Webhouse wouldn't let me fix up any sort of divorce ploy. Possessive, jealous type if ever there was one. So I decided, with or without Mrs. Webhouse's knowledge—all right, Sergeant, I said 'or without'—to kill him. I'd enough acquaintance with the Plas Mawr household to know that Webhouse never missed his walk last thing in the evening, up the cliff path crossing the bridge. I'd blown up bridges and dams during the war."

"Only a harbor wall in evidence so far," put in the irrepressible sergeant. "And that was casual conversation between Webhouse and Mr. Lewker."

"We know—I mean, I, Cattespool, haven't concealed the fact that I know my stuff where explosives are concerned," said the inspector meticulously. "The bridge, a pretty ramshackle affair, gave me my cue. I'm acquainted with a man named Will Evans who handles explosives in Llanerch Quarry. Swearing him to secrecy, I persuaded him to get me a four-ounce charge of rackarock. He served in the same ship with me, and I knew I could count on

him keeping quiet whatever happened. I had plenty of opportunity for preparing the booby-trap, the tools for making a preventive device to act as a
sort of safety-catch, and—if I didn't get a detonator as well as a charge from
the quarry—I was capable of getting some mercury fulminate and making
one myself. Well, I set the trap just as you've said, using—by the way—a
good naval lashing for the nylon cord. Thinking it'd be a good scheme if I
was one of the people who found the body, I picked an evening when I was
dining at Plas Mawr. When I came down the path from changing last night I
pulled away the preventive shield—by kneeling down after I'd crossed the
bridge and pulling on the cord—intending that Webhouse, who would be the
next to cross the bridge, should detonate the charge. Which he did. And I,
Anthony Cattespool, murdered him."

"But," said Mr. Lewker, forestalling Pitt's comments, "did you, then, intend to stay at Plas Mawr until Webhouse took his stroll just prior to retir-
ing?"

Grimmett scowled and rubbed his head. "Why, no. Come to think of it,
that's a bit odd, so it—ah, wait a bit. I intended to walk back to my cottage by
the road, probably accompanying Sir Henry Lydiate. That would have kept
me well clear of the cliff path at the fatal time, though of course it wouldn't
give me an alibi."

Pitt wagged a finger at him. "All right, as far as it goes, but what about
your other shots at rubbing Webhouse out?"

"Ye-es." Grimmett ruminated. "Well, I did try poison first. I was hanging
about the place a good deal and it wasn't hard to shove a bit of something or
other in his morning glass of milk. It didn't work and it made Webhouse
suspicious. Then I happened to be out after rabbits with their rifle one
evening. I saw Webhouse standing just below me and couldn't resist having
a pot at him—I missed, but then I'm not much of a shot. That could have
been the way of it," he added with a glance at Mr. Lewker.

The actor-manager, who was following every word with close attention,
nodded.

"And," he prompted, "on Crib Goch—"

"Yes—I saw a chance again. I'm an impetuous sort of chap anyway, and
there he was again below me on the ridge, and a good-sized rock handy. I
dropped it and missed. As I expected, it was put down to rock falling accidentally."

"You tried to drop a rock on him," Mr. Lewker said slowly, "in spite of the
fact that you had made all preparations for blowing him up that very evening.
A little odd, was it not?"

"I said I was impetuous, sir. I took a chance. It would have been safer, if it
had come off, than the explosive trap."

"Ah!" Pitt said sharply. "That's a point, too. What made you pick a clumsy murder method like mining the bridge, eh?"

"Why shouldn't I, my lad? Don't I know all about mines and such? And won't it go up without anyone but Webhouse being near it?"

Mr. Lewker, hiding a smile at the heat with which the inspector defended his imaginary murder scheme, leaned forward.

"But, impetuous as you are," he said quietly, "you have a certain amount of common sense. How much better it would have been to wait for Webhouse at the bridge and make an opportunity of pushing him over! Surely that would not have been too risky? You might even have loosened the handrail beforehand to make certain. Afterwards you could have pushed the bridge over. Who then could have told that Webhouse had not gone over by accident—having stumbled against the handrail and overbalanced the bridge?"

Grimmett rubbed his head harder than ever.

"Well," he said defiantly, "I'd need an alibi, things being as they are, in case someone suspected. And maybe there'd be witnesses to say the bridge couldn't have tipped over."

"You haven't told us how you managed to pot at Webhouse and fix your alibi in Portmadoc," said Pitt.

Mr. Lewker intervened.

"Nevertheless," he boomed, "you have very prettily incriminated yourself as Cattespool, Grimm. There are several things that remain unexplained, but I fancy Sergeant Pitt will have a hard task making out a better case against himself as Sir Henry Lydiate. Well, Sergeant?"

Pitt grinned rather self-consciously.

"Well, sir," he said, "I'm not a landed gentry but I'll do my best. I'm Sir Henry Lydiate and a little tin god in these parts. This feller Webhouse gets my goat in every sort of way, specially by being the live wire in the move to build hydroelectric works all over my land. I'm sorry for his wife, too. What's more, I've got some pretty high-souled ideas about knighthood, and I reckon Webhouse is about the last bloke that ought to be a knight like me. It gets into my brain—me being a bit eccentric, maybe—that Webhouse is about as ripe for putting away as the dragon was when St. George pranged it. Webhouse killed means the heart gone out of the hydroelectric party, his wife a lot happier, and the knights bachelor—that's right, isn't it?—relieved of a nasty recruit. A sort of conglomerate motive, but it's a motive as far as I'm concerned."

He paused and looked at the others. Mr. Lewker inclined his head, the inspector shook his.

"Righto, then," pursued Pitt. "I've been to Plas Mawr often in Lord Capel's time, and three or four times since. I know all about the cliff path and the bridge and Webhouse's evening stroll, and I know Cattespool goes down to Portmadoc for the day quite often. Got that from my old housekeeper," he added hastily as Grimmett opened his mouth to interrupt.

"We will concede that," Mr. Lewker said gravely.

"Thanks. Well then, I decide to use the bridge as the means. How? Why, shove it over with explosive, Webhouse to do the detonating. I don't know a great deal about explosives, but I'm in a position to get hold of the stuff and no questions asked. Inspect my company's workshops, say, and hook a four-ounce charge. My scheme's to make it look like accident—I don't tumble to the fact that it's bound to be obviously the result of an explosion."

"Thin, lad, thin," said Grimmett. "And what about your idea that Sir Henry spotted Cattespool's device and used it?"

"I've dropped that. No objection, I hope? All right—to rig the thing needs tools, which I haven't got. But I know Cattespool's got some in the hut at his cottage. So—"

"Your old housekeeper tells you that, too, I suppose?" put in Grimmett sarcastically.

"Look here, sir," said Pitt plaintively, "who's committing this murder? Give the boy air, can't you? I've met Cattespool and maybe he's told me about his tools. Anyway, I go up to his place by the field path while he's away and make what I want. I can easy trot up there and set the trap while everyone's away scrambling over Snowdon. I do that, and turn up to dinner in the ordinary way. Oh, and I daren't leave the thing ready to go off in case Mrs. Webhouse or someone goes up there, so of course I shove in that shield. Then I've got to remove that later. Quite easy—I start a row with Webhouse, leave the dinner table all haughty-like, and as soon as Mrs. Webhouse lets me out I cut up to the bridge. Out with the shield, down again, and back to Plas Bach by the road. And Bob's your uncle."

He spread his hands like a stage Frenchman. Grimmett took him up instantly.

"While you were up at the bridge, Webhouse must have come out of the house. He went up the cliff path. You'd meet him, wouldn't you?"

"Right," Pitt countered. "I didn't come down the path, then. After all, I'd fixed the shield so that I could pull it out *after* I'd crossed the bridge. I do just that, and then go on, through the gate above and down the field path to the lane. Okay?"

"Two questions," Mr. Lewker said. "First question, how did you know that Webhouse would cross the bridge before Cattespool, who might be expected to go back to his cottage before Webhouse took his turning-in stroll? Second question, how did you get into Cattespool's workshop? He leaves it locked, apparently, and the paint on the staple had not been scratched until I used my screwdriver there this afternoon."

"Lots of questions, my lad," added Grimmett briskly. "Did you try poison first? And try an air gun shot? No doubt you operated the falling rock by remote control? And as far as I can see, it wasn't you that started the row—it was Webhouse."

Pitt blew out his cheeks, screwed up his eyes, and finally sat back with a shake of his head.

"I could explain some of those with a bit of thinking," he declared, "but not that one of Mr. Lewker's about Cattespool being the one who'd be crossing the bridge before Webhouse." He sat up again suddenly. "See here—we haven't thought of this. Suppose the trap caught the wrong man? Suppose it was set for Cattespool, and Webhouse went up unexpected and caught the packet intended for the other bloke?"

"Use your little gray cells, Sergeant," Grimmett told him. "Mr. Lewker's told us Webhouse was afraid. It was Webhouse that thought he was being poisoned, Webhouse that was shot at, Webhouse that was nearly brained by a roc—"

"All right, all right," Pitt muttered. "I surrender. Let it pass."

Grimmett turned to Mr. Lewker.

"Well, sir," he said, "it's your turn. What's your choice?"

"I," said Mr. Lewker weightily, "will take upon me the part of Charles Feckenham."

The sergeant and the inspector both looked at him sharply. Mr. Lewker's face was benignly inscrutable as that of the Buddha he somewhat resembled; until he began to speak. Then—and Pitt's eyes widened as he saw it—the pouchy features seemed to tauten and become youthful the poise of the big head to change indefinably, so that in spite of the utter lack of resemblance between the two men it was Feckenham, not Mr. Lewker, that Pitt saw facing him across the table.

"Looks as if I'd better come clean," he said, and the voice was the jerky drawl of Charles Feckenham. "Money's my trouble. I've told you the bare truth there. You'd have found out anyway. There's more than that to it, though. Clare and I were always fond of each other. I came back from Ceylon to find her tied to this brute—the man whose death would keep me out of the bankruptcy court."

"How d'you know it would?" Pitt interjected keenly.

"Sound assumption—fellow Webhouse doted on Clare. Bound to have left her all his money." Mr. Lewker's lazily raised eyebrow was a perfect reproduction of a typical Feckenham expression. "And Clare wouldn't hold out on me. Gambling's my only vice, and anyway there wasn't much gamble in that. Right?"

"We'll grant a motive, sir," Grimmett nodded.

"Right. I tried to touch Webhouse on the seventh—last Monday—soon as I got back from Epsom. He refused. At first I thought I'd scare him a bit—slipped some dope in his food. That was on Tuesday. He suspected something, I think, but I could see he wasn't going to give in. I also spotted it was Cattespool he suspected. That gave me an idea. I decided to kill him, leaving a clue or two to point to Cattespool, whom I disliked because of his attentions to Clare."

"No evidence of that," snapped Pitt.

"No? Well, I hardly expected the clues to be picked up, anyway. I knew my stuff on blowing up bridges. Got a charge of rackarock and a detonator—through Cutpursey, whom I bribed to get them—and made the dummy charge in Webhouse's workshop, next door to his garage. I cleared away all traces of my work there and managed to slip the clues into Cattespool's shed when I was up there with him one day. That's why there was no three-eighths bit in the place where the drilling was supposed to be done. You'll find one in Webhouse's workshop."

Grimmett glanced at the sergeant and made a quick note in his book.

"I rigged my mine," Mr. Lewker continued, "when we got back from the Snowdon climb, while Plas Mawr was preparing for dinner and after Cattespool had gone up to his cottage to change. The wooden shield I put in position with the release cord led beneath the bridge to the upright on the other end. I had a hundred-foot length of line with a hook on one end, and this I hooked to the loop under the bridge. Cattespool wouldn't notice it in the fading light on his way back to dinner. I slipped back into the house—no one saw me—got ready for dinner, and then waited in the shrubbery until Cattespool came down. Then I went up to the foot of the ravine and pulled my string. The drag on the loop pulled out the wooden shield, thus setting the trap. The hook and line naturally slipped off and I coiled up the string and later destroyed it. And—but you know the rest."

As he ended, both policemen began to speak together. Mr. Lewker, beaming at them, interrupted in his own booming tones.

"As you say, I have small warrant for Feckenham's movements before dinner on the evening of the murder," he admitted. "I can only say that as far as my own observation goes he did not appear until about five minutes after Cattespool returned from the cottage."

"All right, sir," Grimmett frowned, "but there's more and bigger holes than that. Who shot at Webhouse? Not you, because you were off to the Derby early in the morning of the fourth, the day the shooting took place. And if it was only Tuesday, the eighth, when you decided to kill him—after scaring him with the poisoning trick—that only leaves one day, Wednesday the ninth, to get the charge from Cutpursey, rig the dummy, leave the clues and all the rest of it. Because on the next day you were scrambling around the Snowdon Horseshoe."

"And a lot more too," added Pitt, who had been waiting impatiently for his turn. "How did you work that falling rock? And——"

"A timely accident," murmured the actor-manager.

"—and that gag about pulling out the shield with a hundred feet of string and a hook wouldn't work. What'd happen? Why, when the shield was pulled clear—if it didn't jam, because it wouldn't be a straight pull anyhow—it'd swing out and dangle at the end of the nylon cord, from the upright. Your hook 'd slide down the cord and jam on the shield, which 'd be hanging ninety feet above you."

The inspector wagged his head reproachfully.

"It won't wash, sir," he declared. "Not unless we can get a deal more evidence, it won't. The motive's there, but means and opportunity's as full of holes as a net."

"And the biggest hole, Grimm, is the one we've already noted. If Webhouse—as appears almost certain—was the intended victim, how did the murderer know that Webhouse, and not Cattespool, would be the first to step on the bridge after the trap was set?"

"Unless he was Cattespool himself," nodded Grimmett.

"As you say. What is more, there is yet another curious gap, which I admit I did not see until Sergeant Pitt indicated it a moment ago." Mr. Lewker glanced at the sergeant, who looked puzzled. "But your point about the one day available for the rigging of the trap, Grimm," he added, "is not a complete confounding of my thesis."

"How's that, sir?"

"On that day, Wednesday—the day of my arrival—Anthony Cattespool had gone down to the coast for the day and did not return until late. Webhouse told me that when he took me up the cliff path in the evening. So that if Feckenham, as is possible, had access to the key of Cattespool's shed, he had all day in which to plant clues there."

"But what about the bridge? He'd have to fiddle about with that in broad daylight, so he would."

Mr. Lewker twinkled at him. "Very well, Grimm. Let us leave Charles Feckenham and pass on. You have three remaining possible to impersonate—Mrs. Pauncefoot, Clare Webhouse, and James Cutpursey. Choose thou, and be content."

The inspector frowned at his fingertips and pursed his lips. Plainly he considered further play-acting a trifle unnecessary; Cattespool, to his mind, was the focal point of all the evidence so far adduced. However, he decided to make a second choice in line with his first.

"Well, sir, I'm Mrs. Clare Webhouse," he said; and scowled at Pitt as the latter gave a contemptuous snort. "That's to say, I'm working in with Cattespool. I've got a triple motive for putting my husband away—lover, husband's bullying, husband's money. Cattespool plans the bridge-mine and makes the dummy for testing. While the whole gang are away on Snowdon I set the trap. Previously, by the way, Cattespool—my lover—has had a pot at Webhouse with the airgun, and I've tried to poison him."

"Insufficient evidence for both those statements," said Sergeant Pitt acidly.

"All right, all right! You'll remember, all the same, that she tried—I mean, I tried to kid you my husband hadn't been worried and I said nothing about trouble with his food."

"Just one moment, Grimm," Mr. Lewker interposed. "If my memory serves me, it was Mrs. Webhouse herself, on the evening of my arrival here, who first mentioned in my hearing that her husband had poured some of his milk and soda into a saucer for the spaniel."

"And *that* don't look like she put dope in it," added Sergeant Pitt triumphantly.

"Less of that Yank lingo, my lad," Grimmett said. "Say 'doesn't look as though' and I'll agree with you. Far as I can see, that ends my part—as Clare Webhouse, I mean. Cattespool pulls out the shield when he comes down from the cottage. After that, it'll be my part to see that neither Sir Harry Lydiate nor anyone else uses the cliff path before my husband goes up it to his death. And there you are."

"The falling rock—" began Pitt.

"Cattespool saw a chance and took it, hoping to spare his mistress any part in the murder. It could have been like that, you know," he added, to Mr. Lewker. "The two of 'em working together."

Mr. Lewker made no reply except to raise an eyebrow at the sergeant.

"I'm Mrs. Pauncefoot," said Pitt at once. "Motive, revenge for Webhouse's treatment of my daughter, plus a mad idea I'm the agent of the Lord. I've waited a long time and I've planned the whole shoot. I don't like Anthony Cattespool because he's carrying on something awful with a married woman, so I reckon to be the Lord's agent for two birds with one stone. I plan to frame him for the murder."

"O noble judge! O excellent young man!" murmured Mr. Lewker.

"We can find out if she had the keys to get into Cattespool's shed," said the gratified Pitt. "Seems likely. Well, she—that's to say, I, know a bit about explosives and I can manage a bit of straightforward carpentry. I've plenty of time to do it, too. To make sure my nice line of clues is picked up, I delay the bumping-off until Mr. Abercrombie Lewker, the well-known amateur tec, is here. I fix everything up while the party's on Snowdon. And then—"

He hesitated. Grimmett winked at Mr. Lewker.

"Well, Sergeant?" he demanded. "Cattespool has to come back across the bridge—just in time for dinner, he told us—and you've got to slip out and set the trap after that and before the end of dinner when Webhouse went out and was killed. Stuck, eh?"

"I could've done it." Pitt said defiantly.

"I fancy not," countered Mr. Lewker. "Mrs. Pauncefoot was waiting in the dining room for some minutes before Anthony Cattespool came in. I saw her. And she certainly did not leave the house from that time until the time of Webhouse's death."

Pitt waved his hands. "Okay. I'm finished. But she had means and motive all right. And you're left holding the baby, sir."

"An invisible infant," agreed Mr. Lewker somewhat absently. "An elderly and elusive Ariel. James Cutpursey."

He got up and went to the window. The little room was blue with tobacco-smoke and oppressively hot. He opened the window to its fullest extent and filled his lungs with the scented night air, which had a certain coolness in spite of its continued tension of coming storm, before returning to his seat.

"James Cutpursey," he repeated. "The Derbyshire countryman, the old quarryman, devoted—so we are told—to David Webhouse. None of our five theories have tried to explain why James Cutpursey is missing, or rather— since we may fairly assume voluntary absence—why he has run away. If Cattespool's statement is to be believed, it was probably Cutpursey who fled from the vicinity of Webhouse's body immediately after the murder."

"Might have been Sir Henry," Pitt remarked. " 'Whitish upperworks,' Cattespool said. Cutpursey and Lydiate both have white hair."

"Can you see Sir Henry Lydiate of Plas Bach rushing away into the wood after examining the body?" Grimmett inquired sarcastically. "That old boy hasn't rushed for the last twenty years."

"At least," said Mr. Lewker, cutting short Pitt's retort, "Cutpursey is slightly the more probable of the two. I find it difficult to put myself in Cutpursey's place, because of the entire absence of motive. I shall have to assume that I, James Cutpursey, have recently discovered an urgent reason for killing my employer. Given that motive, I have every means and opportunity for committing the crime. In fact, by June fourth, all my arrangements were made."

"Why by June fourth, sir?" interrupted Grimmett.

"Webhouse locked hisair rifle away after being shot at on that date, and theair rifle was in the workshop where—as I assume we shall find—is the only drill with which I could have drilled a three-eighths-inch hole in the dummy charge."

"Confirm that before you turn in, Sergeant," Grimmett ordered.

Mr. Lewker, methodically filling his pipe, continued his exposition.

"I had every opportunity of setting the trap. I could obtain a charge of rackarock more easily than any of the others, from my old pals at Llanerch Quarry. It is probable that I had keys to the cottage and its shed, but if not I had time and means for making a skeleton set. Alone of all the suspects, I could go up the cliff path during dinner and remove the wooden shield from the detonator. As for the previous attempts, I could have found a way of getting poison into household milk, being no stranger to the kitchen. I used theair rifle occasionally and was the first to be suspected by Webhouse when I failed to shoot him from the path above, as Webhouse himself admitted. The falling rock, Sergeant? An accident pure and simple. In short, I set my trap, waylaid Webhouse when he came out of the dining room for his stroll down to the lodge, persuaded him on some pretext to go up the cliff path instead. He stepped on the bridge and the mine was duly sprung. I hurried through the wood to make certain my victim was dead and unable to tell anyone how I had inveigled him up the path—"

"Ha!" ejaculated Pitt approvingly.

"—and in so doing was seen by Cattespool. Not knowing whether I had been recognized or not, I allowed panic to overcome my better judgment and ran away from Plas Mawr. I fancy," added Mr. Lewker thoughtfully, "that I ran to a hiding place in the mountains, a place already known to me."

"What's that?" said the inspector sharply. "D'you know where this hide-out is, sir?"

"Not I, Grimm. Tell me, how does James Cutpursey look to you, in the character of First Murderer?"

Grimmett stared at him for a moment.

"Well," he said slowly, "if we only had a shadow of a motive, he'd look pretty nigh top of the list, so he would. As you say, sir, he had the best opportunity of anyone to set the trap—and to make certain personally that Webhouse went up the cliff path. So—"

"*But*," Pitt interposed, "Cutpursey couldn't have known that Webhouse would come out of the house when he did."

Mr. Lewker nodded approval. The inspector stood up impatiently.

"The long and short of it is," he said, "we want more evidence. Who got hold of the charge, and where from? What's Cutpursey's past history? We'll have to get moving tomorrow.—Lord, it's hot in here." He went to the window and stood with his hands on the sill, looking out into the night. "But I still say this," he added over his shoulder. "Unless we can find Cutpursey and get some light from him, the evidence we've got points to Mr. Anthony Cattespool as Webhouse's murderer. And that—*hey!*"

He ended with a loud exclamation. Simultaneously the others heard the brief rustle of disturbed bushes under the window.

"Someone listening in—outside," rapped Grimmett, turning. "Sergeant, see if you can get 'em!"

Pitt was on his feet and out of the room in a flash. Grimmett returned to the table and stood tapping his stubby fingers on it and scowling.

"Not that it's much use," he muttered. "Whoever it was 'll be back in his room before Pitt can cop him."

"At least," said Mr. Lewker comfortingly, "he heard a very varied half-dozen theories."

The inspector placed both hands on the table and bent to frown searchingly at his friend.

"Now look here, sir," he said slowly, "I know you. And I know that self-satisfied look of yours. It usually means you've spotted our man. Are you going to tell me you *know*—on the evidence we've got—who killed David Webhouse?"

"On the evidence we have, Grimm," returned Mr. Lewker, beaming at him, "I see only one possible murderer. I am morally certain that person is indeed the murderer."

"Then who—"

"But moral certainty will not do for judge and jury. I must have one more link of evidence. And I fancy that link can be supplied when we find James Cutpursey, Grimm."

Grimmett's comment was forestalled by the entrance of Sergeant Pitt, breathless and with a torch in his hand.

"Well?" demanded the inspector.

"Nobody there or thereabouts," Pitt replied; he looked worried. "But I found footprints in the earth under the window."

"Well?"

"Well," said Pitt, with a glance at Mr. Lewker, "they were pretty small footprints. Must've been Miss Tansy."

CHAPTER XIII

THE WILL

As his wife frequently and exasperatedly observed, Abercrombie Lewker was a creature of habit. It is an unusual trait in actors, but then Mr. Lewker was unusual in many ways. An unfailing habit of his was to read in bed for fifteen minutes before composing himself to sleep; and this evening, having brought with him an old friend in the shape of the Irish R.M., he read the story called *The House of Fahy*. As usual, it brought him (even at this dozenth reading) that satisfying internal laughter than which there is no better preparative for sleep. But when he had finished it, pinched out the candle and removed it from its precarious perch on the bolster, and turned on his side, he was at once aware that sleep was not yet for him. He had not lost a moment's sleep on the night that followed the murder of David Webhouse; but now that he believed he had solved the main problem of that murder he found himself wakeful and uneasy.

Perhaps the heat of his room had something to do with it. It was as airless as if the windows were tight shut instead of open to their fullest extent; the bedclothes weighed upon him like carpets. The night outside was very still, but it was not a peaceful stillness. The whole world of earth and air seemed straining to hold in the demon of storm whose growing strength must eventually burst its bonds. That it would be the very devil of a storm when it came Mr. Lewker had no doubt. He knew that even in summer the mountains can be the center of a violence of weather rivaling the fury of the worst winter storms; and the coming storm looked like being one of those memorable tempests which the mountain-dwellers must fear once in a decade.

He tossed from side to side, and wondered if he should take a blanket and creep downstairs to sleep out on the terrace. He remembered seeing the tents of campers in the upper Gwynant valley; if the storm broke tonight, the lucky ones would be those who could crawl from the ruins of their tents to some convenient barn. The thought reminded him of the old gardener, Cutpursey, crouching (maybe) in some hole of the mountainside. And at once the murder of David Webhouse, with all the events leading up to it and succeeding it, was occupying his restless mind.

He had been perfectly honest in telling Grimmett that he was morally certain who was the murderer. But now he began to doubt. His mind raced and sideslipped with the mad momentum of a speedway rider, checking at dubious points only to accelerate and skid past them and circle back again. He forced himself to consider, one by one, every piece of observed behavior, every action of the persons concerned, every word and inflection of voice. He went over the few tangible clues and tested them against the available evidence. And still they made, together, the one pattern of a pointing, accusing finger.

And yet he was conscious that his theory of the murder, if it were to be put in a single sentence, would sound fantastic. Certainly Grimmett—conscientious, conventional soul!—would find it so. Mr. Lewker could not recall a similar solution to a murder problem in all his experience of crimes factual or fictional. Undoubtedly it was necessary to convince Grimmett beyond shadow of doubt that the thing had been done in the manner he had deduced, and to do that he wanted more than circumstantial evidence—one last confirmatory fact, at least. And if anyone could provide that fact, it was Cutpursey.

How to find Cutpursey? If he had means of sustenance, the man might lie hidden for half a year in the Snowdon glens, in spite of summer trampers and climbers. All the police in Caernarvonshire could not search thoroughly the great hollows of Eryri with their thousands of scattered boulders, peat-hags, unvisited streams and forgotten mine workings. He fell to a consideration of the Snowdon cwms as hiding-places: Cwm Dyli, Cwm Brwynog, Cwm Caregog, Cwm Clogwyn, Cwm Glas, Cwm Tregalan … thirteen of them in all; supposing the man had gone no further than the slopes of Snowdon, he could lie snugly hidden in any one of them. He was beyond reach of any message offering amnesty in exchange for evidence. And why had he gone? Mr. Lewker could still only guess at his reason, and he guessed until he was brain-weary and felt sleep stealing upon him at last.

Tomorrow there were two further points to be cleared up, and something might emerge from those which would set him on Cutpursey's trail. And there was one other thing he must do, tomorrow. Tomorrow—"and in the morn I'll bring you to your ship, and so to Naples" … He fell asleep with a line from *The Tempest* on his lips.

The tempest that threatened Snowdonia did not break in the night. Mr. Lewker, who had overslept, climbed yawning from his bed to find the same atmospheric tension and the same stifling heat. He had intended to make an early breakfast, for there was much to do; but it was nine o'clock before he came downstairs. Grimmett was finishing his toast and coffee in the study with his open notebook beside him.

"No one up except Mrs. P. and the maid," he observed with less than his usual good humor. "I feel like another three hours in bed myself. Pitt's getting the car out."

Dilys brought eggs and bacon, planted them unceremoniously before the new arrival, and flounced out.

"I feel we are no longer welcome here, Grimm," remarked Mr. Lewker placidly. "We must be packed and away by tomorrow."

"That's all very well," began Grimmett sharply; and closed his mouth with a snap. "I hope you're right, so I do," he finished gruffly.

"We shall achieve it, sweet lord." Mr. Lewker poured himself a cup of coffee. "The solicitors, the quarry—and, Grimm, I have an additional call to make, at Bangor University. I would prefer to go there first."

"Just as you like, sir. I suppose it was the dean murdered David Webhouse!"

"My dear Grimm! Do I detect bitterness in that remark? Let me assure you that it was not the dean, and that my only aim is to acquire the evidence that will enable me to say to you 'now I know for certain.' You would certainly laugh at my theory in the absence of that evidence, and you know that I dislike being laughed at. Pray, Grimmett, humor me in this."

"Granted, sir," grunted the inspector. He sounded mollified. "But it's a bit like playing a game with a man's life at stake, the way you take it."

Mr. Lewker became grave. "Grimm," he said solemnly, "please accept my word that no man's life is at stake."

The other looked at him keenly. He knew his Lewker, but he was puzzled.

"No *man's* life," he repeated slowly; but Mr. Lewker made no sign. "All right, then, sir; let it go at that. I've got that note from Mrs. Webhouse to Lloyd & John—she sent it down from her room. I've given it to Sergeant Pitt." He hesitated. "I suppose—look here, sir, I'll have to question the little girl today. Why she was eavesdropping, and that. I suppose she's got nothing to do—in your theory—with this business?"

"Tansy did not lay an explosive booby-trap for her elderly stepbrother, Inspector," returned Mr. Lewker with a twinkle. "I realize," he added more seriously, "that you have to question her, Grimm, but I hope you will deal gently with Tansy."

"Trust me." Grimmett rose from the table. "Now, if you'll excuse me, I'll start on the phone. London ought to be awake by now."

Left alone, Mr. Lewker finished his breakfast with dispatch and went out into the garden. Yesterday's mist had gone, but a pall of darkness hung over summit and valley as though a veil of purple-black gauze had been swathed around the world. He made his way through the shrubbery and up to the fallen bridge, and found the broken upright with the green nylon parachute cord still lashed round it. Thanking the fates that the rain had not come in the night, he untied the lashing and carefully stowed the cord in an envelope. When he returned to the terrace Sergeant Pitt was standing by the big Austin awaiting him.

"Due to bust any time now, sir," Pitt said, jerking his thumb at the frowning skies. "Air's full of electricity. Fair makes your hair stand on end."

"The three-eights bit, Sergeant?" inquired the actor-manager.

"It's there, sir—in the coach-house workshop. No prints on it, nor on the brace or the steel rule or the plan."

"Thank you. I scarcely expected to find any."

Inspector Grimmett came out of the house, mopping his neck with his handkerchief.

"They've been quick at the Yard," he announced without enthusiasm. "Wainwright was on the job. He got Cattespool's records from H.M.S. *Excellent*—Whale Island, naval gunnery school. He was well below average for marksmanship. But that was in 1943."

"He could've picked up since," Pitt commented.

"He could," agreed Mr. Lewker. "And Charles Feckenham, Inspector? Have you anything further?"

"A bit, sir. Subject to confirmation, there's two bookmakers and one or two others ready to put him in the courts for debt. That gets us no forrader."

Grimmett looked so dejected that Mr. Lewker felt slightly ashamed of his own reticence. He took from his pocket the nylon cord.

"This, Grimm," he said, "is what I am taking to Bangor."

Grimmett perked up suddenly. "Aha! The 'curious gap' you mentioned last night, sir—I reckon this is it."

"Yes?"

"The shield, that's where the gap is. Where is it? If it was pulled away as we suppose, it must have hung dangling by this cord until the explosion. Why haven't we found it?"

"Why?" said Pitt, looking up from a close inspection of the cord. "Because the murderer cut the cord and hid it, after he'd pulled it clear. Leastways, that's what could have happened."

"But," said Mr. Lewker gently, "it did not happen. Look at the frayed end, Sergeant. Was that cut, do you think?"

"No-o," Pitt acknowledged. "No knife work there. Explosion snapped it, then."

"It was at the other end of the bridge, well away from the explosion, and hanging eight or nine feet below."

"Let me look." Grimmett peered at the draggled ends. "Looks to me as though this was pounded with a stone or something. Funny, that."

Mr. Lewker, who was watching him through half-closed lids, nodded like a Chinese mandarin.

"I fancy," he said, "that if we could find the shield we should know who was responsible for the death of David Webhouse."

"I'll search that scree today," declared the inspector, recovering some of his enthusiasm. "And there's one or two other loose ends to tie up. That poisoned milk business, for one. I want chapter and verse from the maid and Mrs. P. about that. Meanwhile, sir—if you don't mind my mentioning it—you'd better let the sergeant open the ball with the solicitors, you having no official status, so to speak."

"Of course. And while Sergeant Pitt is engaged in his task at Llanerch Quarry, I will have a chat—a quite unofficial chat—with the quarry manager. But first to Bangor. Sergeant, cheerly to sea—the signs of war advance."

"Yessir."

Pitt opened the car door and Mr. Lewker took his place. Grimmett laid a hand on the door handle.

"One thing, sir," he said diffidently. "I know I'm slow, but what department of this university are you bound for?"

"The physics department, Grimm."

Pitt let in the clutch and Inspector Grimmett was left rubbing his scalp.

The hill-walled seclusion of Plas Mawr had tended to make Mr. Lewker forget the stir that Webhouse's death must make in the world beyond the vale of Gwynant. The sight of a little throng of people in the lane outside the gates of Plas Mawr recalled it to him. Most of the sightseers seemed to be curious holiday makers, but one raincoated young man, who appeared to be sketching the house and its surroundings, yelled excitedly to a companion as the car turned out of the drive, and Mr. Lewker caught his own name. A camera blinked at him as they swept past. Further evidence of public interest was provided by the newspapers, copies of which they obtained in passing through Beddgelert.

"THE BIRTHDAY HONORS MYSTERY," shouted the headlines. "THREE KNIGHTS-TO-BE IN MURDER TANGLE." The details they gave in succeeding paragraphs were vague; but to make up for lack of facts they gave full measure of description, speculation, and biography. The luscious coincidence of murder with the presence of one knight and three prospective ones at "the ancient retreat of the Capels, embowered in crags and trees beneath the frowning precipices of Snowdon," as one paper described it, had given the reporters a chance they were not slow to seize. David Webhouse, Cattespool, Feckenham, had each his paragraph of biographical detail; one acute journalist had emphasized Sir Henry Lydiate's leadership of the anti-hydroelectric protesters and mentioned in apposition David Webhouse's hydroelectric bill. As for Abercrombie Lewker, his name was well splashed across the page together with bold speculations as to the reason for his presence at Plas Mawr. Mr. Lewker, reading these, wondered what Georgie, his wife, was thinking; by now she would be home in London.

The road from Beddgelert to Bangor, which runs along the western flanks of Snowdon past Quellyn lake and through Caernarvon, is not one for fast travel. Sergeant Pitt handled the big Austin well and covered the twenty-one miles in thirty-five minutes. The University College of North Wales stands high above the town. At its imposing doors Mr. Lewker descended from the car.

It was his foible to act a part whenever the circumstances could by any stretch of imagination be said to warrant it. He was now the most distinguished of living biologists paying a visit to a fellow professor. His raincoat flapped loosely round his rotundity, his bald dome glistened with its load of learning, his features conveyed the essence of all professorial arrogance and abstraction. He entered the building with the air of one who spent his life entering larger and better buildings. A succession of awed young men directed him to the Physics Laboratory. A class was in session, but the youthful professor in charge, after one glance through the glass door at his visitor, came out to him. Mr. Lewker demanded an interview in private and was granted it. Perceiving the youthful professor to be a man of humor and intelligence, a man, moreover, who almost certainly read the morning papers, Mr. Lewker threw up his part and adopted a confidential, man-to-man attitude. The youthful professor's eyes widened when he heard what was required and why (he had read the morning papers), but he was young enough to raise no question of regulations and permits. He summoned a biologist into conference; and in due course Mr. Lewker departed in triumph, leaving behind him a few feet of green nylon parachute cord with a frayed end.

By way of the lower road through Pen-y-groes they sped southward again. It was noon, but so overcast were the heavens that they drove through a purple twilight in which the gray stone walls of the road glimmered with an almost ghastly pallor. Through Portmadoc town and across the Glaslyn estuary by the mile-long embankment in whose building Shelley had a hand, past the scarred hill of the granite quarry, they came to the little town of Llanerch. In the gloom its one street looked drab and deserted. Number 51 High Street proved to be a small prim house sandwiched between an ironmonger's and a draper's. The legend *LLOYD & JOHN, SOLICITORS*, in gold letters across its black-painted window, informed them that they had reached their second destination. The office was closed; it was the lunch hour in Llanerch. Mr. Lewker and Sergeant Pitt sought refreshment in the Lydiate Arms across the road, and restored themselves with cold mutton and poorish beer.

At two o'clock they found Messrs. Lloyd & John open and prepared to do business. The gaunt gentleman who admitted them looked, with his shapeless dark tweeds and ragged-edged collar, more like a farmer fallen on evil days than a solicitor. His voice, however, was soft and musical with an educated accent; his flowing gray locks reminded Mr. Lewker that it was at Portmadoc, not half a dozen miles from this spot, that David Lloyd George had begun his career in a small solicitor's office.

"I am Glanmor Evans, gentlemen," he told them, "the present head of the firm. Sit down, if you please, and tell me how I may serve you."

Sergeant Pitt, his Cockney accent quite submerged in official diction, opened the ball.

"From Scotland Yard, Mr. Evans. Here is my warrant card. This is Mr. Abercrombie Lewker, who's assisting the police in their investigations."

"Yes. Yes." Mr. Glanmor Evans' cadaverous face turned from the sergeant to Mr. Lewker, who had instinctively the narrow-eyed inscrutability of a super-Holmes. "Not until this morning did I hear of the decease of Mr. David Webhouse. A bad business, a bad business. There is crime involved, I gather?"

"Foul play is suspected," Pitt agreed. "You seem to have guessed why we're here." He produced Clare Webhouse's letter and handed it over. "This'll explain what we want."

Glanmor Evans opened the envelope and read its contents with care, twice, before raising his eyes.

"This is not strictly regular," he observed, frowning. "But I shall naturally assist you as far as in my power lies. Yes. You do not wish to see the will of the late David Webhouse?"

Pitt glanced at Mr. Lewker. "I don't think that's necessary," he said, "if you can tell us the names of the principal beneficiaries."

"And, perhaps, give us some idea of the amounts involved," murmured Mr. Lewker.

The solicitor's deep-set eyes surveyed each of them in turn. Then his bony frame visibly relaxed in his chair.

"That," he said, "I may do. There is no need for me to sight the will. I shall admit to you, gentlemen, that our business here in Llanerch is not a large one. So large a disposition of estate as is involved in this will does not often come our way, and the particulars—I am an executor—are clear in my memory. Mr. David Webhouse himself was in this office, poor gentleman, with his wife—his widow, I must now call her—a year ago."

"Ah. That'd be just after his marriage, no doubt," nodded Pitt.

"Yes, Sergeant. A week after the second marriage. Mr. Webhouse, very naturally, wished to alter his will."

"In favor of Mrs. Clare Webhouse?"

Glanmor Evans crossed his legs, placed his fingertips together, and closed his eyes.

"Apart from a bequest of five hundred pounds, and some half-dozen minor bequests," he said in a respectful whisper, "the estate is divided equally between Mrs. Clare Webhouse and the mother of Mr. David Webhouse's first wife."

"Mrs. Pauncefoot?" said Pitt sharply.

"Mrs. Anna Pauncefoot, yes."

Mr. Lewker spoke for the first time. "One might hazard a guess, Mr. Evans, that Mrs. Clare Webhouse's influence had something to do with the bequest to Mrs. Pauncefoot."

Glanmor Evans shot a penetrating glance at him.

"One might." he said shortly. "Guesses however, are not within my province."

"Can you tell us the amount of the estate?" Pitt asked.

"Speaking approximately, Sergeant, and using what are known as round figures, I may quote the sum of seventy thousand pounds."

There was a short pause while Pitt made a note. Mr. Lewker broke it.

"May we know to whom the five-hundred-pound bequest was made?"

"To James Cutpursey. He is, I believe, gardener at Plas Mawr."

"James Cutpursey," repeated Mr. Lewker thoughtfully. "And was that bequest made before Mr. Webhouse altered his will a year ago?"

"It was not, sir. Mr. David Webhouse came here to make the further alteration, adding the bequest to James Cutpursey, on May 22 of this year, three weeks ago, that is."

"Thank you." Mr. Lewker paused, frowning. "I wonder," he added tentatively, "if by any chance Cutpursey was with Mr. Webhouse on that occasion."

Again Clanmor Evans' sunken eyes turned their keen gaze on him.

"He was. By Mr. David Webhouse's desire. James Cutpursey saw the alteration made and witnessed."

The actor-manager thanked him again and nodded to Pitt, who had been watching him with a puzzled expression. The sergeant rose to his feet.

"That's all, then, Mr. Evans. Obliged for your assistance."

The solicitor opened the door, admitting a waft of heated air from the street.

"I take it I may call upon my deceased client's widow this afternoon, as I had intended?" he inquired.

"Quite in order, sir," Pitt replied. "Better ask for Inspector Grimmett when you arrive."

Outside, and seated in the Austin, the sergeant drew a deep breath.

"Hell's bells, sir!" he exclaimed. "That clinches motive for Mrs. P. and no error. Thirty-five thou' for her—if she knew about it, and I'd say she did."

"David Webhouse was not the man to keep silence about his generosity," Mr. Lewker agreed. "You note also that Cutpursey gets five hundred pounds."

"Enough to give him motive for murder?" Pitt wondered. "Might be, I suppose. What was the point about him being there and seeing the bequest put in, sir?"

Mr. Lewker beamed at him.

"Sergeant," he boomed, "your own wits should supply the answer. If they do not, I will assure you, in Prospero's words, that 'The approaching tide will shortly fill the reasonable shore, that now lies foul and muddy.'

"Let us on, therefore, to the Llanerch granite quarry."

CHAPTER XIV

THE RACKAROCK CHARGE

Most of the cows in the hilly fields of Hendre Mynydd farm were behaving as cows usually behave when very bad weather is imminent; that is, they were lashing their tails energetically and lowing almost continuously. Some few of them, however, in whom the modern craze for spectacle had doubtless submerged the meteorological instinct, were crowded side by side to stare over the gate into the lane. On the other side of the gate a large Austin car had pulled up, and in the back seat of the car a lanky detective-sergeant was changing his trousers.

"Scram! Imshi! Turn it in, you perishers!" shouted Sergeant Pitt, without making the slightest impression on his round-eyed admirers. "Downright indecent, it is," he added indignantly to Mr. Lewker.

"A cow may look at a copper," pronounced the actor-manager mildly. "Theirs is a dull life, Sergeant. Do not grudge the poor creatures a little amusement."

Pitt, to whom fell the delicate task of locating the man who had illegally supplied a rackarock charge to some person connected with Plas Mawr, had his plans ready. It was only a conjecture, though a likely one, that the charge had come from the Llanerch Quarry, but he was determined to be thorough in his investigations. He had driven the car to a bylane whence (as the map showed) he could reach the quarry on foot, and had there produced from the boot a parcel of dingy but fairly respectable clothes. These he substituted for his neat dark suit.

"Poor but honest working man, that's me," he said as he got out of the car and put on a cloth cap. "Funny thing, sir, how the ordinary bloke nowadays don't consider it dishonest to do a bit of flogging when he can. I'll guarantee the chap as sells me a four-ounce charge—if I find him—is an upright chapel-going bloke. By the way, sir—"

"Yes?" said Mr. Lewker as he hesitated.

"I take it this stunt of mine isn't redundant, so to speak? I mean to say, if you've solved the question—"

"Your stunt, Sergeant, is absolutely essential," said Mr. Lewker firmly. "I am practically certain that the rackarock charge came from Llanerch Quarry, but I must know who obtained it. Confirmatory evidence is what we sorely need."

"Yessir. And was the evidence we got from the solicitor confirmatory?"

"Extremely so."

Pitt lifted his cloth cap to scratch his head.

"And yet I can't see how she set that trap," he muttered.

Mr. Lewker twinkled at him. "All shall be made plain in due course, Sergeant. On stage with you now."

The sergeant moved away up the lane and presently turned along a foot-path leading down through stony meadows in the direction of the quarry. Mr. Lewker, after filling and lighting his pipe, turned the car and drove slowly back to the main road. This he left just short of Llanerch village, taking a very rough lane which eventually brought him to the green flats of the re-claimed estuary lands and headed for the bulky hill where the granite quarry was situated.

Half the hill, he saw as he bumped slowly towards it, had already been quarried away. A 300-foot face of naked granite dropped from its crest to a wide plateau edged with banks of rubble, at the foot of which a cluster of tumbledown buildings huddled above a railway siding. Under that dark and scowling sky the place looked utterly derelict and profitless; yet it was prob-ably a thriving concern. That (mused Mr. Lewker) was typical of the Welsh race. They, and not the English, were the original muddlers through. The English never muddled, being confirmed systematists whose habit was to choose and cling to unworkable systems and make them work by sheer doggedness. The Welsh, abhorring system, punctuality, and all the other business essentials, nevertheless managed very comfortably to make a living.

The road was so bad that he had to change into third gear; it had not, apparently, been repaired in the last decade. That, he reflected, would be attributed by an English visitor to the fact that the Welsh as a nation consisted chiefly of poets and musicians, in contrast to the practical, unmusical, unpoetical English. Yet apart from her singers Wales had produced no musicians to compare with those of England, and her poets were unknown outside their own country. There were historical misconceptions, too; those characteristically brave and tenacious English bowmen who had won Crécy and Poitiers had been, in fact, Welsh archers. Mr. Lewker wagged his head sadly over the ineradicable tendency of the human mind to twist facts into a pattern conformable with some easily-grasped formula. Which led to the reflection that few minds can realize that a fact—even a chain of facts—can point in more than one direction. The otherwise admirable mind of Detective-Inspector George Grimmett, meditated Mr. Lewker, suffered from this latter handicap, the case of David Webhouse's death being a case in point.

The Austin, lurching violently as it crossed the railway line (no gates and one quite illegible signboard) recalled him to his present purpose. He brought the car to a halt beside the first of the tumbledown buildings and got out. The steep bank of rubble rose above, with a runway for trucks descending it from a wire-cable winch at the top and the upper part of the quarry face peering over its crest. A tall and rickety shanty nearby clanged its corrugated-iron roof at every thud of some wheezy engine inside. The whole place had an irresistible savor of Emett, if not of Heath Robinson, and there was not a living soul to be seen.

He wandered along the irregular line of shanties, pushing open doors and finding heaps of scrap iron inside. One door was padlocked, its staple rooted in wood so rotten that a sharp tug would certainly have broken it out. Mr. Lewker discerned the remains of the letters "ER" on the right-hand side of the door, deduced the missing "DANG," and concluded that here was the Explosive Store; a person particularly anxious to obtain a charge of rackarock would have no great difficulty, it seemed, in helping himself. The engine shed seemed to offer the possibility of human occupancy, and he was on the point of entering it when a short square man in a tweed suit and a black felt hat appeared on the top of the rubble bank and began to descend a flight of mossy steps beside the runway. He raised a hand in greeting and smiled a welcome as he approached Mr. Lewker.

"A warm afternoon," he said, nodding. "There will be a storm, it's ferry likely."

Mr. Lewker, replying suitably, scored another point against preconceived notions of national character. The friendly, courteous Englishman—the secretive and suspicious Welshman; so ran the English conviction. Here, it seemed, was a foreman-in-charge; what English foreman, finding a stranger prowling round his domain, would greet him with polite remarks about the weather? The weather, indeed, seemed a favorite subject of the foreman's, and they discussed storms and their probable causes at some length before Mr. Lewker realized that his companion was far too well bred to ask his visitor's business. He broached the matter himself.

"I do not wish to trespass unduly on your time, Mr.—"

"Jones, sir—Prys Jones," said the foreman deprecatingly.

"—Mr. Jones, but I am here to make a few inquiries, on behalf of a client, about a certain James Cutpursey who was, I believe, employed here some years ago. If you can help me, I shall be deeply indebted to you."

If Mr. Prys Jones thought this story needed amplification he was too polite to say so.

"Yess, yess," he nodded. "James Cutpursey—an Englishman, isn't it? He left the quarry three years ago, but I remember him well. An old man, too old for heavy work."

"That is the man I mean."

"James Cutpursey," repeated the foreman, caressing his chin thoughtfully. His rather melancholy brown eyes, which had hitherto avoided Mr. Lewker's, suddenly looked straight at him. "You will be asking in the matter of Mr. David Webhouse's murder," he said with quiet conviction.

Mr. Lewker perceived that he had been guilty of that very sin of preconception for which, ten minutes ago, he had blamed others. Because Mr. Prys Jones was obviously Welsh, not quite at home in the English tongue, and of a good-natured simplicity, he had unconsciously assumed that he was slow in the uptake.

"I wonder how you guessed that," he said with his most genial smile. "You read the morning paper, no doubt, but there was no mention of Cutpursey."

The foreman made a shy gesture that was almost a shrug.

"'Twas easy, sir. You come to ask after a man who was once employed here and is now gardener at Plas Mawr—that has never happened before, indeed. Mr. David Webhouse is killed, and *that* has never happened before. 'Twas easy. Yess, indeed."

He finished with a sharp exclamation in Welsh and pulled an immense silver watch from his waistcoat pocket.

"I will help you if I can, sir," he said rapidly, "but I must go above now. At half-past four we are blasting. Come you with me."

As he spoke the melodious note of a horn sounded its long-drawn warning somewhere overhead. Mr. Prys Jones, with an apologetic wave of his hand, led the way up the steps beside the runway and Mr. Lewker followed. At the top of the bank of rocks they came to a vast level space crisscrossed with narrow-gauge rails, with the vertical face of the quarry rising at its farther side like a gigantic gray wall against the blue-black sky. A score or so of quarrymen, leaving the rusty iron trucks where they stood, were walking away from the face towards several square shelters built of solid rock which stood along the crest of the rubble bank. The foreman hurried his visitor into one of these without ceremony.

"Sometimes the rock pieces will fly ferry long distances," he explained, dusting a wooden bench with his sleeve and inviting the actor-manager to sit. "We take cover, just as in the war."

Three men came in after them, covered with gray dust. They glanced incuriously at the stranger as they sat down, and began to talk in Welsh. A fourth followed, a stocky dark-haired man whose bare forearms were tattooed in blue. A "foul anchor," Mr. Lewker noticed, was the center of the design on the right arm. Acting on impulse, he leaned forward to speak to the man; but at that moment the charges were exploded. A rapid and irregular succession of detonations, like the firing of a 40-millimeter Bofors gun that had somehow mislaid its rhythm, shook the stone shelter. As the echoes of the last explosion died away the man with the tattooed forearms got up and went out of the shelter. The rest sat still until the blast of the horn half a minute later signalled the All Clear, when they filed out to resume their work. Mr. Lewker and the foreman came out last. The foreman spent a moment or two scanning the rock-face and the great flakes and cubes of granite brought down by the blast, shouted something in rapid Welsh to a passing quarryman, and then led his companion back down the steps.

"Were you using rackarock for that blast?" asked Mr. Lewker casually as they descended.

"No, indeed, sir. Rackarock we use to spring the rock, as we say. Then we blast it, with blasting powder. That was blasting powder—but I see you know something of our trade. Perhaps you know Will Evans, too. I saw you make to speak to him."

Mr. Lewker hastened to explain that his acquaintance Mr. Cattespool had mentioned an ex-sailor friend, one Will Evans, working as a "popper" at Llanerch Quarry.

"Ah, Mr. Anthony Cattespool, the book writer," nodded Prys Jones. "Once will brought him here to see a blast fired. A ferry nice gentleman, I thought."

So Cattespool had actually been to Llanerch Quarry in person, reflected Mr. Lewker as he followed Prys Jones past the engine shed; other people would doubtless know of that visit. The foreman ushered him into a low stone building which hid itself behind the engine-shed, and he found himself in a small and dingy office furnished with a table and two chairs and thick with gray dust. A makeshift bookshelf on the wall, he noticed, held a row of green-backed detective stories.

"And fond I am of a good detective," said the foreman, following his glance. "For the English, my reading is a deal better than my speaking." He swept the dust from a chair and invited the actor-manager to sit. "You, sir, I take to be a detective—indeed, you will be Mr. Abercrombie Lewker, I'm thinking, from what the paper says."

Mr. Lewker admitted it and apologized for having omitted to introduce himself. The foreman seated himself and dismissed the apology with a wave of his hand.

"Now," he said with enthusiasm, "you will please, sir, to ask me what you wish to know."

Thus encouraged, the actor-manager wasted no time on subtleties of approach. He produced the newspaper cutting he had brought with him showing David Webhouse and Cutpursey in the group taken at Llanerch Quarry, explaining that as no information was at present obtainable from Cutpursey (an equivocation which, he decided uncomfortably, did not really deceive the other) he was anxious to find out the circumstances in which the old quarryman and "the quarryman's M.P." had become acquainted. He added quickly that he did not expect Mr. Prys Jones to know those circumstances, but had thought that perhaps some useful hint might have been dropped on the occasion of Webhouse's visit.

A faint smile of self-satisfaction wrinkled the corners of the foreman's eyes.

"It's ferry likely I can tell you something," he said modestly. "Being fond of a good detective, now, I'm fond of finding out things. Curiosity, you might call it, I suppose. This will be hearsay, indeed—but you shall judge, sir."

Prys Jones's story was straightforward enough, and not particularly exciting; but with the instinct of the born storyteller he made the most of it. Shorn of much descriptive detail and repetition, it was as follows. James Cutpursey, with a younger man named Tully, had come north from a South Wales quarry where both had been employed, and had been given jobs at Llanerch Quarry. This was in 1944. In 1950 David Webhouse visited the quarry in the course of a political tour of Welsh quarries, to make one of his celebrated fighting speeches. This was the occasion on which the photograph in Mr. Lewker's possession had been taken by a local journalist. The M.P. had noisily greeted both Tully and Cutpursey as old acquaintances; but it was the latter whose response had roused the detective instinct in Mr. Prys Jones.

"Such a surly old ram as he was," he explained, "smiling and fair wagging his tail for Dai Webhouse's attention, that made me wonder, indeed. For neffer a smile did we have of him in the six years he was here, nor a decent friendly word. That photo, now—it shows him all of a grin. Well, sir, 'twas the first time this quarry ever saw him grin. I ask myself then, why is he with

Dai Webhouse like a sheepdog with its master?"

For the sake of finding out, he had found out the reason. Nothing, he knew, could be got out of the old man himself, so he had tackled Tully, with whom Cutpursey had previously worked. And from Tully he got the explanation. It appeared that a year or two before the second world war David Webhouse, then in his thirties, was chief "popper" at the Talgarth Granite Quarry in South Wales, where Tully and Cutpursey were employed as quarrymen. There had been an accident; a big natural rockfall had caught and killed two men working at the quarry face and trapped a third in a pile of fallen blocks. The third man was Cutpursey. By some miracle he was not crushed to death, though one leg was broken, but he was imprisoned beneath a large overhang left by the fall, a jutting nose which was ready to crash down at any moment. Only Webhouse, who had run to the spot with a crowd of others, had had the courage and instant resolution to attempt a rescue. Using his abnormal strength, he had succeeded in dragging away the imprisoning boulders and hauling Cutpursey clear a few seconds before the mass of loosened rock thundered down on the spot where he had lain helpless.

"Even a surly old ram of a quarryman would not forget an escape like that," ended the foreman. "James Cutpursey knew the risk Dai Webhouse ran. Yess, indeed. And that was why his eyes were a dog's eyes, following Dai Webhouse, that time."

"One's life is a very big debt to owe," agreed Mr. Lewker thoughtfully.

"Ferry true, sir. I was not surprised when Cutpursey left the quarry for a job as gardener to Dai Webhouse. That was afterwards, when Webhouse married and bought Plas Mawr."

A prolonged whistle blast reached their ears as he finished speaking. The foreman hauled out his watch and inspected it.

"The knocking-off whistle," he remarked.

"Then I must detain you no longer." Mr. Lewker got up. "I am indebted to you for some useful information."

But Mr. Prys Jones had no intention of allowing his visitor to depart so abruptly. He led him to the shelf of detective stories and demanded his opinion as to the relative merits of Margery Allingham's Mr. Campion and Ngaio Marsh's Alleyn. Mr. Lewker, remembering that Pitt's investigation would be at its crux now, and that the absence of the foreman's eagle eye would help considerably, permitted himself to be inveigled into a discussion which lasted nearly half an hour. After this, he waited while Prys Jones locked up his ramshackle sheds and then gave him a lift as far as Llanerch High Street.

"Slates will lift from the house roofs and branches from the valley trees this night," prophesied the foreman as he got out of the car. "Be ferry certain, sir, that you are indoors, for the storm will be a bad one."

Mr. Lewker thanked him, assured him (in all innocence) that he would take his advice, and drove away. He went to the spot where he had parted from the sergeant and there stopped the car. In ten minutes Pitt's lanky figure, barely discernible in the unnatural gloom, emerged from the footpath into the lane and came towards the car. His brisk step suggested that he had not been unsuccessful.

"What's he approacheth boldly to our presence?" Mr. Lewker greeted him in his deepest bass.

"Hallo, sir—sounds as if you've struck lucky," returned Pitt. He got into the rear seat. "So've I. Here's your rackarock charge, four-ounce, price ten bob. And I hope I can charge it to expenses incurred in course of duty."

Mr. Lewker took the short cylinder, stiff-paper-wrapped, which the sergeant handed to him. It resembled in shape and size the dummy cylinder found in Anthony Cattespool's shed.

"I'll tell you about it ong root," Pitt added, struggling with his trousers. "Best get going pronto. There's the father and mother of all storms dropping on us—made up its mind at last."

He was right. As the Austin, with a reclothed Pitt at the wheel, sped out of Llanerch and down to the estuary embankment, they saw lightning flicker bluely out of the quivering blackness that hid the Snowdon peaks. A waft of cold air, refreshing but ominous, came through the open windows of the car; and the continuous mutter of distant thunder reminded Mr. Lewker of an artillery barrage he had once heard from a hiding place some miles inside the enemy lines.

"You shall have my report first," he said; and told of his talk with Mr. Prys Jones.

Pitt, bent forward over the wheel, switched on his headlights. The reflected glow showed his hatchet face frowning and puzzled.

"May make sense to you, sir," he grunted, "but how about this? It was—but I'll start at the beginning. I prowled round the outskirts of the place first, and got the hang of it. Thought I might spot one of the poppers on the job and tackle him. That blast was fired just as I got on to the edge of the plateau under the rock face. Pretty near shook me out of me skin, I give you my word. Anyway, I decided to wait for knocking-off time. I hung about on the lane ready to—my eye, sir, that was some flash!"

"You had your story ready, I suppose?"

"I had. I was from Barmouth way, just married and bought myself a cottage. Keen on gardening, see? Wanted to get rid of a whacking big rock in my back garden, and wanted to scrounge a chunk of rackarock to shift it. I reckoned to say I'd heard Will Evans might help me out—that's the chap Mr. Cattespool told us about."

"Excellent," commented Mr. Lewker.

"It worked, anyway, sir. First chap I spoke to pointed out Will Evans.

Thickset lad, not much to say for himself. I got alongside him and told the tale as we walked along. At first he stuck it out no one flogged charges in Llanerch Quarry, but I slipped him the whisper it was a chap by the name of Cutpursey who put me on to him, not thinking I was going to hit the target with that little lie. 'Oh,' says Will Evans, 'old Cutpursey Well,' he says, 'it isn't me you want,' and he points out a big chap just coming away from the quarry. Seems this chap was a particular pal of Cutpursey's when he worked there."

"By name, Tully," nodded Mr. Lewker.

"Tully it was, sir—crikey! Looks like we're in the target area. Reminds me of that night in the blitz when—"

The rest of his sentence was lost in the crash of thunder that followed a blinding glare of lightning. They had passed through Portmadoc and were only a few miles short of Beddgelert and the Gwynant valley, heading for what appeared to be the heart of the storm. The nearer flashes, whose attendant detonations interrupted Pitt's report from time to time, seemed to indicate that this was no ordinary thunderstorm; the main storm hung above the mountains, and these outpost disturbances showed how unusually large was its area.

"Well, sir." continued Pitt, his eyes on the twisting road flatly revealed by the headlights, "this Tully turns out to be an easygoing type. Soon as I hint what I'm after, he grins and takes a look round to see if the boss is about. Then he jerks a thumb and we go back again towards the sheds. 'Cost you twelve and a bender,' he says, 'and your Bible oath to keep it dark.' I wasn't going to grab too quick, so I tells him I've had the office the last chap he flogged rackarock to got a four-ounce charge for ten bob. 'Oh,' says Tully, 'that was an old pal who wanted it very special.' We were by one of the sheds by now, and he dodges round it for a minute and comes back with his hand in his pocket. I'd done a quick think while he was away. 'Look,' I says, 'I'm not doubting your word, mate, but the gen I got was that a gent by the name of Cattespool bought a four-ounce charge from you about a month ago, and if you can sell to a gent for ten bob you can surely let me have it for the same.' That riled him a bit. 'You got it wrong, chum,' he said. 'You can have it for ten bob, just to show I'm not doing you down, but I never sold a charge to any Cattespool, and anyway it was a fortnight ago, not a month.' I could see I was mighty close to it now, sir, but I reckoned I'd strike quick. I got out a ten-bob note. 'If it wasn't Cattespool,' I says very casual, waving the note at him, 'who was it?' 'Why,' he says——"

A vivid mauve flash, followed very closely by a violent explosion, cut him short. Immediately after the thunderclap came the rain. It was as though some vast tarpaulin holding an Olympian swimming-bath had been suddenly emptied from the heavens. The headlights flung their rays in vain against a wall of silver water a few yards in front of the bonnet, and Sergeant Pitt had to tread heavily on his brake-pedal and reduce his speed to a crawl. The hissing roar of the downpour forced him to shout the finish of his report.

" 'Why,' he says, 'it was old Jim Cutpursey.' "

CHAPTER XV

DRURY LANE STUFF

It was barely seven o'clock in the evening of June 12th when the Austin splashed to a standstill at the gates of Plas Mawr, but it was already pitch dark. Mr. Lewker had been silent during the last part of the drive from Llan-erch, and Pitt, intent on what he could see of the road through the unremit-ting cascade of rain, needed all his attention for the handling of the car. The sounding of the car horn roused the actor-manager to the realization of their arrival. He sat up, peering out of the car window at the rain-drenched trees by the gate whose leaves reflected the ghastly intermittent flare of lightning. Between the rolls of thunder he could hear the drumming of the rain, and above it a note more ominous—the vibrant growl of a hundred swollen streams racing down the mountainsides.

"Light in the lodge, sir," Pitt explained. "Constable Jones'll open up."

As he spoke a hunched figure stumbled out of the lodge into the glare of the headlights. A white glare of lightning, making the car lights seem yellow as candles, momentarily revealed the stout body of Constable Jones below a hood of glistening oilskin. The gates swung open and the car rolled through.

"Hold on!" yelled the constable above the hubbub, waving an agitated hand at the window. "Mr. Grimmett's down here, sir—in the lodge."

Pitt stopped the car and dimmed his lights, and they-made a dash for the shelter of the lodge. The beat of the rain on Mr. Lewker's bald head was like the smiting of a well-directed hose pipe.

"*Myn diawl!*" said Constable Jones, allowing his emotion to get the better of him as they reached the porch. "It is not often you'll see the like of this mugger, indeed!"

"You'll watch that tongue of yours, Jones," rasped Inspector Grimmett, appearing at the door of a small inner room. "In here, sir—there's a bit of a fire."

The constable took himself and his oilskin to the adjacent kitchen and Pitt and Mr. Lewker followed Grimmett into Cutpursey's parlor. It was a little room, sparsely furnished and lit by a pair of candles, but the fire smoulder-ing in the grate made it a welcome haven in such weather. On the deal top of the small table lay Grimmett's notebook and several sheets of paper.

"Well, sir?" demanded the inspector somewhat defiantly. "Any news?"

His square features seemed to have become squarer than usual and his red mustache bristled as though it had attracted some of the atmospheric electricity.

"We have discharged our errands," replied Mr. Lewker, sitting down in a rickety chair by the fire. "They are complete except for a report from the professor of physics at Bangor University, which I expect to receive by telephone late tonight."

"You've got all the evidence you wanted?" persisted Grimmett.

"No, Grimm. I would not say that. Until I can lay hands on James Cutpursey I cannot—"

"That settles it." Grimmett's voice was unwontedly harsh. "I'll tell you straight, sir, I reckon you're barking up the wrong tree for once. You can keep mum about your Cutpursey theory—just as you like—but I'm going ahead on my own."

Mr. Lewker's heavy brows rose. He perceived that his friend was in an unusually bad temper, some of which might charitably be attributed to the thunderstorm.

"My dear Grimm!" he protested mildly. "Naturally you must go ahead, if you see your way. You have found fresh evidence, I take it."

"I have. Solid evidence." He sat down heavily at the table. "Took me all day to get it, too."

"Let's have it, sir," said Pitt eagerly.

"I'll take orders from you, Sergeant, when our ranks are reversed," snapped Grimmett. "Your report. And make it in decent English, if you can."

Sergeant Pitt, visibly abashed, stood up stiffly from his table corner and made his report. He omitted the details and stated concisely that a quarryman named Tully had admitted selling a four-ounce rackarock charge to James Cutpursey on or about May 28th.

"On or about?" repeated Grimmett sharply. "Can't you get your dates exact, man?"

Pitt looked sulky and said nothing. The inspector blew exasperatedly through his mustache.

"And what's your inference from this, Sergeant?" he demanded.

"Why," Pitt said slowly, with a glance at Mr. Lewker, "we agreed Cutpursey had the best means and the best opportunity for the murder, didn't we? Now we've got proof it was him that got a rackarock charge from—"

"And the motive, man, the motive?"

"I think, Grimm," Mr. Lewker ventured, "you had better hear my report, which throws some light upon the question of motive."

Lightning glared outside, turning Grimmett's scowling face purple as he nodded curt acquiescence. The ensuing thunder, Mr. Lewker noted, was several seconds before it came. He described first his conversation with Prys Jones the quarry foreman.

"But that makes nonsense, so it does," Grimmett frowned. "Webhouse saved Cutpursey's life. We're told he behaved to Webhouse like a dog to his master. That fits with what Webhouse said himself, what Mrs. Webhouse told us, and what Anna Pauncefoot confirmed. He was devoted to Webhouse."

"There is the will to be considered," said Mr. Lewker, and repeated the information given by Mr. Glanmor Evans.

"Had a word with him," grunted the inspector. "He turned up after lunch for a chat with Mrs. Webhouse. Told me he'd instructed his client to keep her mouth shut, blast him!" He slapped his palm on the table. "Five hundred pounds—and Webhouse showed it to Cutpursey in black and white. I grant you a sort of motive there, sir, but I don't believe it. I ask you, is it likely? Lord knows human nature's nasty stuff, but the man who'd saved his life— no, I'll want stronger evidence."

"What did he want the rackarock for, then?" Pitt demanded.

Grimmett rolled up his eyes in mock despair.

"Detectives, they call 'em," he groaned. "When you buy twopenn'orth of violets for your blonde playmates, my lad, what d'you want 'em for? To sit and sniff 'em yourself?"

"Blondes don't like violets," muttered Pitt.

"I'll take your word for it. Point is, there's nothing to say he didn't get the charge for someone else. I say he did. I say he was bribed to get it—or maybe forced to by someone who had a hold over him."

"And who would this someone be?" wondered Mr. Lewker.

Grimmett thumped the table again. "Cattespool, of course. It's no good your coming at me with the old gag that the likeliest suspect can't be the murderer, sir. You can't go against the weight of evidence. I've said it all along and I will say it—every jot of evidence we've got points straight at him."

"Or away from him," said Mr. Lewker quietly.

"Garrh!" said the inspector disgustedly, waving his hands.

As if he had conjured up a demon, a ferocious blast of wind and rain crashed against the window. The candles flickered wildly and a door slammed somewhere in the lodge.

"Proper melodramatic," Pitt commented. "Cue for entrance of unmarried mother with babe in shawl—eh, sir?"

"There is a certain theatrical quality about nature at times," agreed the actor-manager. "This is true Drury Lane stuff, with the effects a trifle over-done. And I fancy the worst of this storm is yet to come." He shifted his chair nearer the fire. "We have yet to hear about the fresh evidence, Grimm."

"All right, sir."

Grimmett turned to his papers and selected a sheet of paper and an envelope. As he began to speak the wind continued to batter at the lodge with increasing violence. The slashing of the rain on the windowpanes drowned the noise of thunder, which was now distant.

"First," he said, taking up the sheet of paper, "let's look at the possibles fair and square, as far as we got last night. Your play-acting game, sir, showed up a thing or two—I'll give you that. But set out properly on paper, what do we get? Why, this." He read from his paper. "*Anna Pauncefoot.* No opportunity to set the trap. *Sir Henry Lydiate.* Very thin motive, unlikely in every other way, could not have been responsible for the falling rock, most unlikely he was responsible for the airgun shot or the attempt at poisoning. *Charles Feckenham.* Opportunity for setting trap very poor if not impossible, did not work the airgun shot, could not have worked the falling rock. *Clare Webhouse.* Opportunity—well, could she have shifted that bridge about? Or pushed the rock down? Suspect only if we take it she was in cahoots with Cattespool."

Here the chivalrous Pitt snorted and received a glare from his superior.

"*James Cutpursey*," continued Grimmett. He looked up. "I've got 'no motive' against him here, and I still think Webhouse's bequest, set against the strong evidence of his devotion to Webhouse, gives no reason to cross it out. What's more, the falling rock wasn't his doing. Lastly, *Anthony Cattespool.*" He put down the sheet and sat forward in his chair. "In his favor, only the alibi for the airgun shot. And that, as we argued it out, isn't unbreakable. As for his poor marksmanship—well, he missed, didn't he? And look this in the face—he's the only one of 'em all who could *easily* have done everything we've got in the charge." He ticked them off on his fingers one by one. "The attempt at poisoning—maybe assisted by the wife. The airgun shot—rubbing out his alibi. The preparation and setting of the trap—he had everything it took for that. And he alone could have pushed that rock down. Nobody else has got so strong a motive. He hated Webhouse, he coveted his wife, he gets a fortune when he marries her. Any objections?"

"There are one or two small points," murmured Mr. Lewker, "but they are very small. You put a strong case, Grimm. I grant that Anthony Cattespool is by far the likeliest of the six, on your showing. But you have something further against him?"

"Yes." Grimmett picked up the envelope and shook it; three small pieces of paper fluttered from it on to the table. "I'll tell you this," he added, covering them with his hand. "I got nowhere with the poisoning business. Webhouse seems to have complained about his food twice, once to the maid and once to Mrs. Pauncefoot. The dog drank the milk that time, so it can't have been poisoned. After that I went right through the house—Webhouse's desk, all the drawers, every place I could think of. I got nothing—until I upended the dustbin. And I found these."

He lifted his hand from the three bits of paper. Methodically he fitted them together. In the short silence as he did so a small branch, blown from a nearby tree, crashed against the window, making Pitt jump and swear beneath his breath. Mr. Lewker, who had risen from his chair to inspect the fresh clue, saw that the pieces formed two-thirds of a typewritten note that had been torn across twice, unevenly. The bottom right-hand corner was missing. The note read:

> Dear,
>   I've rigged it. Zero hour 8 tomorrow
> evening. Daren't leave it lat
> MUST make certain no one el
> path after that time unt
> he does. It would b
> Flora indoors t
>   I lo

"Well?" demanded Grimmett triumphantly. "Plain enough, isn't it? Tells her the time he's pulling the safety-shield out, warns her about seeing nobody else goes up the cliff path after then, even remembers the dog. No signature—that's torn off—but who'd write 'I love you' at the end but Cattespool? And who'd he write it to but Clare?"

"Why'd he have to write it at all?" demanded Pitt rebelliously.

Grimmett ignored him and kept his eyes fixed on Mr. Lewker.

"There is no typewriter in Webhouse's study or library," the actor-manager said slowly, "and there is a typewriter in Cattespool's cottage. This note will be found to have been typed on Cattespool's machine."

"I know, sir—don't tell me," said the inspector with heavy irony. "It's a plant. You'll say—"

"Why didn't she burn the note instead of chucking it in the dustbin?" persisted Pitt.

"Isn't she just the casual type that wouldn't bother?" Grimmett said sharply. He turned to Mr. Lewker. "See here, sir. If it's a plant, who planted it? Not Feckenham, who by every account's fond of his cousin and wouldn't incriminate her as well, as this does. Not Sir Henry Lydiate, the chivalrous old gent. Not James Cutpursey, unless he's a very different character from what everyone and all the evidence tells us. Not Anna Pauncefoot—"

"Why not?" flashed Pitt. "If she got Webhouse *and* Clare out of the way, wouldn't all the money come to her?"

"And when was her opportunity for pulling out the shield, and for all the other things we've gone over? No, my lad." Grimmett swept the fragments into the envelope and sealed it carefully. "This clinches it. Cattespool's my meat, with Clare Webhouse accessory before the fact."

"Your arrest," began Mr. Lewker, frowning.

"Tomorrow. Thorough's my motto, sir, and I want to go over all the evidence again, with everyone present. I'd like to wipe out the points against the others if I can, and I reckon we can get rid of some of them by a bit of careful questioning. Be glad if you'd help me, sir."

Mr. Lewker was rubbing his chin in evident perplexity.

"Of course, Grimm," he said. "But—"

"I knew you would, sir." The inspector, who had talked away most of his ill humor, beamed at him. "Can't be right every time, can we? Now—Sergeant, you'll drive me round to pick up Sir Henry and bring him back. The rainstorm caught me in here just as I was finishing a run-through of Cutpursey's effects," he explained to Mr. Lewker. "Thought I'd wait for the car. And by the way, Dilys says the old man kept a store of candles here. They're all gone—presumably with Cutpursey."

"And have you an explanation for Cutpursey's absence?" asked the actor-manager curiously.

"Fright, sir. The careful Cattespool persuaded him to get the rackarock charge for him. Cutpursey only saw what it was for when he saw his master dead. He remembered the legacy, realized the charge would be traced to him, and reckoned he was in a nasty jam. So he ran for it. We'll find it's something like that when we get hold of him—as we shall in the end."

He went to the door and called Constable Jones, who stumped in and saluted woodenly.

"You'll stay in the big house until I get back, Jones," said the inspector. "Mr. Lewker here will be in charge. No one's to go out. Now, sir, we'll run you up to the house and then push off to get Sir Henry."

Outside in the roaring dark the rain soaked their trouser legs even in the few seconds it took to dash to the car and wrestle into shelter through its wind-shaken doors. As they drove up towards Plas Mawr the headlights held, momentarily, wild pictures—great rhododendron bushes writhing and fighting in the grip of the gale, tall trees bent like bows, clumps of leaves and hurtling twigs borne on the driving rain as on a river flowing in midair. The drive itself was a muddy river. As they came on to the terrace in front of the house the Austin's front wheels bumped and crunched over a long elm bough lying across the gravel. Pitt swung the car round in a wide circle and drew up close alongside the steps of the front entrance. Constable Jones, who was on the side nearest the house, bundled out and dashed for shelter, but Mr. Lewker lingered. He had remembered something.

"You were going to interrogate Tansy, Grimm. What was the result?"

"No interrogation," Grimmett replied. "I left it till after lunch, and then it was too late. Seems she went off on her own and no one knows where. Anyhow, I don't reckon we'd have got anything important from—"

"She went out?" Mr. Lewker repeated. "Is she, then, still out?"

"Well, I suppose she is. Hadn't thought of it. Look here, sir, I'll be back with Sir Henry in twenty minutes. Keep an eye on you-know-who—don't let *him* push off!"

Mr. Lewker, frowning abstractedly, agreed. He got out and ran for the door, and the car splashed away down the drive. In the hall of Plas Mawr he found Constable Jones confronting a difficult situation, surrounded by all the household except Clare and Tansy. Anthony Cattespool, in a black oil-skin and sou'wester, was gesticulating angrily at the constable while Mrs. Pauncefoot, her bony face grim as ever, stood with a goggle-eyed Dilys in the background. Charles Feckenham was sitting at the foot of the stair lacing a pair of heavy boots.

"Damn and blast your orders!" Anthony was shouting, his affected voice shrill with exasperation. "Can't you understand the child's got to be found? People die of exposure in storms like this—"

"You are not leafing here, sir," interrupted Constable Jones, with a touch of Magna Carta in his voice. He glanced over his shoulder. "Here is Mr. Lewker, now. He will tell you the same."

"Look here, Lewker"—Anthony took a stride towards the actor-manager— "tell this fool to let Charles and me get after Tansy. She may be—"

He broke off as the door leading to the telephone in the cloakroom opened and Clare came out. She looked worried.

"It's no good," she said. "The wire must be down or something." She saw Mr. Lewker and came to him. "We must do something about Tansy. I phoned Plas Bach five minutes ago—Sir Henry was in his bath, but his housekeeper said Tansy wasn't there. Now the phone's out of order, and—"

"The kid may be lying out somewhere with a broken ankle," broke in Anthony. "God knows—"

"Steady on." said Feckenham, standing up; his glance went to Anna Pauncefoot, whose thin hands were tightly clasped—her sole sign of anxiety. "More likely Tansy's safe in shelter. All the same, we ought to make sure."

Here Dilys broke in with an excited gabble. Mr. Lewker quelled it by using his most compelling boom.

"I take it that Tansy has been gone some time and that no one here knows where she is. Mrs. Webhouse, will you please tell me when she went out?"

Clare came to stand by Anthony, who put an arm across her shoulders and glared defiantly at Mr. Lewker.

"I don't quite know," she said. "She was mooning about in the shrubbery all morning, and then Anna heard her go up to her room just before lunch.

When I called her to come to lunch she didn't answer, so I went up. She wasn't there."

"That would be about half-past twelve?"

"Yes. She'd taken her mountain clothes, as she calls them, and her nailed boots—she must be up in the mountains somewhere. Oh, we *must* try and find—"

"She's been away seven hours," Feckenham said. "Probably sheltering, of course. Cattespool and I thought we'd better nip round to local farms and cottages."

"We're wasting time," Anthony said impatiently. "Lewker, we've got to look for her."

"Pray give me your attention," said Mr. Lewker ignoring him and addressing the company at large. "Nobody here will leave this house. That is Inspector Grimmett's order, and the constable here will see that it is carried out. I shall go out to look for Tansy myself."

He was halfway up the stairs before Anthony could protest. He had received a measure of enlightenment; and he received more as, while he changed rapidly into climbing boots and breeches, he set his mind and memory to work.

Tansy had been listening outside the library window on the previous night. She could not have failed to hear Grimmett's assertion that unless Cutpursey could be found Cattespool was, on the evidence, undoubtedly the murderer; the inspector, leaning on the window-ledge, must have spoken that almost into the child's ear. And Tansy might very well know where Cutpursey had hidden himself. Mr. Lewker remembered her evasive reply when he had asked her where the gardener went "to watch beasties." Yes, it was at least a tenable hypothesis that Tansy, "mooning about in the garden," had been trying to decide whether she should keep Cutpursey's secret or—to save Cattespool, as she would think—reveal his hiding place to the police. Being Tansy, she would decide to seek out Cutpursey herself.

Granting that (thought Mr. Lewker, stuffing a first-aid wallet and some barley sugar into his rucksack) it could be said with fair certainty that the gardener must be within an afternoon's walking distance of Plas Mawr. Tansy had enough common sense to know that if she did not come back before nightfall there would be a search party out for her. She would not have anticipated the violence of the storm. What else was there to assist his search? The piece of manganese ore Dilys had shown him. That had at least suggested that Cutpursey's hideout was an old manganese working, but even if that were assumed it only helped a little; there were old workings in the hills to north, south, east and west. A cross-bearing was needed, and Tansy was the only person who could supply it, since she—as far as could be seen—was the only person who had been taken into Cutpursey's confidence. If

Tansy knew, she had kept her secret very well for an eleven-year-old. Or—
had she dropped some hint in his hearing? Nagging at the very back of his
mind was the insistent voice of memory telling him that she had.

Mr. Lewker set his remarkable memory to work. He recalled Tansy's first
mention of James Cutpursey, on the evening when she had rolled down the
Gwynant hillside. Mr. Cutpursey put mutton-fat on his head to make the hair
grow. He boiled it first. No clues there. Then the arrival at the lodge, and
Cutpursey himself opening the gates for the Wolseley—Tansy's greeting—
her explanation as they drove up the drive; funny but nice, goes into the hills
to watch beasties, the mutton-fat not effective. But something else. Goes
into the hills—ah! *"He calls it his three-gallon trip"*. Why "three-gallon?"
Did Cutpursey keep a barrel of beer in his hypothetical manganese mine?

Mr. Lewker, with an old gas cape ready to strap round him, stood up,
motionless in the candlelit bedroom. He felt certain that he held the key in
his hand; but it seemed to fit no lock. Why, then, should that nagging voice
insist that the lock was there? Mr. Lewker abandoned memory. He performed
a feat of which few men are capable, a feat which had more than once served
him well: he withdrew all conscious control from his thoughts and allowed
his subconscious mind to take charge.

... He was back in the recent past, a score of hours ago, lying in his bed at
Plas Mawr. Sleepless, he was wondering where James Cutpursey lay hidden.
The thirteen cwms of Snowdon passed again in swift review, his mind's ear
hearing their picturesque names: Cwm Dyli, Cwm Brwynog, Cwm Caregog,
Cwm Clogwyn, Cwm Glas, Cwm Tregalan——

Cwm Tregalan.

There was a 1-inch ordnance map in his rucksack. Mr. Lewker spread it
on the bed. Here was Cwm Tregalan, wildest and least visited of the cwms,
winding up under the very summit-crags of Snowdon, its lower reaches—
Cwm Llan on the map—debouching into Nant Gwynant less than a mile
from the gates of Plas Mawr. But there was no manganese mine marked
there. He rummaged in his suitcase and got out the sheets of the new 6-inch
map. There it was—"Manganese mine, disused"—at the foot of the precipices of Bwlch Main. Mr. Lewker was prepared to wager his head that here
was Cutpursey's "three-gallon trip" refuge.

He threw on his rucksack, wrapped the gas cape round him, and hurried
down the stairs. In the lamplit hall the little party was still gathered, standing
or sitting in attitudes of unease or sulkiness. Cattespool got up to intercept
him, but Mr. Lewker handed him off without pausing in his stride. He passed
Constable Jones, planted immovably near the door, and let himself out into
the storm.

Instantly the wind took him by the throat. Before he had battled his way
twenty yards down the drive he was soaked to the thighs. The abnormal

blackness brought by the thunderstorm had passed over; but although it was not yet eight o'clock the onset of darkness seemed to have begun, and the flailing, spouting rain reduced visibility to a few yards. Bent almost double, he thrust into the gale. In the lane beyond the lodge gates he was to some extent protected by the stone wall on his left and made better progress. He had little more than four miles to cover to reach the old manganese mine in Cwm Tregalan, but most of that four miles was uphill; he must climb from two hundred feet above sea level to two thousand, and the last two miles would be over trackless mountainside. He regretted that he had not borrowed the big electric torch from the hall table. On that last lap it would have been useful.

He emerged into the main road and was blown along its streaming surface like a leaf, in company with twigs and debris. In the turbulent circle of blinding rain he passed the gate on the left, which leads to the mountain track up Cwm Llan, without seeing it, and only realized his error when he found himself ankle-deep in swirling water. The river was already in spate and across the road. He turned back, found the gate, and began to climb.

On his left a steep wood of oaks, roaring and hissing in the wind, gave him some shelter for a while. The track underfoot was solid beneath its surface flow of water. He mounted steeply and came out on the hillside above a deep ravine. The stream in it was invisible, blotted out by the thickness of the horizontally driven rain, but its wild voice came up to him above the bellow of the storm like the noise of a thousand warriors sweeping down to raid the valley.

Half an hour later he entered the mist. It was like walking into a cold sea at night. The rain, he felt thankfully, was no longer so dense (though the change could make little difference to his wetness, which was complete) but it was now impossible to see further ahead than the next step. The track had become a bog, and his best guide was the riotous song of the river, now further away on his left. Huge boulders rose out of the dimness, loomed above him, and disappeared. He felt the crunch of slates under his boots and knew that he was near the ruins of an old quarry-house, where the path ended and he would have to strike up into the heart of the vast hollow which was Cwm Tregalan. In another fifty paces he nearly rammed his head against the ruined wall.

It was too dark to make out the dial of his compass, but the luminous north end of the needle gave him the bearing he required. He left the quarry ruin and struck out into chaos.

Chaos it was, or something very like it. Wind and rain added their full share of violence and confusion, but the earth itself seemed to writhe and swell underfoot as if all order had left it. Jagged banks of boulders rose like waves out of the murk, morasses crept treacherously across the way, deep-cut streams laid their traps at every tenth step. And somewhere above and in front there was a continuous and growing uproar, a sound resembling nothing so much as the voice of a great organ with every stop out and every key pressed down. Before he had gone many minutes across that mounting wilderness of invisible pitfalls Mr. Lewker found the cause of that sound.

He was climbing steadily, glancing now and then at his compass, penetrating further and higher under the summit crags of the great mountain. He had gained the crest of a rock-strewn mound when he felt the first assault of the mightier wind; it sent him flat on his face among the wet rocks. And thereafter he progressed in a series of staggers and falls, like a pygmy chased by a playful giant and smitten repeatedly by a gigantic and irresistible fist. The lower part of the cwm had been to some extent protected from the gale; up here the wind was trapped in a huge blind-alley whose walls were three thousand feet high. In its fury of frustration it flung its gusts in every direction, hurtling along the precipices overhead with a frantic howl that contained every note from a shriek to a bass roar. Mr. Lewker's gas cape was slit from neck to skirt, then torn from him to whistle away into the dark. He was deaf and blind and breathless, bruised by his falls and (in spite of himself) rather frightened. After pitching headlong into a particularly succulent bog he crept into the lee of a great rock to gather his senses. He found it necessary to remind himself that this was, after all, a mere storm in quite small mountains, that in a few more hours it would blow itself out. His compass had been blown from his hands and there had been no hope of finding it again; but he could not be far from the old manganese mine. He most fervently hoped that Tansy was not lying somewhere in the dark among these spouting boulders and streaming mosses.

He had to nerve himself to come out of shelter into the *tourmente* again. The rising ground looming darkly in front of him seemed to sway and heave as he stumbled on, and the storm flung itself on him as a Rugger three-quarter hurls himself at an opponent. Mr. Lewker called Shakespeare to his aid.

"Blow, wind, and crack your cheeks!" he bellowed into the gale. "Rage! Blow! You cataracts and hurricanes spout!"

Lear's mad apostrophe brought him some comfort, but the elements needed no encouragement. They tore and worried at him as he clawed his way up a treadmill-like slope of scree, hosed him with water as he scrambled over its crest, and flung him gasping against a pile of rocks. Mr. Lewker felt that the melodrama was being rather overdone. To go out into the storm to seek a missing child was good theatre; but the rescuer himself to be soaked, lost, and in danger of being the object of a search party was not even Drury Lane stuff. He began to realize that he had now small hope of finding Tansy or the manganese working.

Then his hands, spread flat against the rocks, felt a kind of order in their placing. A tumbledown wall! And the scree slope must surely have been an old "spoil bank." He went on, stumbling along the wall. And then he saw the faint red glow in the obscurity ahead. He shouted, and took three paces more. His boot nails screeched on a steep slab dropping away beneath him and he shot down, clutching vainly at the slimy surface, to land at the bottom with breath and consciousness knocked out of him.

He had little recollection, afterwards, of how he was got out of the old mine-cutting. His first realization that he had reached his goal came when he found himself sitting on a couch of dry heather with his back against the arching wall of the tunnel made long ago by the manganese miners. He was a few yards from its mouth, and nearer the entrance a fire of heather-roots burned brightly, its scented smoke darting and wreathing along the tunnel roof as air currents from the gale that roared outside caught at it. By the fire crouched a gnome-like figure; the craggy features dimly illumined by the glow from several candles stuck in the walls were those of James Cutpursey. Opposite Mr. Lewker, her wide blue eyes fixed anxiously on his face, squatted Tansy Pauncefoot. Mr. Lewker beamed at her.

"He's all right, Mr. Cutpursey!" Tansy cried, smiling back at him. "However did you find us? Were there some clues? I 'spect Mother's worried about me, isn't she? Isn't the storm awful! You *are* wet! Are you quite better now? Did you—"

"Hold, valiant Clifford, for a thousand causes!" boomed the actor-manager. "First let me ask why you, Tough, are here."

Old Cutpursey, hunching himself nearer Mr. Lewker like some cave-dwelling ape, answered.

"She come to seek me, master, that's why. Ah was a fule to run away, likely, an' Ah'm agoin' back soon's Ah can. Ye see—"

"You see," Tansy interrupted, "I heard the red-colored policeman say Uncle Anthony would be captured for the—the murderer, unless Mr. Cutpursey came back. So I went to get him, 'cause I was sure Mr. Cutpursey didn't do it, or Uncle Anthony, and I'd promised awf'ly solemnly I wouldn't tell about Mr. Cutpursey's cave, so I went without telling anyone, and the storm came when we were just going to start, and Mr. Cutpursey says in *course* Uncle Anthony didn't do the murder, nor did he, but he won't say who it was except to a policeman."

She paused for breath. Cutpursey nodded, his sunken eyes on Mr. Lewker's face.

"Ah knaws, reet enough," he growled. "Ah was skeered, d'ye see, bein' how things was. Well, Ah rackon Ah can put all straight when we gets down."

"Can't we go home *now*?" demanded Tansy, swinging her yellow pigtails. "Can't we, Mr. Lewker? I don't mind the old storm—I'm tough."

"Then I," said Mr. Lewker firmly, "am not."

"Miss Tansy," added Cutpursey sternly, "ye'll lie down reet away, on the heather yonder, and get what sleep ye can. 'Twon't blaw itself out afore first light," he continued, addressing Mr. Lewker. "We'm bound to make a night of it here. There's tea, bread, an' a bit o' jam, if that'll do ye."

The actor-manager said gratefully that it would. Tansy was settling herself into the thick nest of heather. Mr. Lewker pulled himself and his sodden clothing nearer the fire, where the old gardener was already preparing a billycan of water for boiling.

"Cutpursey," he said in a low voice, "when you bought that rackarock charge from Tully, for whom did you buy it?"

The other did not turn from his occupation of balancing the billycan over the flames.

"If ye know that much," he growled, "mebbe ye'll tell me who Ah got it for."

Mr. Lewker told him.

"Aye," said James Cutpursey, "thot's reet, master."

CHAPTER XVI

ALL ON STAGE, PLEASE

"By-y-y—*Gum*, sir!" exclaimed Detective-Inspector Grimmett as Mr. Lewker stopped speaking. His china-blue eyes were wide and shining. "It all fits, too—I reckon you've hit it!"

"I reckon I have, Grimm," returned Mr. Lewker modestly.

Grimmett's square face, lit redly by the sun which strove to penetrate the morning mists, wrinkled suddenly. He blew noisily through his mustache.

"Takes a bit of grasping, though," he said, wagging his head. "And there's one or two things aren't too clear."

The two were walking slowly along the path through the Plas Mawr shrubbery on the morning after the storm. The air was still once again and drenched with the scent of earth and wet greenery, and from every side came the sound of dripping water. The path was littered with leafy twigs and branches torn off by the gale; plenty of work here for old Cutpursey, reflected Mr. Lewker.

He had reached Plas Mawr with Tansy and the gardener a little after seven o'clock, having left the manganese tunnel at daybreak. The storm had exhausted its fury by then, and Cutpursey had led the way down Cwm Tregalan in a lightening mist whose slowly-moving wreaths had revealed the gray-green flanks of Snowdon streaked white with the foam of a hundred unaccustomed streams. Tansy had been packed off to bed with a hot-water bottle,

James Cutpursey had made his statement to the inspector, and Mr. Lewker—after being made much of to his satisfaction—had bathed, shaved, and revived himself with a great deal of coffee and toast. With Cutpursey's statement in evidence, he had lost no time in laying his completed case before Grimmett.

"You are still not entirely convinced, Grimm?" he said.

"Oh, I'm convinced all right, sir. But there's a couple of points, one of 'em important. The shield——"

"Ah, yes. There should have been a telephone call from Bangor University last night. That message will, I hope, explain the business of the shield."

Grimmett nodded dubiously. "I hope so, sir. Phone's been out of order all night, though, and it was dead when I tried it half an hour ago. The second point's that falling rock on the mountain. Unless you're going to say that was an accident, it's a tough one to explain, so it is."

"It was not an accident, Grimm, and I fancy I can demonstrate it." Mr. Lewker halted and picked up a fragment of rock from the path. "You see—"

He stopped as Sergeant Pitt came round a bend of the path to confront them.

"All set, Sergeant?" demanded Grimmett.

"Yessir." Pitt's hatchet face split in a grin. "Got 'em all sitting round in the drawing-room—Sir Henry, old Uncle Jim Cutpursey and all. Looking a bit anxious, they are."

"Won't hurt some of 'em," said Grimmett callously. "Very good, Sergeant—go ahead and say we're coming."

Pitt went back down the path and the inspector and the actor-manager followed more slowly.

"I'm leaving all the talking to you, sir," Grimmett said as they went. "If, as you say, you're determined to slide out and leave me with the credit—me, that backed the wrong horse all the way—"

"Nonsense, Grimm. You snapped up every clue very prettily."

"And lined the lot up back to front. No, sir—this was your case from start to finish, and I reckon the final tableau's your pidgin too. Fact is, I wouldn't miss hearing you put across the dinnoomong—not for fifty pound, I wouldn't."

Mr. Lewker beamed at him affectionately.

"Grimm," he boomed, "I believe you are pandering to my weakness for theatre. Very well, then. I will endeavor to give you your money's worth, but I warn you it will not take long. If I am to be in London before midnight, I must leave by eleven o'clock."

They came across the leaf-strewn terrace, where the Wolseley stood waiting, and entered the house. Mr. Lewker's suitcase stood in the hall with his folded raincoat across it. From the direction of the kitchen came the resentful yelps of the imprisoned Flora. Constable Jones, standing stiffly outside the drawing-roomdoor, saluted as they approached, and reported that the telephone exchange had rung through to say that the line was once more in order. The inspector nodded. Mr. Lewker paused to request the constable to take down any message from Bangor and bring it in to him. They went into the drawing room, and seven faces turned simultaneously towards them.

Pitt (who was sitting at the back of the room with his notebook on his knee) had evidently been busy with the seating arrangements. The sofas and easy chairs had been set in a neat semicircle fronting the end wall, against which stood two high-backed chairs with a small table in front of them. There was a short and slightly embarrassing silence while Grimmett and the actor-manager took their seats.

Grimmett cleared his throat noisily.

"You'll be glad to know," he said without ceremony, "that the police inquiry into this case is practically at an end. Thanks to Mr. Abercrombie Lewker here, the identity of David Webhouse's—um—murderer is now known to us. I propose to leave Mr. Lewker to explain."

Mr. Lewker allowed his glance to pass slowly round the half-circle of his audience. It was remarkable, he thought, how invariably that guilt-conscious expression showed itself on the faces of innocent persons in circumstances such as these. Even Anna Pauncefoot, who had brought her knitting and was working busily at it, revealed apprehension in the occasional flicker of her black eyes, though her gaunt face was grim as ever. Charles Feckenham, lounging rather too much at his ease, played nervously with a cigarette; his twisted grin was like a mask. Sir Henry Lydiate sat bolt upright in his chair. He tugged continually at his white mustache, but the action did not hide the slight twitching at the corner of his mouth. Clare Webhouse was pale and undisguisedly anxious as she sat beside Anthony Cattespool with her hand clasped in his, and the aggressive tilt of Anthony's pointed beard seemed to defy laws and morals alike. As for Dilys the maid and old James Cutpursey, who sat side by side at the end of the row, the obvious fright of the one and the hangdog surliness of the other were not suggestive of innocence. As far as present appearances went, seven criminals were facing Mr. Lewker.

The actor-manager made the throaty preparative noise he was accustomed to make before his stage entrances.

"For all except one of those in this room," he began sonorously. "the exposition which Detective-Inspector Grimmett has delegated to me will have a personal importance. You may rest assured that there will be no mistake, no wrongful arrest, no wrong'd innocence that makes the skies to weep. The hand that wrought this singularly shocking mechanism of murder is known beyond the shadow of a doubt."

He paused to smile inwardly a little at his own pomposity; after all, only a voice like Abercrombie Lewker's could deliver a sentence like the last and make it really impressive. His audience was already gripped, and even Pitt was sitting motionless in the background with his mouth slightly open.

"You will forgive me," he continued with a graceful gesture of the hand, "if I begin from the beginning—the beginning, that is, of my own connection with the case. David Webhouse wrote inviting me to come to Plas Mawr. His letter stated that he wished my advice, urgently, upon a very grave matter. It seemed to me that the letter also suggested that the writer was uneasy, anxious—perhaps in fear. That suggestion was augmented and confirmed by a series of slight but significant incidents which began with the evening of my arrival at Plas Mawr. There was Tansy's own impression that David Webhouse was frightened of something or someone. There was the mention of the milk given to the dog by Webhouse, who disliked Flora—a very small matter, perhaps, but scoring its point when later evidence hinted that he was afraid of being poisoned. Further and more weighty revelations made suspicion certainty. Webhouse would not say whom he suspected of firing an air rifle slug at him, but he left me in no doubt as to his meaning. And the rock that fell from the pinnacle on Crib Goch to miss Webhouse so narrowly, the rock that—if its fall were not an accident—could only have been dislodged by one person, assured me that I was not mistaken. If David Webhouse went in fear of death, then the cause of that fear was Anthony Cattespool."

Clare gave a little cry and clutched at Cattespool's arm.

"Webhouse had no cause to fear me," Anthony said jerkily; he had gone very pale. "I've admitted I disliked him. That doesn't mean I proposed to kill the man, does it?"

"You will pardon me for crediting you with sufficient motive," boomed the actor-manager, "and with sufficient initiative. However, let me pass on to the night of Webhouse's death. Certain curious circumstances surrounding that death did not become apparent until Inspector Grimmett and Sergeant Pitt had begun their very painstaking investigation. The evidence that was then brought to light pointed consistently in one direction only. And although James Cutpursey had disappeared immediately after the murder, and someone who might have been Cutpursey had been seen near Webhouse's body after the explosion, this evidence did not point to him."

Cutpursey muttered something under his breath and received a dig in the ribs from the goggle-eyed Dilys.

"I shall not detail the results of the various interrogations," proceeded Mr. Lewker. "David Webhouse—Mrs. Webhouse will forgive me for saying so— was a man who would make enemies wherever he went, even in his own family circle. It will suffice to say that every person here came under the shadow of suspicion, with the exception of Miss Dilys Jones."

Dilys emitted a shrill squeak and clapped her hand over her mouth. Mrs. Pauncefoot stopped knitting for a moment in order to quell her with a ferocious frown. Sir Henry Lydiate shifted his feet irritably.

"I fail to understand why I should be included, sir," he protested in his high voice. "I recent the term 'suspicion' as applied to myself, and I—"

"Pray allow me to continue," Mr. Lewker said severely. "I have said that the discovered evidence did not point particularly to James Cutpursey. Even when consideration of David Webhouse's will revealed that Cutpursey would benefit to the extent of five hundred pounds by his master's death, the fact—as Inspector Grimmett insisted—did not weigh down the scale of probability. And the weight on the other side increased as investigation progressed. Thanks to a brilliant reconstruction, by Sergeant Pitt, of the methods necessary to prepare the explosive booby-trap, we knew what to look for. We looked. And we found it—except a three-eighths bit—in the shed adjoining Mr. Cattespool's cottage."

"*No!*" cried Clare. She took Anthony's arm almost savagely. "Tell them it's wrong—a mistake—"

"It's a damned lie!" Anthony was on his feet and flushed with anger. "There could have been nothing to find! I swear——"

"Mr. Cattespool—" the actor-manager's voice rose and drowned Anthony's—"take Juliet's advice, and mine—do not swear at all. I found this evidence myself. It suggested in the strongest possible way that the explosive trap had been prepared by you. It fell into the lengthening line of other clues, a line pointing always to you. The falling rock. The green nylon parachute cord used in setting the trap, a portion of which was picked up by Mrs. Webhouse in your workshop, as she told me herself."

Clare moaned and clung to her lover, whose bearded face had lost its color again. The impressionable Dilys mopped her eyes with a dirty handkerchief. Mr. Lewker continued.

"There were other and minor points. The nylon cord was made fast to the bridge stanchion with a typical naval lashing. It was, I may say, the release-cord for a species of safety-catch, and was plainly intended for release by pulling from the cottage end of the bridge. But the last and most damning clue was found last night by Inspector Grimmett. It consisted of part of a typewritten note, since proved to have been typed on Mr. Cattespool's machine, obviously intended for Mrs. Webhouse and warning her of the time the murder was to take place."

He paused, expecting an outburst from Cattespool; but none came. Clare's dark head was on Anthony's chest, her face hidden in his coat. Anthony, very pale now, stared back at Mr. Lewker with something like despair.

Mr. Lewker dropped his gaze and rubbed, frowning, at his chin. He had a weakness—not, perhaps, one of his most amiable characteristics—for playing the part of Judicial Chastener. He was reasonably certain that Clare and Anthony had been carrying on an illicit affair, and he considered that punishment was due. Now, however, he relented.

"I may add," he said gently, "that from the first I doubted the evidence against Anthony Cattespool. It was true that he, of all those concerned, had the strongest motives for desiring Webhouse's death. There was evidence that Webhouse knew what was going on between Cattespool and his wife and that Cattespool knew that he knew. But—with apologies, Grimm—the very finding of the material clues made them suspect, for they could nearly all have been destroyed without any trouble. It was inconceivable that a man of Anthony Cattespool's intelligence would not have destroyed them, had he been the murderer. Therefore I inclined from the outset to the opinion that Anthony Cattespool was not guilty."

A rustle of released breath ran round the circle of listeners. Clare made an odd sound between a sob and a laugh.

"It's all right, darling," she whispered brokenly. "It's all right after all."

Anthony held her close. He seemed to attempt to speak, but succeeded only in swallowing convulsively. Mr. Lewker continued his exposition.

"Consider also the other incidents. The business of theair rifle shot presented some odd features, in addition to the fact that Cattespool had an alibi for the time of the shooting—an alibi which would have been at least difficult to break. Surely he was not so ignorant of weapons as to suppose that anair rifle slug would kill at a range of fifty yards? Even if he succeeded in hitting his man in the eye death might not result. The evidence is that he is no marksman, and a man's eye at fifty yards is no easy mark with an ordinaryair rifle. Then the incident of the rockfall, apparently another clumsy and unsuccessful attempt on Webhouse's life. Was it likely that he would risk that? Again, what possible contingency could have driven him to type a highly compromising note to Mrs. Webhouse—the signature, by the way, was torn off—when he had ample opportunity to speak to her privately? My conclusion from all this was the obvious one that this evidence was being manipulated, or had been planted, to incriminate Anthony Cattespool."

Here Sir Henry Lydiate, who had been listening with increasing impatience, interrupted him.

"This becomes tedious, sir. Can you not tell us, without more words, who killed David Webhouse?"

"If I am tedious, Sir Henry," Mr. Lewker retorted a trifle huffily, "it is in your interests. It is necessary that all should be made plain to those who by accident or by their own fault have been concerned in this affair. Pray permit me, like a poor player, to strut and fret my hour upon the stage. I assure you I shall soon be heard no more."

"I am thinking, sir, of the ladies," Sir Henry explained stiffly. "Their anxiety—"

"Shall quickly be relieved. I draw to my point. I have shown how I reached my conclusion that an attempt was being made to saddle Cattespool with the guilt of the murder. Who, then, would do such a thing? Inspector Grimmett himself pointed out that none of those on whom suspicion rested had any known reason for wishing Cattespool's death. It could be argued that Mrs. Pauncefoot, who under Webhouse's will shared the main legacy with Mrs. Webhouse, would benefit if Mrs. Webhouse and Cattespool were convicted jointly of the crime. However, Mrs. Pauncefoot had apparently no opportunity of setting the explosive trap and operating the other attempts."

At the word "apparently" Anna Pauncefoot had dropped a stitch. She raised her black eyes for an instant to Mr. Lewker's face and then resumed her work without comment.

"By this time," the actor-manager went on, "I was, myself, convinced of the criminal's identity. It seemed to me quite plain that if the line of clues and evidence did not point to Cattespool they pointed directly to the person who laid them." He shot a twinkling glance at the inspector. "If I may be obvious for a moment, a line runs in two directions. By putting my eye, so to speak, to the Cattespool end of the line and looking back along it, I saw the criminal at the other end. I was morally certain but I needed indisputable proof. The missing Cutpursey, I was sure, held vital evidence. He had to be found. And then it was ascertained that an explosive charge of the kind used in the trap had been secretly obtained shortly before the murder by James Cutpursey."

Everyone turned to look at Cutpursey. The old man half rose from his chair and opened his mouth to speak. Mr. Lewker waved a prohibitory hand at him and he sat down again. The sonorous voice went on, more quickly now.

"James Cutpursey had witnessed the insertion in Webhouse's will of a large bequest to himself. That was three weeks before Webhouse's death and by Webhouse's own arrangement. Cutpursey was devoted to Webhouse. And Cutpursey obtained the rackarock charge. That set of facts appeared to me to be highly significant. So did another set. David Webhouse had not taken any steps to prevent Cattespool from seeing his wife. He had known for some time of the affair between them. He was—Mrs. Webhouse will forgive me— an exceedingly possessive, vain, and bullying type of man. He—"

Anna Pauncefoot suddenly grunted loudly, dropped her knitting, and stared at the speaker. Mr. Lewker smiled at her.

"I perceive that my point is taken. And"—he turned to Charles Feckenham, who had jerked his lean body upright and was leaning tensely forward—"I fancy Mr. Feckenham is also on the brink of enlightenment."

"The falling rock," said Feckenham, with no trace of his usual drawl. "That was accident, after all?"

"Oh, no. It was a successful effect, simple in the extreme. Perhaps—Inspector, is that someone looking in at the window?"

Grimmett turned swiftly to stare at the window on his left. Mr. Lewker's hand went into his pocket, came out again, and jerked upward. An instant later a small piece of rock dropped neatly on to the inspector's head and clattered to the floor. Grimmett exclaimed and looked up at the ceiling.

"Good lord!" muttered Feckenham, flopping back in his chair.

"Good *lord*!" echoed Anthony more shrilly. "Then it was—"

"Who had the strongest reason for getting rid of you?" demanded the actor-manager quickly. He swung round to face the gardener. "Mr. Cutpursey, will you please tell us why you obtained that rackarock charge?"

The old man got slowly to his feet.

"Ah was proper skeered," he began, looking round him nervously, "when Ah found him a-lyin' there. Ye see, 'twas me got the charge, reet enough, an' Ah knew they'd find out. He made me see the will, an' the five hunnerd pound, which was for me if Ah swore to say nowt about gettin' the charge. Well, Ah swore, but now as he's gone Ah reckon 'tis no matter. Ah got the charge an' made a detonator—not knowin' how he'd use 'em—for Dai Webhouse."

He sat down heavily and blew his nose like a trumpet.

"For Dai Webhouse," repeated Mr. Lewker benignly. "My apologies, Grimm," he added, "for the schoolboy trick."

Grimmett beamed at him. Anthony, Feckenham and Clare all began to speak at once. Anna Pauncefoot's rasping voice cut into the confusion.

"It was like him," she said, nodding grimly. "A vain man and a proud was David Webhouse. He'd never admit, even to himself, that he was losing his wife to another man. No—he'd get rid of the man somehow—Come in!"

The command was in response to a knock at the door. Constable Jones entered with a folded paper, handed it ceremoniously to Mr. Lewker, and stumped out. The actor-manager glanced at the message and passed it to Grimmett, who studied it with knitted brow.

"Mrs. Pauncefoot has begun," Mr. Lewker boomed, "and I may now conclude, the tragedy of David Webhouse. He planned to kill his wife's lover in such a way that it would appear that Cattespool had laid a trap for him and had fallen into it himself. The unnecessarily elaborate deathtrap, which puzzled me from the first, was made necessary by this requirement. The device of the explosive booby-trap was Webhouse's plan, and considering all things it was an ingenious one. He was thorough in his preparations. The carefully hinted fear of poison, theair rifle slug which he had himself fired into the tree, the falling rock on the Snowdon climb—all were designed to make it certain that Cattespool should be suspected primarily when the time came. And I"—the boom deepened resentfully—"I was brought down here to have my nose put upon that red herring trail."

"But I still don't see——" Feckenham began to protest.

Mr. Lewker stopped him with a gesture. "I think Mrs. Webhouse wishes to ask a question."

"I expect I'm silly," said Clare, leaning forward from Anthony's encircling arm, "but I don't understand about that falling rock."

"You see. Mrs. Webhouse, your husband arranged the order in which we should traverse the Crib Goch ridge, and he arranged it with a purpose. When we reached the gap between the pinnacles, while Cattespool was still out of sight on the crest above, he made Tansy and Feckenham and myself face the opposite pinnacle while he took a ciné shot. When we were all looking the other way he took a lump of rock, flung it straight up in the air, and fell flat with a shout. We turned in time to see the rock crashing down and naturally assumed that it had dropped from above—just as the inspector here automatically assumed that my fragment of rock had fallen from the ceiling. I fancy Webhouse hurt himself involuntarily in falling, but the effect was just what he intended."

"But the rest of it," Anthony growled, "didn't work out as the blighter intended."

"No. He had, of course, prepared a number of clues for me to find. I do not think he intended that all of them should be found. He could remove them himself, or direct my attention to them, according to whether the investigation was proceeding too slowly or too easily. The work necessary for the rigging of the trap had been carried out in Cattespool's shed while Cattespool was absent—Webhouse, as landlord, had duplicate keys—but a three-eighths bit, which was required for an essential piece of drilling, was not among Cattespool's tools. Webhouse had one in his own workshop. That small discrepancy served to confirm my tentative suspicions in the actual investigation. The typewritten note"—Mr. Lewker's pouchy face took on an expression of distaste—"was a kind of reserve clue, I fancy, prepared in case Webhouse's singularly low opinion of my detective powers should prove to be too high. And now let us consider the evening of the explosion. Until David Webhouse left the house at the end of dinner, his plans had gone without a hitch. He——"

"Am I to understand, sir," interrupted Sir Henry, bristling, "that his extreme rudeness to me at dinner was a calculated stratagem?"

"That is a correct inference," returned Mr. Lewker approvingly. "The excuse for Webhouse to 'go for a stroll to cool his head' was provided thereby. Of course, it gave him the necessary opportunity to go up the cliff path and set the trap by removing the safety shield. He himself would then see to it that no one else went that way until Anthony Cattespool, returning an hour or so later to his cottage, stepped on the bridge and exploded the charge."

Clare Webhouse shuddered and hid her face with her hands. Anna Pauncefoot got up and unceremoniously pushed Dilys aside so that she could sit beside Clare.

"But look here," said Feckenham, "I grant you Webhouse's intention to kill Cattespool. But you've said nothing to show how the rest of the fake was to be done. Mean to say, it had got to look as though Cattespool was hoist with his own petard."

"Right, Charles." Anthony leaned forward, frowning. "What's more, how did Webhouse come to explode the trap, if he went up there to set it?"

"Webhouse had put the shield in position and had tested it. It was perfectly safe, then, to walk across the bridge—Cattespool crossed it in the morning. Webhouse would therefore step on to the bridge with assurance. But the safety-shield had been already withdrawn."

"Hell and damnation!" Anthony sat up abruptly and glared at the actor-manager. "What are you getting at? That means Webhouse was murdered, after all—there *is* a murderer!"

"Or," said Mr. Lewker enigmatically, "a murderess." He turned to the inspector. "Grimm, I have an unusual witness to call.—Miss Jones, will you kindly bring in the spaniel Flora?"

The flustered Dilys hurried from the room. Mr. Lewker picked up the folded note which the constable had brought in and spread it open before him.

"David Webhouse," he said, "was careful to draw my attention on more than one occasion to Flora's habit of pulling at shoelaces and ends of string, and to the fact that the dog went often up the cliff path. He mentioned in my hearing that he had seen her smelling round the bridge—and, let me emphasize, traces proving that he spoke the truth were found on the cliff path after the explosion. You see the story he was preparing? Flora, he would tell us, must have gone up there before Cattespool, who would be presumed to intend setting the trap as he returned to his cottage so that Webhouse would explode it when he came up on his invariable turning-in stroll. Flora it was, he would insist, who tugged at the cord after her manner and thus pulled out the shield."

"Conjecture," pointed out Feckenham.

"I am reasonably certain that Webhouse would have produced proof."

"What proof?" Grimmett demanded.

"I shall hope to show you in a few minutes. But now comes the irony, the tragic irony, of the affair. Webhouse's fiction became—fact. His fairy tale came true, to his own undoing. And here is our final witness."

Dilys came in with the spaniel in her arms and gave her to Mr. Lewker, who smoothed the silken head and settled the dog on his lap.

"Flora," he said, "you are in the unprecedented position of being at once innocent and guilty." Flora licked his face, jumped down, and ran to her mistress. "I have here," Mr. Lewker continued, taking up the paper, "a laboratory report received by telephone. It deals with the piece of frayed nylon cord found on the bridge, the cord whose other end must have been attached to the safety shield. It reads, in part, as follows: 'Minute particles of a fibrous substance, probably raw beef, were found, together with considerable traces of animal saliva.' "

He looked at Clare, who was nursing the dog. "Mrs. Webhouse, what did Flora's supper consist of?"

"She had a beef bone," whispered Clare.

"And you recall how she came in through the window over here, while we were taking coffee?"

"Good lord, yes!" cried Anthony. "Earth all over her muzzle—it was only a minute or two before we heard the explosion." He sprang to his feet excitedly. "I've got it! The rockery, Lewker?"

Mr. Lewker nodded.

Anthony made for the door and the whole party followed, with Flora barking madly in the midst. Outside in the morning sunshine the spaniel took the lead. She headed for one end of the rockery, where it approached the wall of the house; a corner where such rock plants as remained wore an air of patient suffering and the earth showed signs of frequent disturbance.

"Fetch 'em out, old girl!" urged Anthony.

Flora needed no encouragement. The soil flew between her hind legs as she burrowed frantically. First a decayed bone and then an old slipper came to light. And then, as she began on a fresh patch, a frayed and dirty piece of cord appeared under her paws. Mr. Lewker pounced on it and pulled. Out came a stoutly-made oblong shell of wood. The brass strip on its upper surface glinted in the sun as he held it aloft.

"The safety shield," he announced with satisfaction. "What Flora did with it David Webhouse would have done. It would have been his concluding piece of evidence, as it is mine."

"Flora, you're a naughty, *naughty* little bitch," whispered Clare, stooping to fondle the spaniel.

"But confound it!" said Sir Henry, making a discovery. "This feller Webhouse was a confounded murderous scoundrel!"

Mr. Lewker held up an arresting hand and assumed his most sonorous tones.

"Forbear to judge, for we are sinners all.
Close up his eyes, and draw the curtains close,
And let us all—"

"Oy!"

The interruption came from overhead. Tansy, her pigtails gleaming gold in the sunlight, looked down from her bedroom window like the Blessed Damozel from the gold bar of heaven.

"You waked me up," she said reprovingly. "What are you all looking so pleased for?"

Mr. Lewker beamed up at her.

"Because, Tough," he said, "no one is going to be hanged."

* * * * * * *

Postcard addressed to Miss Tansy Pauncefoot

MY DEAR TOUGH,

The picture shows you Buckingham Palace, and the steps up which I went this morning in very uncomfortable clothes. It was worth it. Her Majesty was most gracious and beautiful. I came down the steps quoting your favourite Viola: "O that I served that lady, And might not be delivered to the world!" And now I have only space left to subscribe myself

Ever your servant and honorary uncle

ABERCROMBIE LEWKER,
Knight

THE END

The Rue Morgue Press has reprinted two other books in Glyn Carr's Abercrombie Lewker series, *Death on Milestone Buttress* and *The Youth Hostel Murders*. These are available from the same bookseller who sold you *Death Under Snowdon*.

About the Rue Morgue Press

"Rue Morgue Press is the old-mystery lover's best friend, reprinting high quality books from the 1930s and '40s."
—*Ellery Queen's Mystery Magazine*

Since 1997, the Rue Morgue Press has reprinted scores of traditional mysteries, the kind of books that were the hallmark of the Golden Age of detective fiction. Authors reprinted or to be reprinted by the Rue Morgue include Catherine Aird, Dorothy Bowers, Pamela Branch, Joanna Cannan, Glyn Carr, Torrey Chanslor, Clyde B. Clason, Joan Coggin, Manning Coles, Lucy Cores, Frances Crane, Norbert Davis, Elizabeth Dean, Constance & Gwenyth Little, Marlys Millhiser, James Norman, Stuart Palmer, Craig Rice, Kelley Roos, Charlotte Murray Russell, Maureen Sarsfield, Margaret Scherf and Juanita Sheridan.

To suggest titles or to receive a catalog of Rue Morgue Press books write P.O. Box 4119, Boulder, CO 80306, telephone 800-699-6214, or check out our website, www.ruemorguepress.com, which lists complete descriptions of all of our titles, along with lengthy biographies of our writers.